A DETECTIVE MAIER NOVEL

"Exuberant writing."
Andrew Marshall, Time magazine

"There's a tremendous – and tremendously fresh – energy to Tom Vater's writing."
Ed Peters, The South China Morning Post

"The narrative is fast-paced and the frequent action scenes are convincingly written. The smells and sounds of Cambodia are vividly brought to life. Maier is a bold and brave hero."
Crime Fiction Lover

Also by Tom Vater

The Devil's Road to Kathmandu
Sacred Skin

TOM VATER

THE CAMBODIAN
BOOK OF THE DEAD

EXHIBIT A
An Angry Robot imprint
and a member of Osprey Group

Lace Market House,   43-01 21st Street, Suite 220B
54-56 High Pavement,   Long Island City
Nottingham NG1 1HW   NY 11101
UK   USA

www.exhibitabooks.com
A is for Asia!

An Exhibit A paperback original 2013

Cover design by Argh! Oxford
Set in Meridien and Franklin Gothic by EPubServices

Distributed in the United States by Random House, Inc., New York

ISBN 978 1 90922 319 6
Ebook ISBN 978 1 90922 320 2

Printed in the United States of America

9 8 7 6 5 4 3 2 1

To the ones of the first hour...
Janey, Lo, Flintman, Rockoff
and Pesey (RIP)

Cambodia: Where the Appalling is Commonplace.
Jerry Redfern

IN THE SHADOW OF ENLIGHTENMENT

In retrospect, Maier could see that the catastrophe in Cambodia had been the turning point. But in retrospect, everything always looked different.

War was never simple. As soon as the first shot was fired, carefully made plans changed beyond recognition. As soon as the first shot was fired, everything was unpredictable, and no one got away scot-free.

Most men were simply blown away by the wilful mayhem, like dry leaves in a fast wind.

Others found themselves in the horror of the moment and got stuck there, making the world die, over and over. A few went by another route, on and on, into themselves, until they experienced a kind of epiphany, a moment of arrival.

War correspondent Maier was about to arrive.

Maier and Hort sat on a crumbling wall near what was left of the railway station in Battambang, or what was left of this once-picturesque and industrious town in north-western Cambodia. Perhaps a school had stood here forty years earlier. A few metres of tired red brick work was all that was had survived the recent vagaries of history. At midday, the wall offered no shade. It was just a structure to sit next to. Better than being exposed, in a world of dust, misery and possible aggravation. A group of men sat next to the two journalists on low stools. They drank rice wine as if their lives depended on it. Perhaps it did.

Garbage and dust-devils blew across the shabby, run-down space between the wall and the railway tracks – scraps of paper, plastic bags, and diapers. Who had money for diapers around here? Where could you even buy nappies in Cambodia?

A young woman with a pinched face served the rancid drink from an old oil canister. There was only one glass, which went around in a circle. People in Cambodia drank quietly and with great concentration. Everyone was waiting. The railway station was a good place to wait. The trains were less reliable than the next glass, as the Khmer Rouge, Pol Pot's feared communist army, frequently mined the tracks between the capital Phnom Penh and Battambang. The Khmer Rouge was the main reason why people were waiting. Despite UN sponsored elections, boycotted by the communists, the war just would not die. Most Cambodians wanted peace, and peace meant waiting.

Hort passed Maier a joint. "The war will be over in a few weeks, Maier. 1997 is our year. At least that what they say in Phnom Penh. Around here, people not so sure."

Hort laughed, as the Khmer sometimes do when they don't feel like laughing.

Maier wiped the sweat from his eyes, rearranged his matted beard and shrugged his shoulders. "Your country is sick of war, Hort. And you are getting married next week, when we are through and you have earned yourself a sack full of money."

The young Khmer was working as Maier's fixer and had been accompanying him for the past four years, every time the German journalist had been on assignment in Cambodia. Four years and six visits to this cursed country. And yet Maier had fallen into uneasy love with this sunny and wicked paradise.

Hort had saved his life on at least two occasions. In a few days, Maier would be the best man at his young friend's wedding, hopefully without making a drunken pass at Hort's attractive sister.

What would Carissa, beautiful and twisted Carissa, say if she found him in the sack with a young Khmer woman? What would be left, when the war really ended, when the international media left this tired land to its own devices? Maier had come with the war. Would he not also disappear with the war? Move on to the next war? Lack of choice wasn't the issue. War was always in vogue.

Hort interrupted him in his thoughts.

"As long as Pol Pot is alive, we not find peace. Why don't UN arrest and kill him?" Hort answered the question himself, "My people no longer have expectation that anyone come and help."

An old woman, her lined forehead almost hidden beneath a faded *krama*, the traditional chequered scarf many Khmer wore, her eyes black and numb like the tropical small hours, passed the two men slowly and silently spat on the hot dusty ground in front of Maier.

Hort's contorted stare followed her.

"I think I could do with a glass of rice wine myself."

Maier and his fixer were waiting for an officer serving with a regiment of government troops. Their contact was involved in peace negotiations with the last remnants of the Khmer Rouge fighters. The civil conflict, which had prevented recovery since the demise of the communists' agrarian utopia in 1979, some eighteen years before, was drawing to a close. The government in Phnom Penh had some control over most of the country, or at least over what was left of Cambodia after a half century of catastrophic politics, war and genocide. Every time he made eye contact with a Khmer, Maier could see that that wasn't much.

The Khmer Rouge had retreated to the west, to the provinces bordering Thailand. Several conflagrations had taken place in Battambang in recent weeks. Nasty, dark stuff.

Maier knew there wasn't much time left. One of the great nightmares of the twentieth century was drawing to a close and Cambodia was moving towards an uncertain but less violent future. He'd come back to find out what that future might look like from the country's last battlefield. Finding out anything in Cambodia usually involved waiting. Maier had been waiting for three days. Today, Hort had assured him, the interview would materialise. Hort had been equally optimistic the previous day and the day before that.

A group of young men in torn work clothes, their dusty, hard feet in plastic flip-flops, walked past the wall, smoking cigarettes and talking quietly amongst themselves. Maier had picked up enough Khmer to understand that the conversation revolved around him. Was the tall foreigner a soldier? Was he looking for a girl? One look from Hort made them shut up.

"What gift are you give my future wife on her wedding day, Maier?"

The young Khmer could hardly wait to return to Phnom Penh. Two extended families were waiting on the groom and his tall, white employer – his protector. They had already put up the marquee.

"If you keep bugging me, Hort, I will buy her a sack of cold, fried frogs." Maier grinned at the young man – for his friend's assurance – as the Khmer did not always understand his sarcasm. How many miles had he already travelled with Hort, how many cruelties had he documented, while his fixer had stood next to him, his face expressionless? How many drunk and triggerhappy soldiers had they passed together at road blocks? Perhaps he really was the young Khmer's lucky charm.

Maier got distracted by a young woman in a bright purple sarong. He noticed the boy as well, but you noticed so many things. You had to choose, and Maier chose the woman. Hort, too, held his breath for a second. The woman passed the wall without looking at the men and crossed the railway tracks. Maier could not see her face, but he was sure that she was beautiful. He followed the languid sway of her hips and let his thoughts meander. The war was practically finished and he felt happier than he had in a long time. His plan to stop working in the war news business had become more appealing in recent months, but since his return to Cambodia, he had enjoyed his work, and after all, a plan was only a plan.

Later, as he sat on the back of a pick-up slowly rumbling towards Phnom Penh, he would suddenly recall the most important moment: the short cropped hair and the fixed stare, the dusty brown baseball cap, which the boy had pulled deep into his face and which had not suited the young Red Khmer at all. But you saw people with fixed stares everywhere, especially in this mad and lost part of the world.

The boy had just appeared on the potholed road. He wore a ripped T-shirt and black trousers and he was barefoot. Why had Maier not looked at him more closely?

The youth dropped his bag next to the woman who was serving the rice wine. She had her back turned to Maier and he barely noticed the brief exchange between the two. It looked like an everyday conversation. It was an everyday conversation. A few seconds later, the boy was on his way and Maier had forgotten him. He stared across the tracks, but the girl in the bright sarong had also dropped out of sight. Maier briefly turned towards the woman serving the moonshine. She had started a heated argument with her customers. He didn't understand a word the woman said. She had a strong accent, and whatever she was saying, quickly fell victim to the mean, silent aggression of the day. He didn't care. The smell of the tropics, saturated with reincarnation and ruin, this hypnotising combination of extremes, of promise and danger, of temptation and failure, had convinced him once more that he'd chosen the best job in the world. In a few hours, when the interview would finally be in the can, he would drink with Hort. He still had a small bottle of vodka in his bag, and they were bound to be able to organise a few oranges in Battambang. No rice wine for Maier. And in a few days, after the wedding, he'd be flying back to Hamburg. That was the plan.

"I'm really looking forward to your wedding, Hort. It will be a special day for me as well."

"The day you ask for my sister's hand?"

The years with Maier had changed the Khmer as well. Occasionally he tried his luck with irony and sarcasm, in a gentle Cambodian way.

Maier replied drily, "Carissa will cut my balls off. Or I'll have to flee and will never be able to return to Cambodia."

"That a shame, Maier. Maybe it better you keep your hands off my sister and follow your western lifestyle."

Suddenly, the three drinkers next to Maier wrested the sack off the wine-seller and jumped up. Hort jerked to his feet and gave Maier a hard push. The explosion killed his friend's warning. The bomb blew most of the wall straight past Maier. The woman who'd been selling the wine was blown to pieces. Screams and smoke. Maier lay flat on the ground for a few long seconds, not daring to move. Even the sky was on fire. Turning his head, he could see twisted bodies through the clouds of black fumes, shapes covered in blood and dust, frozen in black burns. A few small lean-tos that had been built against the wall were ablaze. Maier shook his legs and arms, everything was still there. One of the young men who'd been sitting behind him was alive. Caked in blood, he cried softly, as he tried to pull a friend from under the rubble. It was too late. A wooden beam had completely severed his companion's legs from his torso.

Hort had disappeared. Perhaps he had fallen before the explosion had gone off. But Maier knew that his friend had been sitting between himself and the woman selling the wine and had jumped up to warn him. The sudden realisation that his friend and fixer was dead came as a physical blow, as if some unchallengeable force had risen at speed from the earth below him and was suddenly ripping the skin off his back, racing up his neck as binary code made of needles and knives, and on, into his head where everything contracted in panicked spasms. He sat in debris for a moment, trying to breathe, waiting for something to come back, for time to go on. In the silence following the attack, a couple of dogs barked in the distance and the whine of a motorbike grew louder. Women cried, somewhere to his right. Otherwise, all he could hear was a high-pitched ringing tone in his ears. Maier forced himself up and climbed through the smoke across the strewn-around brickwork. He had to be sure.

The bomb had taken Hort straight through a big hole in the wall of a building that had been destroyed decades ago. A quick look was enough. Hort was dead.

Without a doubt, the bomb had been meant for Maier. The Khmer Rouge hated westerners, especially journalists. And the Cambodian army had known that Maier would be waiting by the station. Virtually anyone with a modicum of energy could get hold of explosives in this country.

Maier moved away from the carnage and disappeared as best as he could into the crowd that was beginning to gather by the railway tracks. He had to get away before the police and the military showed. He ran to one of the nearest shacks, dived into a small shop, pulled his cell phone from his pocket and called Carissa. Then he tied a *krama* around his head and jumped a passing pick-up truck bound for the capital.

He'd call his editor once he'd returned to Hamburg and hand in his notice. Maier was no longer a war correspondent.

PART 1

THE GOLDEN PEACOCK

THE WIDOW

Dani Stricker crossed the Paradeplatz and walked down the Planken, towards Mannheim's historic water tower. It was an old tradition. With Harald, she'd walked down the south German city's shopping mile every Saturday afternoon, no matter what the weather had been like. For twenty years.

The Cambodian could still remember her arrival in Mannheim in 1981. The shops had dazzled her and she'd thought that the fountain in front of the Kaufhof, the biggest mall in town, sprayed liquid gold instead of water into the air. She'd been sure of it. The people were huge. And rich. Today she could see the differences in incomes and lifestyles, but in those early months, she'd almost believed that money grew on trees in Germany. Of course, money did not grow on trees anywhere, unless you owned the tree. She knew that now.

Everything had been strange. Dani had never seen a tram, never mind an escalator. Such things did not exist in Cambodia. In the supermarket, she'd been overwhelmed by the enormous variety of cats and dogs available in tins, which crowded the shelves of an entire aisle. The first *Bretzel* that Harald had bought her had tasted disgusting. She'd felt she was going to suffocate on the heavy, salty dough. But she'd forced herself to eat it anyway, for Harald.

As scary and foreign as her new home had been then, she had not wanted to return to Cambodia. There, death lived in the rice fields and would be able to find her people in their flimsy huts even a hundred years from now, to drag them from their homes into the darkness and make them vanish forever. Dani had been homesick, but she'd understood even then that the country she called home no longer existed. No one had ever returned from the long night that had covered Cambodia like a suffocating blanket for decades. Only ghosts flourished in the rice paddies. Harald had saved her life. Harald was Dani's hero. Everything she had seen and learned in the past twenty years had come from Harald. And now, Harald was dead.

Sometimes, they'd taken the tram from the city centre to Harald's house in Käfertal. Sometimes she'd taken the tram into town all by herself, as Harald had never been keen on public transport. She'd never learned to drive. Now she really needed the tram, was dependent on it for the first time in her life. Now she was alone. She would sell the BMW straight away.

Dani boarded a Number 4 in front of the water tower. An inspector silently took her ticket, looked at it with deliberate, antagonistic care and handed it back, having switched the expression of his sallow face to trained boredom. A couple of rows behind Dani, two youths with coloured hair and buttons in their ears raised their voices against the police state. After the funeral, she would put the car in the local newspaper and hope for a buyer.

The tram slowly passed the city cemetery. Harald had died on October 11th, just a week ago. The poplar leaves blew around the pavement like shiny, copper-coloured bank notes. That looked pretty disorderly by Mannheim's standards, but a municipal employee would soon come with a machine and hoover the leaves out of this world and into another.

One day, Dani's coffin would be laid to rest here as well, thousands of miles from home. She'd promised Harald. Nevertheless, the idea of a burial remained unsettling. How would she fare in the next life if she was not cremated? But promises had to be kept. She'd learnt that as a young girl, working alongside her mother in the family's rice paddy. Without keeping promises, life wasn't worth a thing. It wasn't worth much anyway.

Her parents and her sister had not been cremated either. Perhaps, if she returned to Cambodia, she would be able to locate the mass grave in which they'd been dumped. Her contact had suggested starting some investigations, but Dani had turned his offer down. Too many old bones belonging to too many people lay in those graves and she would never really be certain.

Her mobile rang. The foreign number. The call Dani had been waiting for. She had been waiting for more than twenty years. It was time to let her past bleed into her present life. The past, the present and the future coexisted next to each other. Every child in Cambodia knew that. But here, in Germany, in the West, everything was separated. Now she could finally take steps to take control, to bring closure. Revenge could do that. Anonymous and ruthless revenge.

Dani took a deep breath and answered the call.

"Hello?"

"Everything is ready. Tomorrow I will be in Bangkok to catch a flight to Phnom Penh."

Dani was surprised. The man spoke Khmer, albeit with a strong accent. A *barang*. Dani was shocked at her own reaction. After all, Harald had also been a *barang*, a white man. As a child she'd never asked herself whether the term the Khmer used for Westerners had positive or negative connotations. During the Khmer Rouge years, *barang* had meant as much as devil or enemy. She forced herself back into the present.

"Find him and get in touch when you have learned what has happened to my sister. Force him to talk. When you have proof of what happened to her, kill him."

The man at the other end of the conversation said nothing. He had been recommended by a fellow Cambodian whom she had met on the long journey from a refugee camp on the Thai-Cambodian border to Germany, some twenty years earlier. The *barang* had apparently done jobs like this in Cambodia before.

"If that doesn't work, please kill him immediately."

The miserable ticket inspector passed her again. He was in another world. A world she had learned to love. A world in which you were not pulled out of your house in the middle of the night, to be butchered, because you allegedly worked for the CIA. For a moment, she was back in the rice paddy behind her farm. The feeling of displacement was so intense, she was sure she was able to count the clouds above her family home if she only looked up. She could almost taste *prahok*, the pungent, fermented fish paste, which her mother prepared every day, the best *prahok* in the village. Then the Khmer Rouge, the Red Khmer, had come and killed everyone who had worked for the CIA. Only after she had lived in Germany for some years, had Dani learned what the CIA was.

She was flustered and tried to find the right word to continue the conversation.

"I mean, that's what I hired you for."

"Yes, you did," he answered.

She had no idea what else to tell a contract killer, an assassin. There was nothing to say.

"Be sure to get the right man."

"I have received your money and the information. I will only call you one more time. Please do not worry."

The man had a gentle, almost feminine voice. She knew that was meaningless of course. In the past week she had transferred some fifty thousand Euro, a large part of her inheritance, to the various accounts of this man. Harald would have understood. Or would he? He would have accepted it. But Dani had never dared to tell her husband about her plan. And now it was too late.

The man hung up. She stood motionless and stared at the silent phone for a long moment, unable to disconnect from what she'd just said and heard. Six thousand miles east of a small town in southern Germany, death would stalk through the rice paddies once again, in search of the red devil that had destroyed Dani Stricker's life. She almost forgot to get off in Käfertal.

"Last stop, all change," the miserable inspector shouted. She smiled at the man. He wouldn't beat her to death.

MAIER

Maier, private detective, forty-five years old, a hundred and ninety centimetres tall, perfectly trilingual, single, handlebar moustache, greying locks, currently cut almost short, leaned back in his economy seat, as much as he could, and smiled at the Thai stewardess who was coming his way. Maier had broad shoulders and green eyes and he looked a little lived in. Light boots, black cotton pants, a white shirt with too many pockets and one of those sleeveless vests with yet more pockets – he'd never quite managed to shake the fashion crimes of the war correspondent. At least he'd knocked the cigarettes on the head.

His father had turned up in Germany, from somewhere further east, sometime in the early Forties, despite the Nazis. He'd had green eyes and blond hair, and he had been an attractive man, so attractive that the German girls, who had lost their husbands at the front, fell in love with him. Even in Hitler's Germany, the Other seemed to have its attraction. At least as long as the Other called itself Maier and travelled with the correct, possibly fake papers.

He had survived the war in the arms of young women and had fled to England in the closing months before returning to post-war Germany. In the mid-Fifties he had washed up on Ruth Maier's doorstep in Leipzig, told her just that and hung around. But not for long. After eleven months, he'd disappeared and had never been heard of again.

Sometimes Maier asked himself how many siblings he might have. He wondered whether his father was still alive. And whether he might have worked for the Soviet secret service during the war? And whether he had worked for the Stasi later? Maier had never met his father. His love of women, his restlessness and his looks were the sole assets he had inherited from his father. That's what Ruth Maier had said.

His mother had been right of course. Maier did not enjoy staying put very much. After he'd finished his studies in Dresden, he had worked as an international correspondent in Poland, Czechoslovakia, Bulgaria and Yugoslavia. How he got the job without too much manoeuvring, he never found out. Perhaps his father had had something to do with it.

When East Germany had begun to collapse, Maier had fled across Hungary to West Germany and had eventually ended up in Hamburg. After the Berlin Wall had fallen, Maier had expected to see life with different eyes. Finally he'd be able to write what he wanted. He had been yearning for a new joy, an entirely new existence and he had almost found it. In the new Germany he had, after many years of working abroad, the right connections in the media and was soon hired by the news agency dpa.

But Maier rarely woke up in his small, impersonal apartment in Altona. He was on the road for the most part, on assignment – German holidaymakers from Mallorca to Vegas, German investors in Shanghai, German footballers in Yaoundé. There was always something to report some place. And Maier didn't feel at home anywhere. He'd fallen in love a few times, but somehow he'd never hung around.

The power of money in the new Germany first disorientated him; later it became an irritation. He still felt as if he'd been catapulted in slow motion from the fantastical dereliction of the old system into the depressing realities of the new one. Maier became ambivalent, despite the fact that, for the first time in his life, in the new Germany, he had the freedom to work. But life was too short to wash cars, watch TV or rent a video from the shop down the road. Maier chose the quickest, most radical way out of the German workaday life he could think of: he became a war correspondent.

After eight years down the front of the nasty little wars of the late twentieth century – from the Israeli occupation of the Palestinian Territories to the civil wars in the former Yugoslavia and the high-altitude conflict in Nepal – he'd filed his last story four years earlier in Cambodia, had flown home and, after some soul-searching and a little retraining, had joined the renowned Hamburg detective agency Sundermann. Since then, Maier had been entrusted with cases all over Asia. He had tracked down the killers of an Australian climber who'd apparently had a fatal accident in one of India's most remote valleys; negotiated the release from Bang Kwang Prison, Thailand's most notorious jail, of a man who had fallen foul of the country's draconian lèse-majesté law; and uncovered a paedophile ring amongst Singapore's judiciary, though this most disturbing case had been stopped in its tracks by higher powers before the detective could wrap up his mission. He thought of himself as a fish, passing in silence through a big sea, catching prey here and there, occasionally unable to take a bite out of it for fear of being swallowed whole by more powerful predators. He hardly missed the near-death adrenaline rush he had been addicted to in his last life.

And yet, in his new job, Maier was a pro. The years as a correspondent had left him with contacts in every major city in South and Southeast Asia. He was determined, obsessive even. He always went down to the wire to get his case solved. His work as a crisis journalist had left him hardened, and determined as the hounds of hell. Maier could walk over corpses to get to the heart of his cases. The truth, even if neither palatable nor publishable, was everything to him. Sundermann had not been disappointed by his new detective.

When he was off work, Maier was a directionless romantic
with desert sand in his shoes, a homeless stare and a modicum
of vanity in his eyes. That's how he imagined his father had
been.

"A Vodka Orange, please."

The stewardess's hand touched his arm as she placed the
plastic glass on the collapsible table in front of him. The slight,
barely noticeable gesture made him smile.

She was young, beautiful and, for a few bucks, she risked
her life day in and day out. Cambodian Air Travel, the only
airline that currently flew from Bangkok into Phnom Penh,
ran overworked and ancient Russian propeller planes, dying
wrecks long past retirement that barely managed to clear the
Cardamom Mountains. Planes that crashed over the remote and
heavily mined forests of Cambodia were rarely found. The pilots
were Russian, vets from Afghanistan, who'd once flown attack
helicopters against barely armed resistance fighters. In Cambodia
air space, the Russians' worst enemy was alcohol.

But a cursory glance at his fellow passengers suggested that
the almost forgotten kingdom he was heading for had changed
since Maier's last visit. Young, self-confident backpackers in
search of post-war adventures, a French tour group in search
of temples, and a few old men in search of women, or children,
or anything else that would be available in hell for a few dollars,
had replaced the soldiers, gangsters and correspondents who
alone dared to fly into Phnom Penh a few years earlier.

In those days, he had travelled by helicopter into a darker
place, where men had routinely barbecued the livers of their
enemies on open fires, sitting on the edges of paddy fields in
the shadows of solitary palm trees. They, men that Maier knew
well, had travelled and lived with, had wolfed down the organs
in the belief that they were ingesting their enemies' souls, as
their victims had watched, holding their eviscerated stomachs,
slowly bleeding to death. Just one of a myriad of reasons why

the dead could never rest and the country was beset by ghosts and demons, some of them his very own.

"Do you live in Phnom Penh, sir?" the young stewardess asked him, as she, with her best bit of barely trained elegance, which was breathtaking, placed a small carton, in which Maier could see an old-looking biscuit and an overripe banana, covered in cling film, next to his empty plastic glass.

"No, I am on holiday."

"Another drink perhaps?"

Maier hesitated for a second, and then opened his eyes wide enough to allow the girl a look inside his inside.

"Vodka orange?"

The stewardess's gaze dropped to the floor of the aisle before she rushed off.

A strange case. A case without a crime.

The detective let the one and only conversation he'd had with his client run though his head once more.

"I want you to visit my son and find out what he is up to. You have to understand that Rolf is the black sheep of the Müller-Overbeck family," she had said without greeting or introduction. Her voice had been dead flat.

Mrs Müller-Overbeck, whose husband, a man who could trace his north-German ancestry back for several centuries and who had made his fortune with the first post-war coffee empire in the *Bundesrepublik*, had shot him a nervous, imperious glance. Ice cold and in her mid-sixties. Just like her gigantic villa in Blankenese, built by some Nazi before the war. With a haircut that could have dried out an igloo, silver, stiff and expensive, the woman had simply looked ridiculously affluent. What the rich thought of as low key. The skirt, fashionable and a touch too tight, and the blouse, uniquely ruffled, and finally the many thin gold bracelets dangling from her pale right wrist, almost loud like trophies, had not helped. Yet his client had not projected properly. There'd been something unscripted in her performance, which Maier had supposed to be the reason for his presence in the Müller-Overbeck universe. She'd been agitated. It was hard to be ice-cold and agitated at the same time. How did the Americans say? It was lonely at the top. Life was a lottery. Maier had instinctively understood that this woman's expectations of service were in the rapacious to unreasonable bracket.

"You know the country?"

"I am the expert for Asia at Sundermann's. And I worked in Cambodia as a war correspondent for dpa."

Mrs Müller-Overbeck had winced. "There is war over there? Rolf is caught up in a war? I thought he ran some kind of business for tourists there?"

"The war finished in 1998. The country is currently being rebuilt."

Listening had not been one of the strengths of Hamburg's coffee queen. Another reason for Maier to say as little as possible.

"I do not understand why he wanted to go there. To a country at war. I can remember the post-war years in Germany all too well. I don't understand why he would want to go and look at the suffering of others. But Rolf has always been difficult. An A in English and an F in Maths, everything had to be extreme... Of course the family is hoping that he will come back and take over the reins."

She hadn't offered Maier a drink. Not even a promotional gift, a politically correct cup from Nicaragua perhaps. He pondered whether she ever drank coffee. She had seemed a woman who had never done anything that involved the acceleration of the inevitable ageing process.

"You will find him and watch him. I am paying your usual rate for two weeks. Then you will call me. And I will, on the basis of your meticulously detailed and inclusive report, which you will have sent me by email, prior to our call of course, decide whether you will be recalled to Germany or whether I will make further payments so that you may make additional enquiries."

Mrs Müller-Overbeck had smelled of money and avarice, but not of coffee. It looked as if Maier would become the babysitter to Hamburg's rich heirs. There had been moments when he had wished the Wall back. In his thoughts he had cursed Sundermann, his boss.

"Mr Maier, my expectations are very high and if I get the impression that you are unable or unwilling to fulfil them, then I will mention your agency to my friend, Dr. Roth, who sits on the city council."

His eyes tuned to truthful and trustworthy, Maier had nodded in agreement, and had let Mrs Müller-Overbeck work on him, her scrawny, pale and lonely hands covered in blue varicose veins, fragile as thin glass, held together by gold, coming up and down in front of him to emphasise the message.

"If my son is involved in any illegal or dangerous business over there, then please have his business uncovered in such a way that he is immediately deported back to Germany."

"Mrs Müller-Overbeck, that kind of action can be very dangerous in Cambodia."

The coffee queen had reacted with irritation. "That's why I am not sending a relative. That's why you are going. I expect results, solutions, not doubts. I want to see my son where he belongs."

"I can't force your son to come back home."

"Tell him he is disinherited if he won't budge. No, do not tell him anything. Just report to me. And please be discreet. Rolf is my only son. You never know, in these countries, so far away..."

Maier had only then realised that Mrs Müller-Overbeck was crying. The tears would surely turn to ice in seconds. She'd patted her sunken cheeks with a silk handkerchief.

"Preliminary investigations have told us that your son is a business partner in a small dive shop in a beach resort. He appears to be reasonably successful at what he is doing."

Mrs Müller-Overbeck had abandoned all efforts to save her face and blurted in despair and with considerable impatience, "I could have told you that myself. I want to know with what kind of people he is doing business with, whether he has a woman, what kind of friends he has. I want to know everything about his life over there. I want to know why he is there and not here. And then I want him back."

"You don't need a private detective to find that out. Why don't you just fly over there and visit him?"

"Don't be impertinent. You are being well paid, so ask your questions in Asia, not here. Goodbye, Maier. Please remember every now and then that your agency's licences are granted by the city of Hamburg. That will keep you up to speed."

"This is co-pilot Andropov speaking. Please return your seats to upright position. We are about to land at Phnom Penh International Airport. The temperature in Phnom Penh is thirty-three degrees, local time is 6.30. We hope you enjoyed flying Cambodian Air Travel. Look forward to welcoming you on our flights again soon. On behalf of captain and the crew, have a pleasant stay in Cambodia. Hope to see you 'gain soon."

The old good-bye rap by the deputy captain was barely understandable. The stewardess passed his row, wearing her most professional smile. There was no way to get through now. Maier sighed inwardly and turned to the window.

Cambodia was down there, a small, insignificant country, in which the history of the twentieth century had played out as if trapped in the laboratory of a demented professor.

French colony, independence in 1953, a few years of happily corrupt growth and peace under King Sihanouk, followed by five years of war with CIA coups, Kissinger realpolitik, US bombs, a few hundred thousand dead and millions of refugees – the most intense bombing campaign in the history of conflict was the opening act for the communist revolution of Pol Pot and the Khmer Rouge, that managed to kill off a quarter of the country's population in less than four short years. The genocide was choked off by the Vietnamese, unwelcome liberators, and almost two decades of civil war followed. Finally, UNTAC, the United Nations Transitional Authority of Cambodia, had shown up, organised elections of sorts and had then fled the burnt out, tired country as quickly as possible. The last Khmer Rouge fighters had thrown in their blood-soaked towels in 1997 and joined the county's government troops. Maier had stood right next to them. It had been a painful process.

Since then, Cambodia had known peace – of sorts.

The women were beautiful. It had always been like that, if you were to believe the silent stone reliefs of countless *apsaras*, the heavenly dancers of the Angkor Empire that graced thousand-year-old temple walls in the west of the country. The highly paid UN soldiers had noticed the sensuousness of the women too and had promptly introduced AIDS, which now provided the only international headlines of this otherwise forgotten Buddhist kingdom – a kingdom that had ruled over much of Southeast Asia eight hundred years ago. Past, present and future, it was all the same, every child in Cambodia knew that. Maier was looking forward to it. All of it.

The plane made a wide curve and barely straightened for its landing approach, descending now with the coordination of an uncertain drunk towards the runway. The sky was gun-metal grey. Dark, heavy clouds hung low to the east of the city over the Tonlé Sap Lake. The country below looked dusty and abandoned. Here and there Maier spotted a swamp in this semi-arid desert, an old rubbish-filled fish pond or a clogged-up irrigation canal. Dots of sick colour spilled on a blank, diseased landscape.

The aircraft abruptly lost altitude. Glittering temple roofs amidst the grey metal sheds of the poor that spread like a cancer around the airport, shot past. Beyond the partially collapsed perimeter fence, children dressed in rags raced across unpaved roads or dug their way through gigantic piles of refuse. The Wild East. This didn't look like Prague or Krakow.

The Cambodian Air Travel flight began to shake like a dying bird and Maier could not help but overhear one of the passengers in the seats behind him, a dour but voluptuous Austrian woman. What was he thinking?

"Gerhard, are we crashing? Will we die, Gerhard?"

Maier was just able to spot a few skinny cows grazing peacefully on the edge of the runway. Then they were down.

Welcome to Cambodia.

THE PEARL OF ASIA

"Vodka Orange, please."

The Foreign Correspondents Club, the FCC, was Maier's first port of call in Phnom Penh. As the sun set, Maier sat on the front terrace on the first floor of the handsome French colonial-era corner building and watched the action along Sisowath Quay, the wide road that ran along the banks of the Tonlé Sap River. Since his last visit three years earlier, things had changed. Some of the roads in town had been resurfaced and in the daytime, the city was safe. Amnesties and disarmament programs run by the government and international aid organizations had wrestled the guns from the hands of the kids.

Sisowath Quay woke up in the late afternoon and made a half-heartedly attempt to resurrect the flair of the Fifties, when the Cambodian capital had been known as the Pearl of the East. Half the establishments along the river road were called something like L'Indochine, Pastis was served on the sidewalks and the cute young waitresses in their figure-hugging uniforms had learned to say *bonjour*. The bistros, bars and restaurants did brisk business with the tourists who had, looking for temples, somehow got lost and ended up in the city. A few galleries had opened, offering huge and garish oil paintings of Angkor Wat to less discerning visitors. Too loud for the waiting room at Mrs Müller-Overbeck's dentist back in Blankenese, but just right for the current batch of visitors.

And the anarchy of the recent past remained visible. Small groups of cripples, most of them men, victims of a few of the millions of landmines that had been buried across the country, waiting to blow someone's, anyone's foot off, were gathering on the footpaths. Those with crutches limped up and down the broken pavement, carrying hawkers' trays filled with photocopied books about genocide, torture and the terrible human cost of land mines.

"Only two dollar" was the call that followed tourists brave enough to walk as night fell. Most of the unfortunates merely followed the wealthy visitors with their dead eyes, tried to sell drugs or simply begged for something, anything to get them through the night. To survive in this country could be called fortunate – or not. Those who no longer had eyes were guided in mad circles by orphaned children as they played sad songs on the *srang*, a small, lamenting fiddle whose body was tied off with the skin of a cobra. Emaciated, dried up cyclo-drivers moved their pedal-powered rickshaws along the quay in slow motion as if in funeral processions, while the motorised transport rolled like a dirty wave around them. Thousands of small mopeds, driven by *motodops*, provided the only public transport. Huge four-wheel-drives that had, for the most part, originated with the many NGOs in town and were now driven by heavily armed young thugs, the children of the corrupt upper classes, of government cronies and the upper echelons of the military, or Toyotas smuggled in from Thailand, with the steering wheel on the wrong side – you drove on the right in Cambodia, on the left in neighbouring Thailand and any which way you preferred on Sisowath Quay after dark – rarely displayed number plates. Some of the drivers were too young to look above the steering wheel. The countless bars on the side streets branching off from the river were filled with young women in tight clothes. For a few dollars you could take any one of them back to your hotel.

Directly above the steep banks of the river, the municipal authorities had built a wide promenade where the inhabitants of Cambodia's capital could enjoy the fresh breeze while the tourists could get excited about photographing the resident elephant. The US dollar was still the main currency in circulation, if the price list on the FCC's was anything to go by. The riel, the country's currency, wasn't worth much. Only the poor used it.

Maier found himself getting depressed. Here on Sisowath Quay, as the sun sunk into the slow moving, broad river, dotted with small fishing barges, a shoot-out before dinner was wholly imaginable, just as it had been four years earlier. Some change.

"Hey Maier, long time no see, mate. You're missing the boom."

Carissa Stevenson had once been the best and most attractive foreign journalist in Phnom Penh. After UNTAC had packed up its tanks, the media types had left and the country had slipped from the international front pages, Carissa had stayed on. She had stayed, after Hort had died and Maier had said goodbye to his old life. Now, as he got up and put his arms around his former colleague and sometime partner, he noticed that the four years in the sun of a country the world had forgotten had given her a positively golden bloom. Carissa radiated life force.

"Hey Carissa, you look great, better than anyone I've seen lately. The heroin must be getting better in these parts."

"Well, it's getting cheaper all the time, Maier."

The woman from Nelson, New Zealand broke into a slightly lop-sided and gorgeous smile. Rings around her fingers and bags under her dark eyes, lined with kohl. Dressed all in red. The skirt was tight and short. The long frizzled hair was white. White!

Maier remembered Carissa as ash blond.

"I don't suppose you've come to Phnom Penh for a holiday? And you're not here for me either. And there's no big story to be scooped. Apart from the daily rapes and murders, rampaging elephants and the occasional drug overdose by some third-tier member of the European aristocracy, it's pretty quiet. The good old and wild times, when Cambodia could shock the world are long gone. Hollywood's coming in the shape of Angelina Jolie soon. I don't suppose you have become a reporter for the stars? So what are you doing here?"

"I haven't worked as a journo for years, Carissa. I'm a private detective now. And I'm here on business."

Carissa laughed drily and, with a languid, studied gesture, waved for service. The waiter, at the far end of the teak top bar, nodded. It was as it had always been. Everyone knew what Carissa wanted. For a moment Maier remembered the exciting weeks in Phnom Penh – nights on the terrace of her colonial-era villa, crushed by sex, amphetamines, alcohol and marihuana, as gunfire rattled through the darkness around them. Life had been uncomplicated then. You just had to react to whatever had been going on.

The trips up-country were just as vivid in his memory. He'd often travelled with soldiers loyal to Hun Sen, the country's new leader, a young and ruthless ex-Khmer Rouge who had gone over to the Vietnamese, had helped liberate the country from the madness of stone-age communism and had since reigned with a single eye and an iron fist, most recently in the name of democracy. The soldiers had gone out to hunt Khmer Rouge. Looking danger in the eye had become habitual, like smoking, and had given Maier the illusion of eternal life. Somehow he'd lost that later. On the day the bomb with his name on it had killed Hort, it had disappeared altogether. Now, as he looked at his old partner, he could see his past in her familiar, so-familiar face clearly.

"I don't fucking believe it. A private detective? I'll call you Holmes from now on."

"There are better private detectives."

He gave her his card.

"Marlowe is probably more appropriate."

Carissa expelled a short, mocking laugh. She had lost none of her charm, or cynicism. She smelled good too. She leant dangerously close to Maier and for a second he turned his eyes away from the street and fell into hers, like a fever.

"And how can I be of assistance to solve the great detective's case?" she whispered with the broadest Kiwi accent he'd heard in years.

"I am not sure I can let you in on the confidential aspects of this case," he replied just as softly.

Carissa pulled a face and began to search through her handbag, until she'd found a half-smoked joint.

"You won't convince me with that. Is Cambodia the only country left in the world where smoking weed is still legal?"

"No longer, at least not on paper. The Americans put the heat on and parliament has passed the relevant laws. But what does that mean here? There are three restaurants in town that have happy pizza on their menu. One slice is enough to take you straight back to the good old UNTAC days. You can even choose, appropriately for the consumer age – happy, very happy and extremely happy. I've just covered it for *High Times.*"

"Shame, that's not why I came back. But it's great to see you."

Carissa looked at him impatiently and passed the joint.

"So tell me what brought you back to Phnom Penh. I'll promise not to publish a word without your permission."

"I am looking for a young man who runs a scuba diving business in Kep. You know, the beach place near the Vietnamese border."

"Yeah, I fucking know the place. We had sex in an old ruined church there once, remember? A pigeon shat on your arse."

Maier did remember.

"There's only one dive place. It can only be Rolf or Pete. Rolf's German, Pete's a Brit. The outfit is called Pirate Divers or something original like that. Pete's in town at the moment. Those two aren't hard to find."

Maier took a quick drag and passed the joint back to the journalist.

"Well, if Pete is here already, I would like to meet him. Where does he go at night?"

"The English guy? But your case surely has to be about the German? Has he done anything wrong? I hope he's not a child molester, but I suppose he wouldn't have slept with an old lady like me if he went for the young ones."

"As far as I know, he is nothing of the sort. But I don't know much and that's why I am here."

"Is there a warrant out for him in Germany?"

"No. How long have you known Rolf Müller-Overbeck?"

Carissa grinned with only a modicum of embarrassment.

"Don't sound so formal, Maier. I picked Rolf up in the Heart of Darkness bar. On his first night in town. That was six months ago, in April, around New Year. You know, when everyone throws water and talc at each other and everyone gets wet. Rolf's the kind of guy who's straight in there, no hesitation. He poured a bucket of ice water over my head and I took my revenge. The Heart of Darkness is a pick-up joint."

"How did he seem to you?"

Carissa laughed, "Quite flexible for a bloke, especially for a German. Spontaneous, friendly and naïve – as far as Asia's concerned. He hadn't caught yellow fever yet. Then I was down in Kep in May to celebrate my birthday. I saw Rolf again that night and he still hadn't been infected. But that has, as far as I know, changed now. What do you want from him?"

"Confidential. But as far as I know, he has not committed a crime. Yellow fever?"

"Oh, you know, the unhealthy fixation on Cambodian women so many male foreigners acquire here. They think that Cambodian girls are the most beautiful females in the world, which has a lot to do with the fact that they don't talk back. As long as the money keeps rolling in. Once the boys become infected, I'm out of the race, completely. Naturally. I talk back."

"And the English guy?"

"...is kind of a smooth operator, a wide-boy as they'd say where he comes from. But the dive business seems to be going good since Rolf got in as a partner. He invested and manages to get German customers via their website. The dive industry's in its infancy here. Those two are real pioneers."

Maier was suddenly exhausted. The long flight and the short joint, the unfamiliar heat and the city air, saturated with petrol fumes, the anarchy on the street, and on top, his old lover –he liked to keep the word girlfriend locked up deep inside – it was simply great to be back in Cambodia and float in clouds of nostalgia. This case would be more fun than Mrs Müller-Overbeck had had in her entire life.

Carissa raised her glass, "So, Mr Private Detective, if you don't come home with me tonight, I'll do everything in my power to make your case more complicated."

INTO THE HEART OF DARKNESS

By 9 o'clock, the city burnt out. For a few short hours the daily struggle for survival of almost all the city's inhabitants ground to a halt. As soon the sun disappeared into the Tonlé Sap River, the shops closed and the pedestrians got off the river promenade. The opposite side of the slow-moving water had already fallen into silent, mosquito-sodden darkness. Perhaps the river was not to be trusted: after all it changed direction twice a year. Yes, Cambodia was a special place.

Even the one-legged entrepreneurs slowly faded from the sidewalks and soon only hardened *motodops*, pushing ketamine, brown sugar and girls, all at the same time if desired, cruised up and down Sisowath Quay. Homeless families, perhaps just in from the countryside looking for jobs in the construction industry, were camped in front of closing restaurants. These people had to share the concrete floor with cockroaches and rats, for as long as it took to find employment and a roof over their heads.

Maier sat on the back of Carissa's 250cc Yamaha dirt bike. The Kiwi journalist drove like the devil down Street 154 and didn't hesitate to take a cop's right of way on Norodom Boulevard.

"If you drive too slowly at night, you still get harassed by kids with guns."

Phnom Penh remained a wonderful, frightening backwater. If the Cambodian capital had been safer, investors would have built a sea of chrome-and-glass monstrosities. But there were enough buildings from the French colonial days and the optimistic post-independence era of the Fifties left standing to get a feeling for the city's history, even at sixty miles an hour.

The Khmer Rouge had laid siege to and finally taken Phnom Penh in April 1975. In the following weeks, the victorious revolutionaries emptied the city of its people. The entire population was driven into the countryside onto collectives to work as rice farmers. The stone-age communists were trying to stop US imperialism in particular and the entire capitalist system in general in its tracks. Overnight, schools, post offices, banks and telephone exchanges were made obsolete. Money no longer existed. The Pearl of Asia became a ghost town. For three years and eight months, the city stood empty. Only S21, a school turned prison camp, showed any sign of activity. Here, more than seventeen thousand people were interrogated and tortured, before being taken to the Choeung Ek, farmland fifteen kilometres outside the city, where they were beaten to death with sticks and thrown into shallow graves. The Khmer Rouge kept just a few government ministries open and a handful of friendly countries including China, Cuba and Yugoslavia continued to maintain embassies. Apart from a handful flights to Beijing every week, Cambodia was virtually cut off from the rest of the world. As a nation amongst nations, it ceased to exist.

The forced exodus of the Seventies and the lack of investment in subsequent decades saved the city's character from demolition. As neighbouring Bangkok grew into a *Bladerunner*-like cityscape, Phnom Penh remained provincial, because much of Cambodia's urban population had been butchered in the Killing Fields and many of the capital's current inhabitants were really landless farmers who'd drifted into town since the end of the war in search of work.

The side streets were deserted. After dark, dogs, cats and rats, all about the same size, ruled the garbage dumps, which

spread across almost every street corner. Here and there, fairy
lights glimmered in the darkness, beacons of hope and all its
opposites to guide the night people towards countless massage
brothels which could be found in the small alleys off the main
strips. The red light was Phnom Penh's only vital sign at night.
The best party going was at the Heart, as the *motodops* called
the city's most popular bar without a great deal of affection.

"How d'you want me to introduce you to Pete?"

"As your victim. And as a potential business victim. You can
tell him that I am on the way to Kep and that I am planning
to invest there."

On Rue Pasteur, close to the nightclub, a small traffic jam
clogged the road. Rich kids, the sons of the families who
plundered the country, were trying to park their king-sized SUVs
with horns blaring, while mouthing off to their compatriots. It
appeared to be a fairly well-established and reasonably safe ritual
– the children of the privileged were all surrounded by their
personal teams of bodyguards. The street was in a permanent
state of détente, yet just a few small steps short of apocalypse.
With these people around, there would be occasional fuck-ups.

A food stall was mobbed by prostitutes – taxi girls. The
young Khmer seemed to eat all day long – perhaps a reaction
to periodic famines, which had many villages in its grip,
even today. Ever since the Khmer Rouge had taken over the
government and had begun to beat all educated Cambodians
to death, there'd not been enough food to go around. Some
Khmer had not had enough to eat for twenty-five years.

The music in the Heart of Darkness was loud. The bar was
packed three deep. A small laser, the first in Phnom Penh,
swished like a searchlight across the crowded dance floor to
the sounds of Kylie Minogue's "Can't get you out of my head"
– the vaguely futuristic dazzle caused a slight culture shock.
The Heart was a different world. Backpackers, worn out, sleazy
ex-pats – leftovers from the UNTAC years – and young, rich

local thugs gyrated in front of the massive bass bins. Everyone danced in his or her own personal hedonistic movie. Taxi girls threw *Ya-ba* pills, cheap methamphetamines from Thailand, into each others' mouths. Bowls of marihuana graced the long bar. The smoke of a hundred joints hung above the cashiers like a storm cloud.

The Heart was a Cambodian institution, a collection point for all those who couldn't sleep at night and had money to burn.

Carissa made her way towards the bar. Maier followed her through the dense throng, her white head guiding him like a torch. The pool table was run by shredders, young and beautiful taxi girls who played the tourists for their wallets. On the wall above the table, a faded photograph of Tony Poe, a CIA operative who'd made his name collecting the heads and ears of his communist enemies during the Secret War in Laos in the Sixties, faced onto the dance floor. Maier had heard the stories from UN soldiers. Poe had been so awful, he'd eventually become the template for Marlon Brando's Colonel Kurtz in *Apocalypse Now*. Maier smiled to himself. That was how small and post-modern the world had become. The Heart of Darkness was probably the best-known watering hole in Southeast Asia.

But you had to take care in here. The squat Khmer bouncer who was in charge of bets at the pool table was not the only man who carried his gun more or less openly in his belt. Maier was keen to avoid trouble. After all, he'd only landed a few hours ago.

"Shit, it is loud in here."

"You're getting old," Carissa laughed over her shoulder and passed him an ice cold can of Angkor Beer.

Maier didn't like beer. Nor did he like *Ya-ba* and disco music. *Ya-ba* meant mad medicine. Just the right kind of drug for Phnom Penh.

"Holidays in Cambodia" by the Dead Kennedys blasted from the speakers. Maier could at least remember this one. Good sounds to kick back to and watch the dance on the volcano. And what a dance it was. Jello Biafra screamed "Pol Pot, Pol Pot, Pol Pot," and the girls, who'd probably never heard of the man who'd killed their mothers and fathers, uncles and aunts, gobbled more pills as the sweat of three hundred drunks dripped from the ceiling onto the dance floor.

By the pool table, a life-size sandstone bust of Jayavarman VII, the greatest of the ancient Angkor kings, stood, softly lit, in an alcove. The thousand year-old god-king sucked up the chaotic scene in the room with empty eyes. Maier sympathised. In the Heart, he felt as old as a Khmer god-king. An even older French man, his shirt open to his belt buckle, had climbed the bar with two girls and waved at the crowd, a bottle of red wine spilling from his right hand. The hair on his head and chest stood in all directions and he looked like an electrified dancing bear. Perhaps he'd once been a butcher or owned a tanning studio in the *banlieu*. And one day that had suddenly felt like no longer enough.

Maier understood the man, though he had no desire to swap places. In the clouds of marihuana smoke behind the pool table, one of the young shredders began to open the trouser belt of a helpless, drunken and equally young tourist. Maier had just read in the *Phnom Penh Post* that the staff of the US Embassy was banned – by the US government – from entering the Heart. He had to laugh. Had this decision been made for security reasons or out of prudish concern for America's brightest?

"The English guy is already here, at a table behind the bar. And he's with bad company."

"With some of these nouveau riche thugs?"

Carissa leaned heavily into Maier and tried to make herself understood above the din of the music. "No, with real gangsters. People who don't belong in here."

Maier shrugged and pulled a face. "So what are we waiting for? Introduce me."

"Hey Pete."

"Wow, Carissa, babe, you look stunning, as always. May I introduce to you, gentlemen, Phnom Penh's classiest import from New Zealand."

Maier immediately saw that all the chairs were occupied by problems. The skinny Brit with the bright red hair and the sunken cheeks, a tough little pirate, had jumped up and embraced Carissa. Maier guessed him in his mid-thirties. Perhaps he was from Essex or some shitty London suburb, where he had probably burnt all his bridges. The silver chain around his wrist was heavy enough to sink a water buffalo. He wore a Manchester United shirt, with the collar up, and moved in a cloud of cheapish deodorant. He counteracted this with a strong-smelling Ara, the cigarette of choice for taxi girls and *motodops*, stuck in his nicotine-stained fingers. Two full packs and three mobile phones lay on the table in front of him. So this was the business partner of Rolf Müller-Overbeck: the wide-boy from the mean streets of Britain. Not completely unlikeable, but definitely not trustworthy.

The other two men at the table, both Khmer, were of a different ilk – one was young, the other old, though they came from the same dark place. They were smoking Marlboros and looked at Carissa as if she were a piece of meat. These days, Maier did not encounter men like these very often. There weren't that many. Both of them had been defined and moulded by war. They were men who killed and thought nothing of it.

Maier noticed that his presence had been registered. He could almost physically feel being observed and judged. Was he a potential danger or an opportunity to further their interests? What was the English guy doing with guys like this in a cosmopolitan filling station on a Saturday night?

The older man was in his mid-sixties. He had glued his short hair to his square, box-shaped head with gel. His neck was nonexistent. He wore a black polo shirt and looked too casual in a grey pair of polyester slacks. Like a toad on a golf course. This man had worn a uniform for most of his life.

The youngster next to him was his son, mid-twenties, wide hip-hop jeans, a Scorpions T-shirt, and a baseball cap, worn back to front on his equally square head, his thick, hairless arms defaced by backstreet tattoos. The boy had been born and had grown up during the civil war, a stark but no less assuring contrast to his formerly revolutionary father.

Luckily, all the chairs were taken. It was better to stand, around people like this.

Carissa exchanged kisses with Pete. "My old friend Maier is on the way to Kep, guys. He wants to poke around down there, see if there's anything worth investing in."

Pete's handshake was hard and dry. His dark eyes sparkled frivolously in his sunken face, which seemed deathly pale, despite a deep suntan. Pete looked like a guy who had nothing to lose and loved playing for huge stakes. Maier thought him largely pain-free.

"Maier, mate. Come and visit. An old friend of Carissa's is always welcome. And my partner is a Kraut too, just like you. At least you look like a Kraut."

Pete winked at him as if they were secret co-conspirators and whispered in a hoarse tone, "Kep was made for people like us. Nice beach town, built by the French, who are long gone, thank fuck. It's a bit shambolic down there, but things are getting better. Haven't you heard? Cambodia's booming. Now's a great time to get your investments in, mate."

The old man had got up. Pete threw him a few clunky chunks of Khmer. The son had also stood up, showing off the pistol in the belt of his low-slung ghetto pants. The older man bowed slightly.

"My name is Tep. I am number one in Kep. My friends call me Tep."

Maier couldn't imagine that this man had friends. The handshake was soft and moist, like creeping death. Did number one expect a round of laughs? Maier extrapolated a little – the man had Khmer Rouge and genocide written all over his face. The old comrades from the politburo, those who had survived the vagaries of history, had become investors. The price of peace.

The younger man with the gun did not introduce himself, but that was OK.

For a long moment, Tep smiled silently at Maier. The sonic sins of a Britney Spears song hung suspended between the two men, creating a strange, trivial backdrop to the encounter. What was a man like that doing in a place like this? Tep should have died in the jungle a long time ago.

"I run a few businesses in Kep. I can help you if you need anything in Kep. Come to visit on my island. And bring your girlfriend."

The old man's English was simple and barely understandable. Carissa pulled at Maier's sleeve, as the detective tried to look as uninformed as possible.

"Beer?"

Pete had already ordered five cans of Angkor Beer and banged them on the table. Tep sat back down, a shadow of irritation shooting across his face, and turned to Carissa. The antipodean journalist was waiting for him.

"Aren't you a former Khmer Rouge general? And aren't you the guy who blew up the Hotel International in Sihanoukville? Perhaps you remember, a tourist from New Zealand died in that attack, General Tep?"

For a split second, the old man's eyes burst into flames. Pete laughed nervously, "Wow, Carissa, babe, Carissa, we aren't here to reheat old rumours, are we? It's great to see you, babe."

Pete, Maier decided, was capable of balancing a tray full of landmines, which was just as well in this place, at this moment.

A young Khmer with a skinhead, dressed in an immaculate white silk suit, dead drunk and sporting a slight similarity to the bust of the god-king, had pulled his gun at the next table. A flat-footed tourist had just stepped on his brand-new, imported Nikes. Enraged the young Khmer had spilt his beer onto a row of green pills he'd lined up on the table in front of him, which he now tried to rescue from the ash-sodden slop directly into his mouth. The hapless tourist had already disappeared into the throng.

There'll be trouble in a minute, was the only thing that came to Maier's mind.

The bald playboy swallowed his last pills and got up to scan the crowd for a likely scapegoat who was going to pay, one way or another, for someone else's clumsiness. Someone would have to pay. With a theatrical gesture he whipped his gun from his belt and waved it around the room.

Sometimes things happened quickly. The skinhead climbed onto his chair and began to scream hysterically. Tep nodded to his son and turned to Maier, "Don't make any problems in Kep. Investors are welcome, snoops and stupid people are not. You see."

The first shot, the one to drive up the courage, went straight into the ceiling. The Heart stopped in its tracks. The DJ cut the music. The house-lights flashed on, illuminating a few hundred twisted, strung-out faces in mid-flight. Carissa grabbed for Maier's shoulder and pulled him to the sticky ground. Pete had already vanished. Punters rushed for the exit. The old general made no effort to move. His son had got up and walked a few feet away from the table, behind the fashionable rebel who stood on his chair, turning round and around, levelling his gun more and more towards the surrounding tables. From the floor, Maier had a perfect view of the young man's next moves.

Pop, pop, pop

The tourists screamed in panic. The playboy skinhead was dead by the time he hit the table in front of Maier, which collapsed in a hail of bottles, cans and cigarette butts.

Tep's son had shot him in the back.

Blood, beer, pills and broken glass spread across the tiled floor. The dark red was striking on the immaculate white silk. That's how easy it was to die in Cambodia.

The boy helped his father get up and made a path for the old man to get behind the bar.

"Follow them." Maier grabbed Carissa. "There must be another exit."

The muggy night air felt good after the two beers he shouldn't have drunk and a murder he hadn't wanted to witness. But outside there was only Cambodia. Shots rang down the street. Car windows were smashed. A small gang of *motodops* raced down Rue Pasteur, into the darkness. Girls screamed. Saturday night in Phnom Penh.

"So this is the most popular nightclub in the country," he said, more to himself than anyone around him.

The windows of the police station that stood, hidden behind a high wall, directly opposite the Heart, remained dark, despite the gunfire. No policeman who earned twenty dollars a month would get involved in this weekend orgy of adolescent violence unless there was money to be made. The situation would eventually bleed itself to death.

The general pulled his polo shirt straight and stared down the road, an expression of faint amusement on his flat features. The old man did not seem overly concerned about his son's state of mind, after the youngster had just killed a man in cold blood in front of several hundred witnesses.

"Thanks, Mr Tep, your son saved our lives."

The general looked at Maier for a moment, his eyes fixed and devoid of message.

"Kep is a quiet town. You can relax. Come and visit on my island. Ask local fishermen how to get to my villa on Koh Tonsay. Germans always welcome. And forget what happen here tonight."

His car pulled up.

Carissa had freed her 250 from the chaos of parked bikes in front of the Heart and Maier lost no time jumping on the back. A few seconds later, they crossed Norodom Boulevard.

"Fucking hell, Maier, as soon as you turn up, the bullets start flying. The article I'm going to write about this tomorrow will be sensational. Son of former KR general shoots son of oil executive in Cambodia's most cosmo nightclub. That'll make waves. You'll have to drink beer without me tomorrow."

"I don't like beer."

CHRISTMAS BAUBLES

Carissa's heavy breasts floated above Maier's equally heavy head, as seductive as the baubles that his mother had fastened to the Christmas tree forty years ago. In his drunken state this absurd association made passing sense, a few heartbeats before sunrise. Gram Parson's "Hickory Wind" was playing on Carissa's laptop. The song, which she'd always liked, took Maier back to his early assignments in Cambodia. Another job, another life. Dangerous thoughts percolated in his mind.

"The nights were never long enough with you."

"What nights, Carissa? Mostly we did it on the roof of your villa in the mornings, because we were working at night or because we were too wasted."

"Nothing much's changed with ten years having passed then."

"Probably not."

"Then I still turn you on?"

"Yes, you do."

"Everything's all right then."

Carissa rolled out from under the mosquito net and stretched in front of the open window of her apartment.

Life wasn't easy in the tropics, but a sunrise that you could never witness in Europe was about to point its first light fingers across the horizon, and get caught up in a decadent play of glittering sparks on the golden roof of a neighbouring temple before beginning to dance around Carissa's neck and shoulders. Maier groaned.

"Why didn't you stay?"

"For the same reason I will go to Kep alone."

Carissa turned towards Maier in the faint light. Now she looked like the Hindu goddess Kali, irresistible and merciless.

"Why?"

"Because I do not like to watch my best friends die. And this country finishes off even the best. Especially the best."

"So you expect problems on the coast?"

"I do not expect anything. I don't even really know why I am here yet. But I am sure that the son of my client is up to his neck in shit."

"I survived quite well without you for the past ten years, Maier. You're just commitment-shy."

"That I am. But that has nothing to do with me going to Kep alone."

"Then you love me a little bit and want to save me from the evil in this world?"

Maier sensed the sarcasm in her voice and replied as calmly as he could. "That I do and that is what I want to do."

"All men are the fucking same," she hissed, lifted the net and fell towards him.

Maier was alone in his dream, crossing the country on foot. Everything was on fire. The air was filled with the stench of burned flesh. The smell was so bad that he seemed to be permanently retching. The corpses of lynched monks, policemen who had been skinned alive, dismembered teachers, postal workers, rotten and hollowed out by maggots, of engineers who'd been half eaten by stray dogs, artists who'd been shot, judges who'd been beaten to death and decapitated students whose heads grinned from thousands of poles that had been rammed into the rice fields, piled up by the roadside and slowly slid into shallow graves that they themselves had dug earlier. Except for a few farmers with closed faces, virtually all the adults had been killed. General Tep and his horde of undernourished, angry humans, clad in black pyjamas and armed with blood-soaked machetes and sticks, marched with torches across the dying land and burnt one village after another to the ground.

Maier reached one of the villages, a typically dysfunctional cooperative on the verge of starvation, destined to fail, because no one had any tools and all the tool makers had been killed.

Tep had caught a woman who'd been grilling a field rat over a smouldering, badly smelling fire. Angkar, the mysterious and powerful organisation that fronted and obscured the communist party of Cambodia, had forbidden the private preparation and consumption of food. What Angkar said was law. And all those who opposed the laws or broke them, were taken away for re-education or training and were never seen again. Angkar could not be opposed.

There was good reason for this. Those who ate more than others were hardly exemplary communists and were not completely dedicated to help Kampuchea rise from the ashes of its conflicts. Those who ate in secret had other things to hide. With traitors in its midst, Kampuchea had no chance to fight the imperialist dogs. The enemy was without as well as within. And the CIA was everywhere.

Tep had no choice. He beat the woman to death with a club, split her head right open. As the woman's skull cracked, a small noise escaped, "Pfft," and the world lay in pieces.

The woman had two daughters. The girl in the rice field had watched her mother's murder and was running towards her father who was working under a hot sun with his second, younger daughter.

Tep, soaked in blood, the liver of the woman in his fist, followed the girl. He listened as the father shouted to his daughters to flee. When he finally reached the man, he tried to kill him with a hammer, the last hammer in the village. Tep hit the man in the face, again and again, but he would not die. Tep began to sweat. Maier stood next to Tep. He was sweating as much. He was witness. He couldn't stop a thing. The younger daughter stood a little to the side. She wore her hair short and like the rest of her insignificant family, wore black pyjamas. She was a product of Angkar and had grown up in a children's commune. She hardly knew her father. She was a child of Angkar.

"What is your name?" Tep smiled gently at the girl.

"My name is Kaley."

"Your father is an enemy of Angkar, Kaley. He works for the CIA."

The girl smiled and looked down at the broken man, who lay beside her, breathing in hard spasms. Tep handed the hammer to the girl. She might have been twelve years old. After she'd done as ordered, he shouted for his men to cut the man open and devour his liver.

The older girl had run and reached the edge of the forest beyond the paddy fields. Maier was also running. The teenager had left her younger sister behind, a daughter who had stayed next to the father she had just killed. Maier looked back across his shoulder.

Tep's men were queuing up to rob the little sister of her innocence, life and liver. Some had leathery wings and hovered above their victim like attack helicopters. *Flap-flap-flap-flap.*

A white spider, as tall as a house, appeared on the edge of the village. The men shrank back and made a tight circle around the girl and her dying father. The white spider moved slowly towards the circle. It did not hesitate, it just took its time. Maier ran on, his mind locked in terror. He no longer dared to turn. The fire rolled across the family, the village and the land. Maier's tears were not sufficient to put out the flames.

"Maier, are you crying in your sleep? Have you missed me that much or did you go soft back home in Deutschland?"

The morning breeze ran coolly across his sweat-soaked back and he crept deeper into the arms of the girl who'd become a woman. Carissa lifted her head, her white hair alive like the tufts of the Medusa.

SELF-DEFENCE

Pete's hair looked more fiercely red in bright, merciless daylight than it had in the damp flickers of the Cambodian night. It didn't look natural. The Englishman was just devouring his very English breakfast at the Pink Turtle, a pavement restaurant on Sisowath Quay – scrambled eggs, bacon, sausage, baked beans, toast and grilled tomatoes, all of it swimming in a half centimetre of fat.

Despite the previous evening's shooting and a royal hangover, the dive shop owner was in a good mood. A can of Angkor Beer sat sweating next to his delectable culinary choice.

"So this French guy walks into a bank the other day. The newest bank in town. Just opened. Air-con and all. And he walks up to the cashier and pulls out a shooter. There are three security guys in this bank, armed with pump actions. But they don't know what to do, they're so fucking surprised. A *barang* robbing a bank? How mad is that? But then the French geezer makes a mistake. As the cashier hands him a bag full of dollars, he puts his gun down on the counter. He just lost it for a sec. That's when they jump him. It's just too easy. Fucking prick's in jail, looking at twenty. Had gambling debts and they threatened to cut his girl's throat, only she was in on it. Great Scambodian fairy tale, so fucking typical."

Carissa ordered two coffees. Pete was on a roll.

"The dive business is going good, mate, it really is. We have great dive sites a half hour from the beach by long-tail boat.

Our customers get to see turtles and reef sharks, and there's plenty of titan trigger fish and large barracuda out there. As long as they don't overdo the dynamite. But I'm an optimist. We're searching for new dive spots all the time. There are hundreds of wrecks down there. And every year, more and more tourists come here. The first real beach resort only just opened. That's Tep's of course."

"And what else does Tep do?" Maier asked, his eyes recovering behind a pair of mirror shades.

Pete shrugged his narrow shoulders. "Yeah, I agree, mate, that didn't look too cool last night. It was well ugly. But luckily, this kind of thing doesn't happen too often. Almost never." The Englishman must have noticed a shadow of doubt cross Maier's face. "It was virtually self-defence."

Maier smiled. "Virtually."

Carissa laughed throatily. "The boy shot the bald guy in the back, Pete. Only in Cambodia is this called self-defence, and only if you know the right people and have sacks full of cash."

"You were always very principled, babe. You know exactly how things stand and fall here. In a small dump like Kep everyone knows and respects the boss. Otherwise you can't run a business or do anything. In Cambodia, you need good connections and a strong will to live."

Carissa, resigned boredom painted across her face, shrugged lazily.

"Always the same excuses. And you screw the taxi girls because you are really humane employers who believe in equal opportunities and don't want to see them exploited by Gap in the garment factories."

Pete stopped concentrating on his beans for a moment and winked at Maier. "Some get bitter as they get older. Others realise what they've missed. Life's a short and meaningless trip crammed with suffering and emptiness. I knew that when I was five years old. You don't need the Buddha to realise that. I think it's best to fish for as much money and pussy as possible. Come on, babe, Carissa, you're not so different."

The journalist rolled her eyes in silence and lit a crinkled joint she had fished out of her handbag. How quickly you got used to the small rituals of friends, Maier thought.

"Does Tep have enough connections upstairs in the government to suppress the incident in the Heart completely?"

"Yeah, he does. He's got a few old mates in government. The bald playboy in the Armani suit went mad on drugs and shot himself. There are witnesses who swear he took a bunch of pills before he pulled his gun, put it to his chest and pulled the trigger. Over and over, apparently. That ketamine is strong."

"Then I don't have a real story. Just a suicide on drugs won't do." Carissa complained.

The Englishman grinned at her.

"No you don't, unless you want a shed load of trouble."

"So what else does your influential friend do?"

"Tep's a businessman. He knows he can't be too greedy. He needs us foreigners as much as we need him. And unfortunately the country also needs can-do guys like Tep. Together we create employment opportunities. And not just for taxi girls, as Carissa likes to think."

"This doesn't really answer my question."

"You're a pretty curious type, Maier. Normally the Krauts are a bit more reticent."

Maier let the remark pass, almost.

"Before I invest anything here, I want to know how much disappears in the quicksand. And that didn't look too good last night. I have read good things about Kep, but I have also heard good things about Koh Samui in Thailand."

Pete relaxed, pushed his plate away, lit an Ara and laughed drily. "Maier. Don't be so German, so pessimistic. Come down to the coast and meet my partner, Rolf. He's just as much a true human being as you two, and still, he's happy. And anyway, people shoot each other on Samui all the time. Every month, people go awol and are found later, half-eaten and drifting in the Gulf. I know, cause most of them are countrymen of mine. That's how it is in these parts. That's why we're here and not at home."

Pete beamed at his breakfast companions.

"But in contrast to the overcrowded, unfriendly beaches in Thailand, Kep is stunningly beautiful and quiet, just totally fucking idyllic. We have a few hours of electricity a day, no traffic, no disco, no Internet. And on top of that, Kep has plenty of traces of this country's sad history, something you Germans usually go for, no?"

Maier had gotten tired of the Englishman's jokes and had withdrawn into himself. "Two world wars and one world cup" appeared to define Pete's idea of Germans. He was hardly unique. Southeast Asia was a favourite destination for the UK's piratical and lawless white trash underclass. But the little red-haired, wrinkled man had still not finished.

"Just one thing, mate, a friendly piece of advice. People who get too curious about how things work in Cambodia, people who ask too many questions, are in danger of giving the impression that they might not be around for the reasons they say they are. If Tep gets this impression of visitors, it can have really heavy consequences for them. It's better to let life roll along at its natural pace down there and to roll with it, then most questions will be answered anyway. I'm sure you understand me."

"I must be lucky then that I let life roll at its natural pace last night." Maier laughed.

Pete reached across the table and slapped Maier's shoulder like an old friend. "You're a fun guy to be around, Maier. That's why my advice comes flowing your way. Our community down there in Kep is so small that every newcomer is looked at, like under a magnifying glass. It's just a local reflex. We don't mean anything by it. And anyway, you come with the best of references."

Maier looked across at Carissa. Was this skinny little Englishman threatening him or was it all just talk? Maier did not want to fall in love with his old colleague again, but now he was worried and that was never a good sign. The detective rarely worried. Worries made life, this short and meaningless journey of suffering and emptiness, more complicated. The Buddha had been right about most things.

But Maier had no time to philosophise. The young waitress of the Pink Turtle appeared with a tray, loaded with three whiskeys, on the rocks.

Just like the freebooter he was, Pete had remembered the most important thing of all. "I know, Maier, you don't like drinking beer. I already noticed that. It makes you very likeable somehow. Let's drink Jack Daniels to the man who doesn't like beer! Cheers."

Maier did not like whiskey much either but he lifted his glass. He was on duty.

ON THE BEACH

Maier was the day's first drinker in the Last Filling Station. The ramshackle bar stood on the edge of a beach in a palm orchard, a few hundred metres west of what was left of Kep-sur-Mer. More than a hundred villas slowly crumbled into the brush along the coast towards the Vietnamese border. Kep was a ghost town about to be reconquered by the jungle. Even the Angkor Hotel, near the crab market, was in a pitiful condition, its pockmarked walls protected by downwardly mobile shards of sheet metal. Maier had taken a room right under the roof. During the night, the rain had roared all around him, loud enough to drown out the noise of the television, which, powered by a car battery, had run at top volume in what passed as a lobby until dawn. Just as well all good roads in the world led to a bar. And the Last Filling Station was special. It was the only bar in Kep, and in the mornings, it served the desperate.

"This town has seen better days."

"It has. But the impression of total collapse is misleading, buddy. Kep has had a demanding history and it ain't done yet."

The old American behind the counter gave a friendly nod and lit a joint. The moist and pungent smoke rolled through the heavy air towards Maier. The proprietor was a small, fat man with hairy, tattooed arms that stuck out of an old, sleeveless Bruce Springsteen T-shirt. Born in the USA, no doubt about it. His lumpy face, in which two beady eyes threatened to drown, descended to several ridges of double chins. His voice had crawled out of a Louisiana backwater and forgotten to dry off. The thumb on his right hand was missing. He was a character.

The establishment's décor perfectly reflected its owner's personality. In the Last Filling Station, the Vietnam War was celebrated like a nostalgic road trip. Behind the counter, the shelf crammed with mostly empty liquor bottles had been welded together from machine gun parts. A torn cloth of the Rolling Stones' tongue hung like a pirate flag from a wooden pole that had been lodged, with the help of a couple of CBU bomb cases, into the ground in the centre of the small square room. The ceiling fan squawked like a tired seagull and barely managed to turn the air in the bar. Around the fan, spent mortar shells and hand grenades hung suspended from the ceiling. *Willie Peter* canisters, once the receptacles for white phosphorus, which burned through skin like napalm, served as ashtrays.

It was too early to smoke and drink. Maier had only just started working.

"First time in Kep?"

"Yes."

"But not the first trip to Cambodia, right?"

The American had a good eye for people.

"No, I was here a few times between '93 and '97, came as a journalist."

The American's tiny eyes lit up.

"Is there anything to report from Kep that the world might be interested in?"

"No idea. I no longer work in the media business."

The man behind the counter shrugged.

"That's probably for the best. Folks who ask too many questions around here end up floating in the soup pretty damn soon."

"You've already asked me three questions, be careful." Maier laughed and offered the American his hand. The bar owner's thumbless paw was huge and badly scarred.

"Maier."

"Les. Les Snakearm Leroux."

"Really?"

"Really! My momma called me Lesley Leroux. And they called me Snakearm in Vietnam."

"Snakearm?"

"Because I could squeeze the life out of a python with one hand."

"No shit?"

"No shit. Made a heap of money in some dark places in Saigon, right up to the day we abandoned ship and honour. That was three questions, buddy. One more and I'll shoot you dead."

"Vodka Orange?"

"Bang."

The war vet was an instantly likeable guy. And the Last Filling Station was the perfect place to drink your troubles away on a lonely near-equatorial morning. Not that Maier had anything to be mournful about. Not yet. He was only just getting started on this case. Perhaps, in the absence of empathy or depression, he could drink his soul's soul.

"So what happened here? Was the town destroyed in the war?"

The American shook his head.

"Kep was the Saint Tropez of Cambodia. The French showed up in the late nineteenth century and started it off with a few hotels, churches and brothels between the jungle and the sea. In the Fifties, Kep became popular with Khmer high society who came down from Phnom Penh and built weekend villas. They had it all just the way they wanted it – waterskiing and cocktail parties, barbecues and rock'n'roll bands on the beach. But the good life ended with Sihanouk's departure. Rich folks boarded up their houses and stopped coming. The KR were here from '71 to '77 and they did kill quite a few locals, but there wasn't much fighting here. Then in '79, when the Nam invaded, the harvest didn't happen. People broke into the houses and stripped them, even chiselled the steel out of the walls. Whatever they got, they exchanged with the Vietnamese for rice. Hard times."

Les coughed thick clouds of smoke across the dark, scratched wood of the bar.

"But that was all a long time ago. Now we got three hotels in Kep and the first scuba diving outfit opened some while ago. At weekends it gets really crowded with locals who come for the crabs. The crabs are fucking delicious, you should try them. About a dollar a kilo. Otherwise, backpackers, weekenders from Phnom Penh, adventurers and lunatics. Which crowd d'you run with, Maier?"

A young Vietnamese woman with a closed face and short black hair that was trying to grow in several directions at once appeared silently in the door between the bar and kitchen and handed Maier his Vodka Orange. Les had his hands full with his joint.

"That's the fashion in Vietnam these days. The girls want to look like the guys in the boy bands."

Van Morrison's "Brown-Eyed Girl" poured from the speakers that hung amongst the ordnance from the ceiling. The wall facing the sea had been almost completely destroyed and replaced by thin wooden slats. The other walls, in which various calibres had left their marks, were covered with framed photographs of the American wars in Vietnam, Laos and Cambodia.

Les pointed at a faded image of a young man in jeans, sporting a huge moustache, posing in front of a helicopter. "I was a pilot. First I flew Hueys out of Danang for the Navy. Later I worked for Air America in Laos. Black Ops. Top Secret. This shot was taken in Vientiane. We flew weapons, troops and drugs for the CIA. Then, from '73 on, I was here, until the KR took over."

"You must have been on one of those last buses full of foreigners to leave Phnom Penh, which the Khmer Rouge accompanied to the Thai border?"

"No, wasn't there. Just prior to that, I evacuated employees from our embassy. I flew an overloaded Huey to one of our ships. After the last flight, we tipped the bird off the ship and into the sea, just like my colleagues did off Saigon. You can't imagine how that felt."

"So why did you come back?"

Les Snakearm Leroux looked around his bar as if he'd just entered it for the very first time.

"I ain't a historian or anything. But I saw a lot in the war. I saw a lot of war. Not all of us were junkies, at least not all of the time. I knew even then that politics was behind the rise of the KR. We ran an awesome air campaign against suspected Vietnamese positions inside Laos and Cambodia. We killed thousands of civilians and carpet-bombed their fields. How is a Khmer farmer supposed to understand that a plane drops from the sky and burns his village to the fucking ground? Just think, one payload dropped from a B-52 bomber destroyed everything over a three square kilometre area. Everything. Nothing's left after that. We atomised people. We vaporised them. Hundreds of thousands died. And that was before the KR ever took over."

Les lit the next joint. Maier was sure that the pilot had shared his story, his trauma, his life, with anyone who came through his door with open ears. It was a good story.

"Anyway, buddy, the war years were my best. We lived from day to day, hour to hour. We drank through the nights and learned Vietnamese, Lao, Thai and Khmer from the taxi girls. Many of us also consumed industrial quantities of opium, heroin, LSD, amphetamines and marihuana, uppers and downers. And in the morning we were back up in the mountains to pick something up or drop something off, to set fire to some village, to carry on killing. As I said, my best years."

A bout of coughing interrupted his nostalgia. "When it was all over, I had no desire to go back home. The New Orleans that I'd left more than ten years earlier no longer existed. That's how it goes in war, I guess. It changes the perspective, and stands everything that you learn about life on its damn head. Back home everything was too much and too little at the same time. And every fucking hippy I passed in the street shouted abuse at me. I had to ask myself whether I qualified as a war criminal or not. How much of your responsibility can you shift to others? I had changed into something else in the East. I was burnt out from being burnt out. I couldn't face queuing up in a supermarket. Never again."

Maier nodded and lifted his glass.

"I would like another Vodka Orange."

Les seemed to be adrift in reminiscences, and stood nervously fumbling with the napkins on his bar. Was there a signal or did the Vietnamese have the ears of a bat? Maier was not sure, but seconds later, he had a second glass in his hand and the young woman was already disappearing back into the kitchen.

"You know the rest. We never forgave the Vietnamese and that's why we supported the KR in the Eighties – embargo, famine, civil conflict – that's the American way of war. Until UNTAC turned up, with guys like you in the luggage."

The American laughed without malice.

Maier'd had enough history lessons and changed the subject.

"And how long have you been in Kep?"

Les looked into his eyes for a second and lowered his voice.

"Black op, buddy, you catch my drift. I may be an alcoholic, but I ain't stupid. You're no tourist and in a second you're gonna tell me that you've come here to buy land. And then you carry on asking questions."

Maier did not think too long about his answer. It was too early to make enemies in Kep.

"I am looking for a piece of land. I have heard that Kep will soon participate in the national economic boom."

"Soon." The old vet laughed. "Maier, if I stumble across a piece in the dark, I'll keep it warm for you. Ha-ha. You're all right, aren't you?"

"I am alright. And an old friend of Carissa Stevenson."

Les passed Maier the joint.

"If you'd told me that earlier... Carissa celebrated her last birthday in this shack, back in May. Carissa is my soul sister. As long as my joint is open, she's got credit."

A *barang* entered. Within a split second, the light in Les' eyes faded.

"Howdy, Maupai."

The new arrival pulled a sour face. He looked like a man who'd recently retired to a life of leisure and had not yet worked out what to do with free time at his disposal. He was about the same age as Les, in his mid-sixties, but he was a different type altogether. A man who'd probably spent his entire life in the same job and the same marriage. If such people could live here – the man was obviously not a tourist, he was wearing a worn but reasonably clean linen suit, a white shirt, the three top buttons undone – then Cambodia was on its way. But where?

Maupai had thick grey hair that fell in a lock that was too heavy for its own good across his forehead. A gold chain hung around his neck. A French bank director perhaps, used to the good life, who had aspirations to be a bit mid-career Belmondo or late-career Cassel. More like Belmondo with a season ticket for the opera.

"My wife is not well. And the doctors talk about the sea breeze."

"Your wife's not well, cause you're always in a foul mood and because you screw the local girls."

"A beer."

Les shrugged. The Vietnamese woman handed the man a can of Angkor. *My Country, My Beer*, it said on the can. He looked across at Maier, lit an Alain Delon, Cambodia's fanciest cigarette, and raised his can.

"Be careful if you are considering buying land in Kep, monsieur. Many of the documents of the old properties which you will be shown are fakes."

Maier tried his most respectable smile.

"Is real estate the only subject people talk about?"

The man nervously brushed his hair from his eyes and laughed defensively. "The only subject that is safe to speak with strangers about. Everything else our little community talks about is so evil, you will not want to know."

He put special emphasis into the evil, like a real estate salesman or a priest talking up an unspeakable product to keep consumers tied to their own shoddy wares.

"Maier."

The hand shake was slack and moist. His English was perfect, but for the pronunciation. His voice was full of pride he took in his own importance.

"Henri Maupai, from Paris. I was regional director of Credit Nationale, but I got out of the rat-race early. Life is too short for working only, *n'est-ce pas*?"

Maier grinned at the Frenchman. That's exactly what he looked like. Like a man who wanted to get something out of life, but had somehow missed the boat. Really a good-looking guy, but way too boxed in. Here, he could let go. Maier tried to imagine Madame Maupai.

"Well, you don't look like much of a backpacker, Monsieur Maupai."

"Ha," the man laughed drily. "This *Lonely Planet*, the *Guide de Routard*, they should be banned. The people who travel with a book like that, they leave their brains at home. The little bastards come and destroy everything. They fuck on the beach and upset the locals. They drive their bikes too fast and sleep in the old villas, so they are not paying anyone anything. They hardly bring any money into the country anyhow and they bargain for every riel, and if the room price in the guidebook is lower than offered, they have a fit. This generation is a weird one, incomprehensible. And just think, we put them into the world. We gave them life, everything."

His second swig finished the can and he waved at Les. The Vietnamese silently put another can on the bar. She smiled, but not at her customer. Maier didn't like the man much, but you couldn't fall in love with every-one.

"I have retired here with my wife. My children have left home. I grew up in a France that no longer exists. In my time, one might have bought a little holiday house or apartment in Provence, but these days, too many Arabs and Africans live there. They steal your car while you are sitting in it. The concept of the Grande Nation is dead, completely dead. There's a McDonalds, Burger King or kebab on every street corner. If the Arabs don't burn our cars, the Americans force their fast food down our throats."

The second can was empty.

"*Ca m'enerve*. Compared to that, the Khmer are just great. Here the communists killed everyone who could think, but at least the Cambodians have respect, and they smile when I ask them something."

Maier silently played with the bar mat and tried to look neutral.

"Maupai is our village racist. He doesn't enjoy life."

"You just enjoy life because you fuck your little Vietnamese and take drugs all day."

"You hit it on the head there, buddy." Les chuckled, trying to diffuse the Frenchman's aggression.

"Have another beer, Maupai, and enjoy the unique ambience of the Last Filling Station. Soon you're gonna die from misery."

"Enjoy, enjoy, you are just running away from something. One day Kep will be returned to its former glory and guys like you will be thrown out. Kep will bloom, I tell you. Just like it did fifty years ago. A little island of civilization in this tired country. Imagine if we had kept l'Indochine. There would be hospitals, schools, roads, electricity and good coffee."

Les sighed and turned to Maier. "People travel around half the world because they don't like their own country and then they complain about how things are done in their adopted home."

Maier was content everywhere. Maier never spent enough time anywhere to get bored. But the Frenchman was drunk and wouldn't let it go.

"That's all just talk. You know as well as I do, how mad and murderous the Khmer really are. How can one be happy in a country like Cambodge, a land with so much sorrow? Look at what happened to Monsieur Rolf. A pleasant countryman of yours by the way, Monsieur Maier. A young man from a good family, that much was immediately clear. He came with great ideas and ideals. He wanted to help. And look what happened. And then take a good long look in the mirror."

"One day I will bar you from the premises, Maupai, because you have a big mouth. You can go sit on the beach, converse with the dogs and get eaten by crabs."

The retired bank director laughed loudly, his bitterness gurgling in his throat like long suppressed bile. "By then there will be a bistro and a wine bar here and only the rats will visit you. Until that time, you need my money. See you tomorrow. Salut."

Maupai slammed a handful of dollar notes onto the bar and walked out into the sun. Les shrugged while the Vietnamese gathered up the money. ZZ Top played from the speakers overhead.

"Don't ask me about the young German straight away, otherwise I might really think you're a snoop, buddy."

Maier also paid. There was no sense in putting a man like Les under pressure during a first meeting. The conversation would continue another time.

"Nice to meet you, Les Leroux. I will be in the area for a while, so I will drop by again. Great bar."

"You alright, Maier, ain't you?"

"I am, yes."

"Then take care. And don't believe everything you hear. Kep is a small place. Everyone knows everyone else and everyone thinks they know everything there is to know about everyone else. Almost everything. It's wonderful, really."

KALEY

A sandy potholed track led from the Last Filling Station to the crab market. To the north of what passed for town, the densely forested Elephant Mountains rose into a gun-metal grey sky that had conspired with the jungle to fall down and bury everything. You always had to fear the worst in Cambodia. And usually it wasn't too far off the mark if you did.

Kep was no exception. The villas of the rich and gone stood on overgrown plots of land, demarcated by crumbling concrete fences and grandiose entrance gates. The side streets that branched off from the coast road had been claimed by tall grasses, and, following the rains, the former streets had turned into ponds and small streams, in which millions of black tadpoles flicked about, hoping to grow four legs before the water evaporated. Kep was an untapped archaeological dig of the very recent past, waiting to be rediscovered by twenty-first century history students. Cows grazed in the middle of traffic crossings. Twenty-year-old palm trees had replaced the street lamps and grew from the foundations of the old buildings. If nature had its way, all traces of human activities would disappear within a few years. No buildings, no streets, not even thoughts. Maier suddenly felt hopeful.

But Kep had not yet recovered. In 1994, a train had been attacked nearby. A number of Cambodians had been killed, while three foreigners had been kidnapped and taken into the mountains along the coast where they had later been executed.

Cambodia found it hard to rid itself of its old revolutionaries. Maier walked from property to property, aimlessly at first, in order to think, and to get the vodka and the joint out of his system. He hadn't smoked for a long time. In Germany it no longer suited his lifestyle. But here... he laughed at himself, anything was possible in Cambodia.

Maier took a closer look at some of the abandoned properties. Some of the buildings were occupied by penniless Khmer – most of these casual tenants had no belongings and simply strung a piece of tarpaulin between walls that remained standing, to find refuge from the rain. Feral-looking children grew up beneath the improvised plastic roofs. But for the squeal of a child or the squawk of a chicken, the silence amongst the buildings was complete. Lizards slid silently across hot stones. If not for these occasional signs of life, Maier thought, Kep might have been the perfect town to encounter a ghost. For the Khmer, ghosts were as real and commonplace as the monsoonal rains. And down here in the blinding humidity of an inebriated morning, it was easy to empathise with their superstitions.

The crab market, a long row of wooden sheds, which lingered under palm trees in front of a ruined colonial rest house, appeared abandoned. Young salesgirls dozed in their hammocks, dogs scratched themselves on the broken tarmac and the surf slashed hesitantly across the narrow, dirty beach. A few hysterical seagulls circled above heaps of rubbish by the shacks. Maier bought a bottle of water and sat in the shadow of a tall coconut palm. His mind replayed the Frenchman's drunken speech. What had happened to Müller-Overbeck?

The woman appeared silently, like a cat. Maier's eyes had fallen shut for just a second. Now they were open and the detective held his breath.

The famous, impenetrable smile of the Cambodians, the *sourir Khmer*, a phrase the French had coined a hundred years earlier, was shining down on him like a floodlight at the Millerntor-Stadion, and flushed over him like a hot, lazy wave. She was the most beautiful woman Maier had ever seen. Not quite perfect, in fact, not perfect at all. But breathtakingly, stunningly beautiful.

"Hello, Maier."

The detective was lost for words. That didn't happen very often. The woman was well informed.

"My name is Kaley."

She stood in front of him, stock-still, tall for a Khmer, wearing a colourful sarong with flower patterns and a black blouse. Her hair fell straight down to her hips, like a waterfall of black pearly drops cascading in the midday sunshine that just touched her face, fragmented by palm leaves overhead. She studied him.

Maier recalled old Cambodian ghost stories. Perhaps Kaley was a vision. Had someone slipped something into his vodka? The detective swore never to drink or smoke in the mornings again. Eastern promises.

Kaley was barefoot. Silver rings curled around her toes, the toenails painted in a garish red. Her hips were broad, perhaps she was a mother. The black blouse was buttoned up, her prominent breasts vibrated slightly underneath the worn cloth. Her neck was delicate and thin, fragile even. Maier guessed she was between thirty and forty. But he found it hard to guess. Perhaps she was two thousand years old. Maier pulled himself up and looked into her face with care. Through the pitch-black eyes of this woman, you could see all the way into the heart of the world. Or at least into the heart of this unhappy country. A risky business.

She put her hands together in the traditional greeting and slowly, ever so slowly, and with the utmost elegance, sat down, two metres away under the next palm tree, and stared at him. Directly, openly, vulnerable, invincible. Maier felt his balls contract. Some men would kill for a woman like this one.

"I am looking for my sister, Maier. Can you help me?"

Her English was pretty good. But Maier could hardly focus on what she said. He was completely captivated by what she looked like. A long red scar crossed her right cheek, which gave her a crude and mystical aura. A broad white tuft of hair cut across her forehead and across her face like a knife, parallel to the mark on her skin. Her extraordinary physical uniqueness reinforced his first impression: he was facing a formidable, exceptional being.

Maier had been around long enough to evolve from atheist to agnostic. The Khmer lived in a different world to the *barang*, a world in which ghosts were as real as a cup of tea. This enabled curious visitors to open doors in their heads through which they could peer into this other world, which was subject to different laws. Maier enjoyed looking. His ten years hopping from conflict to conflict had led him somewhere else. Borderline situations were always crowded with ghosts. Kaley was different from any other woman he had ever met. For the first time in his life, Maier felt fear in the presence of an unarmed, friendly woman. A strange, foreign feeling and one he relished. Mostly it was her black, so very black eyes. The expression in her eyes made him want to offer her some commitment, a promise, a finger, anything, even if it would bind them to the bitter end.

Her end, not his.

Maier felt callous for a second. Then he remembered to breathe slowly and enjoy life.

"How do you know my name, Kaley?"

"Les told me. Les my friend."

"Was your sister just here a moment ago?"

"No."

"When did you last see your sister?"

Her expression remained impassive. She just kept looking at him. He had the feeling that she was very close to him now and that she could sense something in him that he had no conscious knowledge of.

"When I am little girl. In our rice field. But now she is coming back to come and get me. I think that maybe you see her?"

Maier shook his head.

"What gave you that idea?"

"Les told me that you are good man with good heart."

"I am a man."

"I know." Maier began to sweat, sitting in the shade.

"I have to go."

"Where do you have to go, Kaley? Stay another moment." As soon as the words passed his lips, Maier knew he shouldn't have asked.

"Les said you are good man," she said stubbornly. But she stayed. And smiled at him. He'd be responsible for what was to come. He'd asked her to stay.

Maier knew she'd go with him. He only had to ask. And then she would never be able to sit in front of him as she did now. He remained silent. Her first question had been her last. You were only asked this question once in a lifetime, or at all. It was like a Grail. He offered her his water. She took a swig and handed him the bottle back. A few drops ran down her chin and fell onto her black cotton blouse where they turned into steam.

"I tell you a story. An old Khmer story that people tell in the village at night."

Maier nodded to her with encouragement.

"A long time ago, a rich woman live in Kep. Her name Kangaok Meas. She very cruel woman and treat her husband and her slaves very bad. Kangaok Meas have slave called Kaley. Kangaok Meas beat and curse Kaley every day. Even Kaley work in the field all day, she hardly have enough to eat. When Kangaok Meas find out Kaley is pregnant, she send her husband away to the harvest and make her work harder. On the day Kaley get her pains, Kangaok Meas beat the girl with a yoke and shout, 'Because you love your husband, you forget that you are my slave. I will kill you and your child.'

"The husband of Kangaok Meas felt sorry for Kaley but he scared of his wife. When she angry, she bite him, scratch him in his face and kick into his balls, so he almost fall sick. Soon Kangaok Meas died and was reborn the child. The people in the village hated the child. Not even Kaley like the child. Ten years pass and one day, Kaley tell her daughter to work. Now Kaley daughter work in the sugarcane field from morning to night time. Then she marry the man who is no good, always drunk. When the girl get pregnant, the husband beat her and she die with her child."

Somehow, Kaley took something like a bow in front of him as she rose and for a split second Maier could see into her blouse. Her breasts shifted with the rhythm of her sparse, elegant movements. Kaley moved so slowly that he could enjoy the eternal second. These were forbidden fruits. You did not look at the cleavage of a ghost, a goddess or a cursed being.

"Thank you, Maier."

Kaley departed as silently as she'd come. He was alone. More alone than he'd ever been in his entire life. In a sudden flash, helped along by her outlandish tale, the monotonous, lazy rush of the surf and the shrill squawking of the seagulls, he was acutely aware of the terrible transience of life's most wonderful moments. He sat in the shadow of the palm tree, as if paralysed, desperate to stop time.

A long while later, Maier shook his head. He'd made a promise to a vision, he knew that much. He smiled. Now he was in the story, in the case and on the case, now the action could begin. Now, he was sure, he had the case of a lifetime to work on.

And who had named her Kaley?

DOG LOVER

The policeman was in his mid-fifties. Maier was standing on the first floor of a dilapidated villa when he saw him approach on a small motorcycle. He was fat and every time he drove through a pothole, the rusty vehicle beneath him bounced around like a balloon. An old German Shepherd ran behind him.

The ruined villa stood on oddly angled concrete pillars, had round windows and a spiral staircase with aspirations that extended beyond the first floor. The building, which stood in the centre of a long-abandoned palm orchard, looked like an unlikely prop from a war movie.

The policeman, now stationary and sweating heavily, waved up to Maier. He took his cap off to wipe his broad forehead and, and, with these few gestures, he managed to convey the impression of an officer who'd not worked this hard in a long time. Maier jumped down the broken stairs and met the man halfway.

The handshake was moist, almost wet, like his eyes. The man sweated so hard that he seemed to cry permanently. He also chewed betel – periodically, he spat huge blood-red gobs of juice onto the floor. A well-oiled side-arm hung from his belt. Otherwise, this cop looked scruffy.

The dog had caught up and sniffed his way around Maier. Maier liked dogs and the policeman's companion quickly lost interest.

"Police dog. Very good dog."

The policeman patted the head of the exhausted animal. People in Cambodia rarely showed this much affection to their domestic animals. Maier got the impression that the cop and the dog were very close.

"*Soksabai.*"

"Do you want to buy this house?"

His English was not bad, nor was it very clear.

"I am just looking around."

"This property for sale. But you go quick. Prices go up every year. Fifty percent."

The officer of the law swayed back and forth in front of Maier and for a second it looked as if he was about to embrace the German detective. The two men stood, silently facing each other. The cop looked at Maier with crying eyes. He'd lost the plot.

"Where you from?" he managed after a while.

"From Germany."

"Germany is rich country."

It sounded like "I want to fuck you". Maier let the statement stand.

"My name Inspector Viengsra."

"My name is Maier."

Inspector Viengsra pulled a small red pill from his breast pocket and pushed it into his mouth. His teeth were almost completely black, perhaps that's why he didn't smile much.

"*Ya-ba*?" Maier asked innocently.

The policeman nodded gently and grinned, without showing teeth.

"You are friend of Mr Rolf?"

"No."

The inspector pulled a face and then pulled Maier onto a broken stone bench in the shadow of an old mango tree.

"If you want to buy land in Kep, you need friend. No friend, no land. Very difficult. Many people not honest, many document not right."

Maier shook his head in shock.

Inspector Viengsra was recovering from the ordeal of his very recent activities, somewhat. Maier did not feel the need to ponder what this man did in his spare time. The public servant nodded solemnly and, wincing and with some difficulty, pulled a document from his hip pocket.

"Here you see. This is real. For this beautiful house."

Maier turned around. The ruin which he had just wandered through was about to collapse. The armed real estate man next to him was going the same way.

"Just fifty thousand dollars. Good price. The *barang* buy. We build Kampuchea again. Every year more."

"I will think about it."

The policeman leaned over a little too far towards Maier. "And be careful if you see the beautiful woman with the cut on her face."

Maier nodded respectfully.

"I fight many years. I fight Khmer Rouge. I fight many battle and massacre."

Maier sat, waiting for more.

"Death is a lady, monsieur, I tell you. Every time I fight the enemy, I see the woman. Death is a lady. Every time she come, we all know, someone die. But you never know who goes with the lady. Sometime the enemy, sometime my friend. Maybe me next time."

The policeman yawned and scratched his balls.

"Why is the woman with the scar so dangerous? The war is over now."

Maier was not going to get an answer. Despite his intake of amphetamines, Cambodia's finest had fallen asleep on the broken bench.

Maier left quietly. The dog didn't budge.

Police dog.

Nice dog.

THE REEF PIRATES

Reef Pirate Divers was an appropriate name for Kep's only scuba-diving outfit. Tourism in Cambodia was limited to the temples of Angkor. Beyond the magnificent ruins, the country was still waiting for wealthy foreigners. You could tell in this shop.

The office of the dive business was located in a small traditional family home that rested on high stilts on Kep's main beach. A few hundred metres to the east, a long stone pier stretched into the shallow water of the Gulf of Thailand. A large sculpture of a nude woman, recently painted in glistening white, rested regally at the end of the pier.

The compressors were located in a concrete shed. The bottles, wet suits, BCDs, regulators, masks, fins, snorkels and weights hung in a long wooden pavilion, underneath a grass roof that didn't look like it would survive a rainy season. Reef Pirate Divers was a modest enterprise.

A few tourists, geared up to dive, were just clambering onto a long-tail fishing boat. A young Khmer was loading the bottles.

Kaley stood on the beach, talking to Pete, who was shouting into two mobiles simultaneously until he recognised Maier.

"Our German hero and investor! Hello Maier. Hey Rolf, the other Kraut I told you about has turned up."

With his Porsche shades, his torn T-shirt and a pair of faded shorts that sported stark prints of white skulls on black cloth, Pete looked like a man intent on spending the rest of his life on a beach. Rolf on the other hand looked the stereotypical involuntary heir to an industrial fortune. Maier couldn't imagine this instantly likeable, good-looking young man sitting in an office to count coffee beans. But he was no pirate either.

Rolf was more than ten years younger than Maier, and he looked like he'd enjoyed a healthier life. He had a deep golden tan from working outdoors. A couple of decent tattoos of sharks circled one another between his shoulder blades. His dark straight hair fell just over his broad shoulders. Around his waist, he'd wrapped a red karma, like a belt. He was half a head taller than his English partner. A tiny earring sparkled on his left lobe, but that didn't make him any less acceptable for a visit to grandmother. Rolf Müller-Overbeck was one of those who'd always been lucky in life. Until the day he had decided to visit Cambodia.

"Hello Maier. Pete already told me about the mayhem at the Heart. You're an old friend of Carissa's? I'm Pete's partner, Rolf."

Strong handshake, chiselled features, open smile, steel-blue eyes. He looked more like Till Schweiger than his mother. With long hair. Maier's gaze drifted to Kaley, whom Pete had not introduced. For a second Maier could detect a moment of insecurity in the eyes of the young German who continued, "My girlfriend, Kaley. She's helping us with our business."

Seeing the girl for the second time, Maier was still mesmerised.

Kaley had changed her sarong and now wore cool silvery green. She had put up her hair with a couple of wooden chopsticks. She looked like a mermaid, so beautiful that men might construct a pier in her honour. Kaley nodded politely and offered a cool hand. How could she have such cool hands in this heat?

"Nice to meet you, Maier. I hope Cambodia is beautiful for you," she said in broken English. She smiled as you smiled when meeting strangers. Maier smiled back, hesitantly. He was finding it hard to get used to the young woman's hypnotic eyes.

"Hey, Maier, we have a spare space on the boat, why don't you hop on? Know how to dive?"

"I have not dived for a couple of years. But yes, of course, that could be fun."

For some reason, the Englishman was upset and lit a cigarette before throwing it into the surf a few seconds later. Rolf on the other hand was relaxed, almost glacial. The very definition of the successful German. Perhaps he was trying to make a good impression on his clients, three girls and a boy from Frankfurt, barely out of their teens and heavily tattooed on legs and shoulders.

"You can dive with me, I don't have a dive buddy. We go out beyond Koh Tonsay, there are some good rock formations and swim-throughs."

Ten minutes later, Maier sat, zipped into a wetsuit, next to Samnang, the captain, in the stern of the open boat which slowly slid out into the Gulf of Thailand. He tried to remember how to operate his equipment. Koh Tonsay was the largest island off the coast off Kep, partially forested and almost uninhabited. King Norodom Sihanouk had called it L'Île des Ambassadeurs – the Island of Ambassadors – and thrown extraordinarily decadent, private parties on its beaches. Countless criminals had later been imprisoned on this speck of paradise and were then called upon to defend the coast from pirates. Today, a few families, the former inmates' offspring, lived in a modest fishing community on the main beach. The island's royal residence had long been swallowed up by the jungle.

The locals called Koh Tonsay Rabbit Island. Apparently, seen from the air, it looked like a rabbit. How the fishermen knew this was a mystery, but Maier had a harder case to crack.

"Where do you come from in Germany?" Maier asked Rolf, who sat on a wooden plank in front of him and was playing with his dive computer.

"I was born in Hamburg where I grew up and where I started and terminated my university education. Prior to coming here, I'd never really been anywhere by myself."

That sounded like almost like a crime, but the young German grinned across the water, barely a worry on his face.

"And how long have you been in Cambodia?"

"Well, about six months or so. It's hard to believe, but I was at the dentist a while back, sitting in the waiting room and reading these articles about Germans who emigrated. One story was about a man from Bottrop who settled in Kampot. Kampot is a small town thirty kilometres up the coast towards Sihanoukville. That read a lot better than my studies and the constant hassle from my mother to take over the family business. It's not easy growing up in one of the typically traditional Hamburg trading families. I mean, they, we, are just very conservative," Rolf explained. "I had some money and I basically dropped everything – my girlfriend, my studies, my apartment, and my mother…especially my mother. And now I'm the owner of a dive shop in Kep."

"The dream of the German emigrant has come true?"

Rolf turned again and looked past Maier, across the water back to the receding shore.

"Well, not quite."

Maier saw conflicting emotions cross the prominent features of the young coffee heir from Hamburg. But Rolf said nothing more and began to tap away at his computer again. "I live in Hamburg as well. I rent a flat in Altona. But I am hardly ever there. I have come down to Kep to talk to the local expats about the economic climate. I might even buy something. Plenty of nice properties around."

The young man was himself again and swivelled around.

"To be really honest, I wouldn't bother. Kep is a little brothel town, a seedy hole on the beach."

Rolf laughed, his voice filled with undisguised bile. "A ghost town turned into a whorehouse. The dead rise again to get in on the boom. Can you understand that? I thought about selling my shares in Reef Pirates, but what would happen to Kaley, if I closed shop and disappeared?"

"Ah, women, always complicated."

The younger German turned towards Maier, his face twisted with worry, his eyes drilling into the detective like dark blue, dying stars. "I can't leave her. Impossible. That would be the end of her. And morally speaking, me as well."

That sounded almost like a confession or some long-learned, infinitely melancholy statement. Maier kept his thoughts to himself. He decided to provoke the younger man. "Well, you don't have to take it so seriously, I am sure. She would not be the first Cambodian girl a white man has left behind. Women get over this kind of thing. And the way she looks, she would find a new friend soon, no?"

Rolf replied angrily, "You want to fuck my girlfriend, Maier? You another sleazeball washing up in Cambodia? Kaley is not a taxi girl, she no longer works in that business."

Maier raised his hands in defence. "Hey, Rolf, sorry, I misunderstood completely. You have a serious relationship here and you can't just leave her."

Maier felt a little cheap. But only a little. Of course, under different circumstances, he would have attempted to bed Kaley in an instant. But the moment of opportunity already lay in the past.

A pod of dolphins played in the dark blue ahead of the boat. The tourists from Frankfurt craned their necks in excitement and Samnang revved his engine in order to keep up. The dolphins were game and dived under the boat, jumped clear of the placid water and did pirouettes ahead of the divers. They had no problems outrunning the long-tail.

Koh Tonsay lay just a few kilometres off the Cambodian coast. A little further east a much larger island loomed from the sea – Phu Quoc. Rolf pointed to the fog-laden ridges of the huge landmass.

"The Khmer say it's theirs. The Vietnamese say the same thing. But the Vietnamese have the upper hand, as usual."

The colour of the water was changing as the boat got closer to Rabbit Island. And Maier, who was looking over the side of the boat, could see the sandy sea floor broken up by small rock formations. Rolf got busy checking his customers' equipment. A few hundred metres ahead, a small fishing boat had just pulled anchor and was leaving.

Rolf shook his head in frustration. "No one is allowed to fish around here. Even the governor is keen to save the coral and I will report these idiots later."

Samnang slowed down and let the boat slide on under its own momentum. The dolphins had followed them into the shallow water and were now circling the spot the fishing boat had just abandoned. What was there to see for a dolphin?

Rolf was asking himself the same question.

"Friends, we have reached the first dive site, but before we all jump into the water, I'll check with my friend Maier what the dolphins are so curious about. They must be attracted by something down there. Otherwise they would not be circling over one spot. So make yourselves comfortable for a few minutes. Our captain, Samnang, will put up an umbrella. Drinks in the cool box. On the house."

The young coffee heir had already checked his gear and opened Maier's bottle.

"Everything OK? Ready for the jump into the unknown? No fear?"

Maier shook his head, "No problem, scuba diving is like cycling... Once you have learned it..."

"Let's go."

BLUE, RED AND DEAD

Samnang had dropped a small anchor. The boat bobbed about in the clear water as Maier wrestled into his BCD, pulled his fins over his feet, donned his mask, checked the regulator and dropped backwards into the Gulf of Thailand.

The sea floor loomed barely ten metres below them. The water was warm and crystal clear. Maier could see about twenty metres. The water crackled in his ears as he descended and equalised. The dolphins had disappeared. Rolf hovered below Maier and waved to him to follow.

Maier had learned to dive in Cuba in the Eighties with a bunch of crazy KGB guys and after his last big case in Thailand he'd travelled on a liveaboard to the Burma Banks to dive with hammerhead sharks. But he'd never been on duty, on the job, so to speak, underwater.

Dark rocky pinnacles rose like stalagmites from the gently descending sea bed. Maier felt he was swimming through a park of miniature cathedrals. As soon as he reached Rolf, a solitary great barracuda came to check the visitors out and lay perfectly still next to them in the water. The predator looked like an expensive sports car. Maier got so close, he could almost count the razor-sharp teeth in its open jaws.

Rolf lost no time and followed his compass, swimming a few metres above the sea floor. Maier followed suit. While no coral grew here, the variety and volume of fish was surprising. Lobsters waved their long white feelers from the nooks and crannies of the rocks, a moray eel and countless small colourful reef fish vied for his attention. A shoal of squid suddenly appeared in front of them, lined up in formation like a squadron of fighter jets. Seconds later, they shot away into the deep blue, in one single coordinated movement. Maier paddled hard behind the young man from Hamburg and tried to concentrate on his breathing. They weren't deep, but he was going to have to do the second dive with the same bottle. He slowly inhaled, slowly exhaled, until he found his rhythm.

The sea floor began to fall away steeply below the two divers. They were about to slide into a cauldron-shaped depression, littered with rocks as large as minibuses. Rolf stopped at the edge of this abyss and moved closer towards one of the rock formations.

Suddenly, two dark shadows appeared out of the blue – and moved lightning-fast directly towards the two divers. That had to be the dolphins. But there was something wrong. The two animals seemed to be bumping into one another as they got closer. Rolf pulled Maier's wetsuit and pressed him against the rock.

The reef shark, its head swinging wildly back and forth, shot a few centimetres past the detective's arm. A young dolphin had pushed the predator off its course. Amidst an explosion of bubbles Maier briefly caught Rolf's eye. The young German was alert but remained completely relaxed. He moved further into the rock and pointed in the direction from where the shark had attacked.

Maier had dived with reef sharks many times, but he'd never seen one race towards a diver so aggressively. Reef sharks hunted more modest prey. There had to be blood in the water, a lot of blood. Perhaps another, injured, shark, hooked on a line, was driving his predatory brothers and sisters mad. Maier looked around, but the shark had not returned, not yet. The detective pointed to the surface, but Rolf shook his head and began to search the pockets of his BCD. Seconds later, he pulled out a red plastic hose, unrolled it and filled it with air from his regulator. The two-metre-long safety buoy shot to the surface like a rocket.

Rolf grabbed Maier's arm and they descended further into the cauldron. Maier checked his air, his bottle was half full and they were at twenty-four metres. No problem, yet.

Rolf urged him on, as close as possible to the large rocks that made the area look like an abandoned scrap yard. After twenty metres, the younger German stopped, slid, as best he could, into a narrow cave and pointed ahead.

They were very close. Maier suddenly felt cold. Fear spread through his wetsuit like ice water. The centre of the cauldron was a hellish place.

Twenty to thirty reef sharks had gathered and were nervously cruising around their find. Ten metres ahead of the two divers, a man floated, his feet chained to a stone, dressed in a torn shirt and jeans, upright in the water. One of the sharks had already ripped away his right arm and part of the shoulder. Blood formed small clouds around his injury.

The man was dead.

Maier was ready to retreat, but Rolf shook his head again and pulled Maier deeper into the cave he'd found.

The next time Maier looked up, the reef sharks had gone. The scene in front of the two divers was ghostly. The man hung in the blue water, all alone, almost elegant, as if waiting for something. Maier could not see whether the corpse was Khmer or foreign.

A large, dark shadow appeared at the opposite rim of the cauldron and descended, like a malignant avalanche, down the slope towards the dead man. Maier was not sure what they were facing – a blue shark, a tiger shark? He had no idea. Whatever it was, it was monster size. Definitely not friendly. Definitely wound up by the blood.

The shark was bigger than many of the rocks in its way and seemed in no hurry to reach its prey. But its slack movements were deceiving. Within seconds, the huge creature had passed the dead man and was gliding straight towards the two divers. Maier could feel the blood pumping in his temples. The shark had reached the cave. Black, dead eyes. Mouth, jaws, teeth. Maier had heard that some sharks closed their eyes seconds prior to taking a bite while dislocating their jaws. But this shark kept its eyes open. It must have been close to four metres long, as large and as heavy as the hammerhead sharks in the Burma Banks. And a lot meaner.

As the shark reached the narrow cave, Rolf pressed the buttons of both his regulators and the water filled with clouds of bubbles. The shark, irritated, changed course and disappeared behind them. Maier thought he could hear the boat engine above them, but Rolf grabbed hold of his jacket and shook his head. Maier understood, they could no longer ascend safely. They had dived too deep for too long to go to the surface without safety stops. Rolf checked Maier's bottle and shook his head again. Maier no longer had enough air.

Maier tried to bend his head back. The fissure into which they had squeezed led deeper into the rock and widened above them. Rolf had the same idea. They pumped up their BCDs and slowly ascended while pushing deeper into the rock. Rolf had found Maier's alarm buoy, filled it with air and let it rise to the surface.

At eight metres, they had reached the upper lip of the rock. Maier could see the boat clearly above them but he did not dare raise his head above the rock. He turned slowly.

The large shark had forgotten about the two divers and was slowly circling the man below them. A few reef sharks had returned but they kept cautiously to the rim of the cauldron. A metal clunk distracted Maier. Samnang had lowered a full bottle, tied to a weight-belt onto the rock. Rolf carefully pulled the precious air into their crevice. Maier's bottle was almost empty and he changed regulator. Rolf had enough air and calmly watched the drama below them. Maier sucked on his new bottle greedily.

The shark swam in a wide curve and coiled, like a tightened spring. As the huge fish came face to face with its victim, it sped up. Then it was upon the dead man. In the last moment before impact, the shark turned on its side and shot forward like a rocket. Maier had no idea whether the fish shut its eyes or dislocated its jaw. The water filled with blood.

Rolf pulled him up then, his computer had indicated a safe ascent. The reef sharks were back and fought over the legs of the man.

Maier had never climbed into a boat as fast. Samnang pulled him out of the water. The young tattooed tourist from Frankfurt asked, "So, are we going in now, or what?"

ONE HOT, ONE COLD

"You still want to invest here, Maier?"

Rolf Müller-Overbeck leaned drunkenly into the bar of the Last Filling Station. His long hair dripped with sweat. The young German's question did not sound sarcastic. Maier was counting his dollar bills for the next round of drinks. There had been many rounds already.

The Last Filling Station was packed. Even Les Snakearm Leroux served beer tonight. It looked like the entire foreign community was present. Maier looked around – a pretty strange life you led here, isolated from the locals, but, he knew, that was the norm all over Asia. Unbridgeable culture gaps and huge income disparity precluded integration. The Khmer sat on the floors of their huts and drank illegal rice wine that had been distilled in the jungle. The foreigners sat on plastic chairs and drank beer. To make things worse, Kep's resident expatriates sat in segregated clusters, divided by nationalities, at several metal tables.

Still, the entire room had murder on its mind. Murder talk in at least four languages. And with every translation, the details became increasingly sketchy, the truth more flexible, the shark ever larger.

The French, including M and Mme Maupai, sat in the centre of the action. A second table was occupied by a noisy group of Scandinavians tourists. They had heard about the killing from the German kids and kept away from the local *barang*. As if murder was contagious. Perhaps it was in Cambodia.

"What kind of shark was it?" was Maier's first contribution in a while, a change in subject without changing the subject.

He'd decided by now that he would have to keep his true intentions in Kep secret. He had a feeling the murder in the Gulf was in some way connected to his new young friend, the coffee heir from Hamburg. Luckily, nothing brought men closer together than the shared survival of dangerous adventure. Hanging out with the man he was hired to shadow now came natural.

"It was a tiger shark. I've done more than four hundred dives off the coast of Kep, but I've never seen a monster like that. Tigers don't usually show up in such shallow water, but perhaps El Niño has something to do with it." Rolf swallowed hard. "A friend told me that he saw a big shark off the west coast of Thailand a few months ago, while snorkelling! I didn't believe it then. Maier, we were fucking lucky. A tiger shark! Luckily, I didn't see how it finally mauled Sambat, poor bastard. But I'm still in shock."

"The fact that such a big fish came into shallow water must have had something to do with the victim and all that blood. Sharks can smell blood for miles. Who was the victim?"

"Guy called Sambat. Worked with his sister for an NGO in Kampot, a few miles down the coast. The NGO looks after orphans. The two of them were orphans themselves – and one of their parents was a *barang*. They were born shortly after the Vietnamese invasion in '79. It's a kind of miracle they survived at all. I didn't know Sambat well, but he was a nice guy."

"A great guy," Les added.

"He often came on his half-dead Yamaha from Kampot for a beer. He was really a serious man, reflective and pragmatic, really amazing for his age. Just like his twin sister. In fact, he dropped in yesterday and talked about abductions of children to Bokor."

"Bokor?"

"The old French hill station, stuck up on a plateau in the Elephant Mountains, buddy. Maier, if there's a building in this world that's haunted, the Bokor Casino is it. As I said, built by the French as a pleasure palace in the Twenties and full of ghosts, just crammed with'em, like no Hollywood haunted house ever could be. The area around it is a national park."

Maupai suddenly stood next to Maier. "And today it is all fucked. *Ca m'enerve*. Bokor was a French institution and one of the most exclusive hotels in l'Indochine. Guests came from all over the world to lose their money in Le Bokor Palace."

He leaned past his wife towards Maier. "If Kep-sur-Mer was once the Côte d'Azur of Asia, then Bokor was the Monte Carlo of Indochina."

The Frenchman's eyes had glazed over, he was badly drunk.

"Believe me, Monsieur Maier. Bokor is a monument to our greatest days. And perhaps to Cambodia's greatest days too."

"Chérie, please sit down with Hervé and Celine, otherwise they will think that we don't want them here. They came all the way from Paris."

Madame Maupai did look poorly. She was about ten years younger than her husband and might once have been a great beauty. Now she was in her mid-fifties and she'd probably bought her skin-tight dress in a children's clothes store in Paris. The high heels didn't help, as she had the legs of a stork. Her face was deeply lined, the march of time barely disguised by a thick coat of make-up underneath which she sweated. Her eyes lay deep in dark caverns beneath darker brows and she wore her hair short. Her illness had progressed so far that the attempts to hide it were pathetic. Despite all this, she exuded more dignity than her husband.

Maupai gestured impatiently.

"Let me drink my beer in peace, Joséphine. You hassle like a bloody Arab."

Madame was obviously used to the tone and, without another word, she returned to the table of their friends.

"Everything is broken. *C'est comme ça.*" Maupai groaned, without turning around.

The silent Vietnamese girl pushed two cans of beer across the counter at him. Maier waved briefly to the young woman. A few seconds later he had another Vodka Orange in his hand.

Rolf did not look as if he wanted to talk to the Frenchman and turned his back on him.

"Maier. Let's drive up to Bokor tomorrow. Great place. Change of scene. My customers from Frankfurt have left for Kampot. After our experience yesterday, they aren't going to dive in Cambodia. I could do with a break from the business, working is hard work. And I have to go visit Mikhail."

"Mikhail?"

"Mikhail. Mikhail is a true original, an exceptional guy and a free spirit. A Russian who has been doing guided tours through Bokor Casino for the past weeks. Nothing official, but I'd like to offer his service to my clients, as long as there's no development up there. That man is an enigma. Never answers a question directly. Knows more about Kep than all of us put together, even though he has only been here once, and very briefly. But he tells a good story. He's an interesting guy. Sits in the clouds and drinks with the park rangers. And no one knows whether he's a real Russian. He does seem Russian though. He drinks like a Russian."

Maier drifted away, wondering about what abductions of children might have to do with his case. He was missing far too many pieces to form any assumptions. And Maupai didn't like being ignored.

"You probably want a break from your luxury slut? Isn't that a bit of an extreme swing, from Kaley to the homo Russian on the hill?"

Rolf suddenly looked stone cold sober.

"Waiting for the Man" by the Velvet Underground came to an end and for a second one could have heard a pin drop in the Last Filling Station.

"Maupai, you're a drunken asshole, a real pig. My 'luxury slut' told me that a guy like you would never get near her, not even for a thousand dollars. So shut up, my friend, before you really offend someone."

The Frenchman had gone pale and looked ready to counter with another hate speech, but Hervé, Céline and Madame Maupai pulled him back to their table. Dylan's "Subterranean Homesick Blues" started up and the Scandinavians paid and left.

Maier felt like relaxing after his dive, but he hesitated taking his glass to the beach and letting them fight it out. He'd find out more if he stayed around until the community began to throw punches at itself.

Pete had chosen the right moment to arrive. The wiry Englishman stood in the door of the Last Filling Station, flanked by two young women.

"Yes, friends, my old lady couldn't make it tonight, so I brought my secretaries, Mee and Ow. I will be giving some language lessons tonight."

Pete propelled the two girls, both Vietnamese, towards the bar.

"Only joking of course. They already know more than enough English. What would you like to drink, dears? Beer, whiskey, Coke, juice or maybe a glass of soya milk?"

The silent waitress pushed two glasses of Coke across the counter at the two girls. She had nothing to say, even to her compatriots.

Les leaned across to Maier. "My girlfriend hasn't said a word since she was five years-old. She saw the ghost of her mother in her father's bed. The next morning the father was dead. Since then, she's been stumm."

"How do you communicate?"

"Ah, well, you know, buddy. She's been working for me for the past three years and she sleeps in my bed. I provide a roof over her head. She doesn't have anyone else. I think we communicate OK. If it's something important, she can write some English. And I do remember some Vietnamese."

The two young girls began to dance to the sounds of the Doors. For an instant Maier felt transported into a bad American war film. Capitalism had won. Capitalism had won anyway. So this was what the Wall had fallen for.

"Pete, where did you find these two fine ladies? Did you drive all the way to Kampot to get them?"

"Maier, mate, you haven't had much of a look-see, have ya? Seen the two huts above the Angkor Hotel? That's our very own village brothel, poorly disguised as a barber's shop. One large, one small. You must have seen the handmade signs. The large hut is home to my two friends and a few of their compatriots. In the small hut, we had Kangaok Meas, our very own peacock girl. But she's not present now."

"Kangaok Meas?"

"Yes, Maier, the golden peacock. Never heard the story? You are usually pretty quick, aren't ya?"

Somewhere in the back of his head, new wheels began to spin, but Maier wasn't sure whether they were turning in the correct direction. The redhead had not finished yet.

"Probably the same Kangaok Meas that caused poor Sambat to drown. The police in Kep have decided to ignore the incident as there's no corpse, no crime scene. No need to make statements. And the dive business is saved. Long live Cambodia."

Rolf stared angrily at Pete. Maier gently held the young man's arm and said quietly, and in German, "Obvious that would happen. Whoever wanted to get rid of the young man had already cleared it with the local authorities. They dropped him right on a dive site. Don't start an argument with your business partner over this."

Marvin Gaye came on and Pete became distracted by the bored gyrations of his companions. With the girls in his arms he looked ten years older. One of the girls wore a jacket.

"Are you cold or do you have a machine gun under there? A machine gun?"

The girl did not understand a word.

"One hot, the other one cold, not bad, eh?"

Before Rolf could open his mouth, Pete stepped forward and embraced his partner. "Come on, Rolf, it's Friday night. The night is warm, the girls are willing and if you screw one of these two, it won't rain."

He winked at Maier. "The entire village goes there. The fishermen can only afford short time on a wooden bunk under a leaky roof. Our good friend Maupai, on the other hand, could enjoy a Friday night sandwich, just like me, if he only understood that his covert afternoon excursions aren't particularly discreet."

Maupai had been listening to the Englishman and now stood up, dropping his Alain Delon.

"Here, Maupai, one hot and one cold," the Pete taunted.

Before the furious Frenchman could lash out, Les had already stepped around the bar and grabbed Maupai from behind. The old American looked ready to crush the Frenchman. Maier almost burst out laughing – old men impatient as young pups, doing a hundred eighty miles towards their own demise. The return of Snakearm Leroux, gambler of a thousand Saigon nights. The bank director itching for a fist fight. You only got that here.

Les squeezed until Maupai had gone red like an overripe peach. Maier looked across at the French table but there would be no help for the village racist from his own quarter.

Les finally let go, disgusted, "No fights in the Last Filling Station. And you're much too old for this."

He turned to Pete. "Take your guests away with you. No one likes you today."

"Why, are you going to shoot me with your M-16 if I don't?"

The American laughed, "Of course, buddy. I've been looking for a good reason ever since you first came into my bar. Now I got one."

THE CASINO

Maier rode ahead. There wasn't enough road left to be able to admire the landscape. He concentrated on the potholes and sandy ridges that had carved the old mountain road into a rutted graveyard trail.

The first thirty kilometres led through dense jungle. Maier didn't see a soul by the roadside.

He tried to circle each pothole, some of them, half-metre craters, in order to get through the mud, gravel and sand as quickly as possible. Every now and then he could hear Rolf rev his bike behind him. Both sides of the road were hedged in by giant ferns and tall grasses. Small streams ran through the brush and underneath old, partly-collapsed bridges. The canopy threw long and deep shadows. A few tigers were said to survive here. The birds, unseen, managed to create enough song to occasionally filter through the roar of his machine. Politicians, business tycoons and the military, public servants of the finest order to a man, were depleting Cambodia's natural resources as quickly as the country's infrastructure would allow, but the jungles around Bokor had so far escaped this redistribution of wealth campaign.

On steep curves, the road had washed away altogether. During the rainy season, the red lateritic soil turned into an ocean of rust-coloured mud. Maier gripped the handlebars hard to avoid losing control of his machine and continued to slither up the mountain. Sweat ran down his back, despite the shade.

An hour into the drive, it got noticeably cooler. The wet, impenetrable forest loosened up, light looking like dirty milk poured through the trees. Quite suddenly, on a sharp corner in the road, the blackened ruin of a large house loomed into a grey sky. The sun had vanished behind thick wisps of cloud.

Maier stopped in front of the once handsome building and cut his engine.

The Bokor Plateau lay right ahead, a highland area of shrubs and low, gnarled trees, dotted with twisted rock formations. A cold wind made his vest stick to his sweaty T-shirt and blew black clouds across the sickly horizon. An old water tower and a copper-coloured chateau-style building stood on a barren cliff a few kilometres away. Beyond the two buildings, there was nothing. That had to be the end of the road. As Rolf pulled up next to him and killed his bike, Maier felt as if he'd gone deaf: the silence, but for a whisper of wind, had a finality, like death.

"This ruin here is the Black Villa. The building used to be one of Sihanouk's residences, when he visited Bokor in the Fifties."

The royal villa stood empty and windowless, the floor tiles had been smashed and partly carted away, and the walls were covered in obscene graffiti. Nature was going about its business to reclaim all it could. The squat servants' quarters had already been swallowed by the jungle. Nobody lived here.

"Quite a trip up here, no? A vibe away from the beach."

Rolf grinned and looked like a man without a worry in the world, as he used his *krama* to push his long wet hair from his face.

"The casino hotel over there was opened in 1924. Only the super-rich could afford to come all the way up here."

Maier was taken by the landscape. The plateau, with its eerie remnants of long-faded frivolity and privilege, looked like a post-apocalyptic archaeological dig. The rolling monochromatic grassland lay dotted with concrete ruins as far as he could see.

It did have a vibe. A malign current ran straight through this place. Maier was not a religious man, but the word godforsaken crossed his mind for the second time since getting off his bike. Bokor was perfect to burn a witch or two.

"You are the history expert, Rolf. Did the Khmer Rouge reside here as well?"

The coffee heir shook his head.

"The communists came in 75' but never stayed for long. In the Eighties, the Cambodian military occasionally had shoot-outs with the KR up here. The rebels would walk up through the jungle, kill a few soldiers, drop a few mines and disappear the way they'd come."

Heavier, grey clouds crawled up the mountain behind them. Seconds later the view across the highland had been swallowed up by dirty white fog. The milky nothing brought the ghosts of war. He felt like he could almost hear them march. The ghosts of the French, the Khmer Rouge, the Vietnamese, the ghosts of victims and perpetrators. It was time to move.

Maier got back on his bike. Suddenly, he heard steps behind him. A young, broad-shouldered man in uniform, a machine gun casually slung across his shoulder, peeled out of the fog. Rolf approached him.

"*Soksabai*, Vichat. How are you?"

The park ranger answered something in Khmer. The closer he got, the smaller and less dangerous he looked.

"This park full of poachers and ghosts," the Khmer laughed, when he saw Maier looking at the gun.

Vichat was around twenty. His uniform was worn and he wore cheap plastic sandals. His weapon was in working order though.

"The poachers shoot deer, boar, sometimes the elephant. Or they come with chainsaw and steal the tree. But ghosts very bad. Last week one ranger disappear. Before, he tell me he talk to three young girl, all dress in black."

The young ranger whispered, "Like Khmer Rouge."

Vichat pointed to Rolf's bike and into the fog.

"My bike break down. Take me to ranger station. Not safe out here, alone."

A few hundred metres along the road, they came across the ranger's motorcycle, marooned in a ditch with a flat tyre.

The fog got denser the further they rolled across the plateau. Maier opened his throttle and slithered across moist rocks and broken tarmac. For a moment the clouds lifted around them and Maier spotted a church tower ahead. A few hundred metres on and the road split once more. The fog had already swallowed Rolf. Maier could no longer hear the young German's engine and took the right turn. He passed several overgrown plots of land, fronted by opulent gates that appeared to lead nowhere.

Bokor must have once been one of the most exclusive and beautiful holiday destinations in the world. More than a thousand metres above sea level, the colonial rulers of Indochina had forced their subjects to build a magnificent, almost paradise-like resort, a French Shangri-La, surrounded by tropical forests teeming with tigers and elephants.

There wasn't much left of that glory now.

The road ended abruptly and a huge, dark shadow loomed out of the fog. He got off the bike, pushed it to the side of the road and walked the last fifty metres to the Bokor Palace. As he got closer, the casino peeled out of the mist like a Victorian ghost ship. He slowed and stopped. This was some building. It had personality. The black, cavernous windows of the erstwhile luxury hotel stared at Maier like the dead eyes of long-fallen soldiers. The roof was topped by four crumbling towers. A wide moss-covered stairway led up to the main entrance. The grey, bullet-riddled walls were overgrown by a red, luminous fungus, which looked like a torn and bloody carpet hung out to air a hundred years ago and forgotten about. Spent gun cartridges, evidence of past wars, crunched underneath his feet as he stood at the foot of the stairway.

Maier had not planned to go in, but he suddenly thought he could hear someone walking. He looked around. There was no one within his limited field of vision. A few crows circled above Maier, the first animals he had noticed since emerging from the jungle. A dog barked behind the building.

Maier began to ascend the stairs. He felt exhausted. It was hard to take each step, as if walking uphill against a strong wind. This building was tired of visitors. At the same time, the yawning entrance door at the top of the stairs appeared to try to suck him into the building.

A half century ago, people had lost their money and perhaps their lives in Bokor Palace. During the war, hundreds if not thousands had certainly lost their lives here. He reached the top of the stairway and passed the threshold.

The lobby was smaller than the detective had expected. The reception lay behind a kicked-in dark window, a tiny and barren office. Lamps and fittings, light switches and furniture had long been removed. From both sides of the lobby, long corridors stretched away into darkness. The yellowing, damp walls were covered with the traces and thoughts of earlier visitors. A few obscene drawings could still be made out. Maier stepped into a ballroom. Some joker had carved the sentence "Everyone will die" into the moist plaster above the door frame. The heavy, castiron fireplace lay smashed by the door. Otherwise, the room was empty. Fog haemorrhaged through the large broken windows on the opposite side of the cavernous hall No one had danced on the tiled floor for decades.

The wind picked up and began to whistle through the old building. He could hear a girl call. On the first floor. Suddenly he heard a loud bang.

Bang, bang, bang, bang.

The noise came from above. It didn't sound like gunshots. Maier walked back to the entrance door and looked up the stairs. The narrow, worn steps were deserted. The afternoon light was fading. Soon it would be dark.

Bang, bang, bang, bang.

He scrambled up the stairs as quickly as possible, trying to avoid garbage and lose tiles. Empty rooms, dirty and dead. The tubs and washbasins had all been smashed. The tapestry had peeled off the walls. Traces of war lingered everywhere – many rooms were connected by holes, large enough for a man to step through. Rusty cartridges and shotgun parts lay amongst other debris. Dark water stood in muddy puddles everywhere.

The noise came from the west wing of the sprawling building. As Maier stopped in one of the rooms, catching his breath, he heard a noise, very close, behind him and spun around. Out of the corner of his eye, he sensed, more than he saw, a shiny purple sarong rush past, but he'd been too slow. He stepped into the corridor. Maybe it had been a child. He couldn't see anyone. But something was wrong. He walked towards the noise, towards a large dark room next to the stairway, towards its door and the black beyond. Now it sounded like a machine, though not regular enough.

Bang, bang, bang, bang.

Maier stepped through the door.

The room was empty. Large holes had been hewn into the floor.

Maier could see down to the ballroom below. A weak light flickered nervously though the holes. At the far end of the empty room a second door opened into a second darkness. The noise which had turned the empty room into an echo chamber originated in the next room.

Maier crossed the broken floor carefully and looked into darkness. A cold night wind blew in his face.

The last room was empty.

A plastic bag had been caught up in the tiny bare place and blew jerkily from wall to wall.

Bang, bang, bang, bang.

Maier let the plastic bag continue its madness-inducing racket and returned to the first room. He lay down by the largest hole and tried to peer down into the ballroom. He could still see the flickering light and began to crawl forward in order to push his head further through the unlikely window to the scene below.

A light flashed and suddenly he could see clearly for a split second, but there was no time to take in what he saw. Someone yanked him from his lookout with massive force. He tried to turn and kick, but it was too late. He felt his ear rip open as he passed the rim of the hole, a second later the proverbial blunt object connected with the back of his head.

Loud voices woke Maier. He could not have been unconscious for long. It was pitch dark and the wind had calmed, but the detective could hear heavy raindrops hitting the roof of the casino. He still lay in the room in which he'd been attacked. He slowly turned on his back and touched his head. Nothing broken. His ear was still there as well.

Voices poured up from the ballroom. Maier looked around. He was alone. Whoever had clubbed him over the head was an amateur assassin or no friend of the people in the ballroom. They certainly wouldn't have left him alive if they'd caught him spying. What he'd seen for just an instant was hard to digest. Life-changing. But not for the better.

Maier, riding his stubborn streak, crawled up to the hole a second time while trying to keep an eye on the door behind him.

The ceremony, if that's what it had been, had ended. Kaley and Tep's son stood together, talking. The woman had washed the blood off her chest and now wore a white T-shirt. He couldn't see anyone else. Maier had a headache. The plastic bag behind him began to do the rounds once more.

Bang, bang, bang, bang.

Kaley looked up to the ceiling, towards Maier, before quickly dropping her gaze again. She had seen him. He snuck out of the room as quietly as possible and felt his way along the corridor to one of the stairways in a far wing of the casino.

The stairs he found had partially collapsed, but he had no choice. He had to get out but escaping via the main stairway he had come up on was too risky. Maier climbed as carefully as possible into the gloom below him. Metal bars reached like petrified snakes out of the torn walls, ready to impale careless passers-by. On the ground floor, Maier saw another shadow rush from the corridor into a room as he emerged but by the time he'd come to a halt and held his laboured breath, he couldn't hear a thing. He turned and carried on until he reached the basement. The water stood up to his ankles. Something stank, but he wasn't sure what it was. A few metres ahead, Maier could see another set of stairs that led out into the open. He waded slowly towards the weak light, trying not to stumble in the cold, dead water. Several times he bumped into large soft objects. He didn't stop, but tried to remember why he'd come.

Maier climbed the slippery stairs as quietly as possible. As he emerged from the basement, he spotted Inspector Viengsra, the policeman he had met in Kep, on the balustrade that encircled the casino property, sitting in the rain, next to a four-wheel drive. He had his back turned. The dog sat between the policeman's legs.

As Maier passed, the cur raised its head and looked briefly in his direction. But Maier was every dog's friend.

He found his bike, snapped it into neutral and pushed it as quickly as possible back to the last crossing. The fog was slowly drifting away and he could see the roof of the ranger station, barely a kilometre below. Lights twinkled down there. Maier let the bike roll.

MOTHER RUSSIA

The giant stood on the wide steps of the station and toasted Maier with his bottle and a wide, mischievous grin across his face.

"Tourists get lost around here regularly and it's a miracle that no one has fallen off the cliff down into the jungle. Some, I have been told, are thrown off by the ghosts of the casino. You were too heavy for the ghosts?"

Maier had not expected a welcoming committee, much less a camp, quite possibly drunk Russian with a poetic bent. For a second he was tempted to throw the few phrases of Russian he remembered from school at the man, but then he decided to say nothing.

Mikhail had charisma. His command of English was perfect, even playful, his accent that of a Hollywood bad guy.

"Well, young man, have you been rendered speechless? Let's start at the beginning, dear. What's your name, and what dark power propelled you to enrich this godforsaken part of the world with your delightful presence?"

The Russian wore shorts and a big shirt that flopped open over his huge, smooth belly. His long grey hair framed an unshaven, beetroot-red face and he looked like someone who tried to give an impression of sloth and laziness. The eyes of this freewheeler were sharp and alive though, sober in the extreme, and reminded Maier of his own – eyes you could switch on and off. The Russian was a few centimetres taller than Maier. Next to the park rangers, he was humongous.

Maier felt that the Russian was a man with a mission, just like himself, and that Cambodia was merely a stopover for a man like Mikhail. This old Soviet hippy was, despite his extrovert drunkenness, nowhere near the end of his line yet.

"Leave it be for a moment, Mikhail. I just came off my bike."

Rolf and the young ranger had appeared behind the Russian.

"What, my name travels ahead of me? You heard of me in Kep and defied the dangers of the jungle just to come and see me? Perhaps you heard of me as far away as Kampot or Sihanoukville? Or did someone whisper my name to you in the capital? I mean, young man, there's not much to see up here except for me."

Rolf and the young ranger looked carefully into his blood-encrusted ear.

"What happened?"

Maier realised only now that the right shoulder of his vest was soaked in blood.

"I fell off the bike at the last crossing. I had taken my helmet off, started driving, puddle ahead, deep pothole, and bang, I fell flat on my face and must have passed out. The rain woke me up. But the bike would not start again."

The Russian translated into Khmer.

The ranger seemed to understand at least part of what Mikhail said and shook his head in disbelief.

"Vichat thinks that you were up in the casino, fighting with ghosts."

"Is he serious?"

"Serious, young man. He also suggests that we sow your ear back to your head. Vichat is the only man here who knows anything about first aid. He told me he even amputated a leg once."

The Khmer looked at Maier questioningly and pulled a small mirror from his pocket. In the weak light of a single bulb, the detective did not need a thorough self-examination to decide that something had to be done.

"Is there any vodka?"

"Tonight, you will have to make do with whiskey, Maier. Otherwise there's the always reliable local rice wine, a drink that makes good people very bad."

"Is there any ice?"

Rolf handed him a full bottle.

"Be a man, Maier."

Vichat began to clean the wound with alcohol. Maier took a swig.

The four men sat outside the ranger station. Vichat spoke quietly on his radio set to a girl in Kampot, far below them on the coast.

"You want to offer guided night safaris though the casino?"

The Russian looked across at Maier and nodded, his voice dripping with sarcasm.

"I have been doing this for a while, with people who come up here by themselves. But I don't know what to do if something happens to a tourist. Some people fall off their bikes before they have even seen the casino."

Rolf shrugged in frustration.

"It was just an idea Pete, Mikhail and I had. Mikhail does a great tour through the hotel, it's a total ghost ride. I almost shat myself."

The Russian grinned with mock malice and showed yellow teeth.

"While Pete wanted to bed a couple of girls in the casino the first night he was up here. How is our happy-go-lucky British pirate? Does he still dream of infinite power and undeserved wealth?"

Rolf did not answer.

"Come on, Rolf, you are not stupid. You know how to run a business. You are good-looking. You still have a nice character. Be careful that you don't get stuck in the wrong country with the wrong people. Cambodia really sticks to some."

"Are you going to tell me Kaley is a slut as well?"

Mikhail laughed and poured himself another glass.

"Deep inside, you know what she is, Rolf. Just be careful that you don't end up in the rain one day. You never know. But the local slut she is not – that's me! That is my privilege."

Rolf didn't answer.

Maier coughed into the silence. "Well, are you going to let me in on something?"

"Only if you sleep with me tonight, young man."

Mikhail laughed himself into a coughing fit.

"So here comes a well-preserved German of young middle-age with an alleged sack of gold and tells anyone who will listen that he wants to invest, though he has not looked at a single piece of land. And he wants to be let in on something? Into our dark secrets?"

"Why would I invest in a country like Cambodia if I didn't know who pulls the strings, at least locally? Especially in a small place like Kep."

"You are right, Maier. Don't be so touchy. You don't need to justify yourself. You know how it is in Cambodia. People react to people who ask questions. Hardly anyone does, so it is noticeable. In time, you will make best friends here. Kep is full of nice people."

Rolf interrupted the monologue.

"So nothing's going to come of it?"

"Of what, dear? Of us? Nothing, I think. You are too romantic. And you like the ladies too much. And the sad thing is, Rolf, that most of the women around here are so skinny that they almost look like men. Isn't that depressing? The poor suckers come from Moscow, Berlin and London, frustrated and fragmented by their luscious, voluptuous *devotschkas* and fall in love with these passive shrimps. Not with me, but with these skinny nothings, who have no tits and no asses. No opinions either. It's all about power. None of these girls are any good in bed. You need brains, imagination to be any good in bed. You have to be a bit of an artist. Like me. The tough guys from the West, they only come here to load one of these little mice on the back of their rented chopper cycles and drive around like apparatchiks."

Maier was definitely amused. Mikhail was a freak, a prophet of the damned. A man not to be interrupted.

"But power is something very temporary, very transient. The moment these men look away from their shrimps, they are being ripped off. It was just the same with the French. Look around. This place was once a dream destination. And what happened? After fifteen years, it was all finished. The casino closed and the power evaporated. Even the Khmer, Sihanouk and Cambodia's elite could not save the dream. That's why I love it up here. Man defines himself here. The French played around with the country, the Americans flattened it, and the communists had graves dug for the entire population, socialist mass graves. Those exist in my part of the world too. What about yours, Maier?"

The Russian burped quietly and stumbled on without waiting for an answer. "And now the business types turn up. People like you. Do you really think you can help this country? Wouldn't it be better to throw all the foreigners out for five years, so that the brothels close and golf courses aren't built in national parks?"

"Is anyone building a golf course up here?"

Vichat increased the volume on his two-way radio. The girl on the coast started to sing. The Russian fell silent and listened to the young Khmer woman's love song. The moon had risen above the casino, clearly visible above them. The church and several other buildings rose out of the darkness like tombstones. North of the casino, the old water tower appeared to walk, like a UFO from a Fifties sci-fi movie, across the darkened highland. The voice sounded eerily metallic through the tiny speakers, but it dripped with genuine emotion. Words of love amidst war of the worlds.

The voice of the girl brought movement into the tall grasses beyond the station. Maier remembered good times in the old communist Germany, long walks with young women who'd also had beautiful voices. Even his headache was subsiding. Vichat smiled himself into a quiet daze. The song ended and the girl on the coast, a thousand metres below the plateau on which the four men sat, whispered good night.

"So what about the golf course?"

"Maier, you are a Prussian hunting dog. The tears have not dried yet and you are already asking again. Was it not full of love, young man?"

"I can imagine how we could spoil a place so remote and lovely, and a national park to boot, but I would like to know firsthand of course."

The huge Russian slapped his back

"Haven't you noticed yet, that we can spoil anything? Not just here, but in our backyards too. Why bother with Cambodia? Our backyards are legendary. Or is this just your roundabout way of asking more questions about what you are really after but don't want to tell us about?"

Mikhail had dispensed with his glass. He lifted the bottle to his mouth and took a long swig before he continued. "You will find strange bedfellows in Kep if you are looking to invest. Some people think the town is a gold mine. Others think the casino is a symbol for past glories. As I said, there are a million ways to spoil the world. And in Cambodia, they have all been tried. All of them."

Maier turned to Rolf. "A golf course, up here? Who will pay for it? They would have to rebuild the road first, that would take years."

The younger German did not answer.

Mikhail changed the subject.

"Rolf, I would love to do the tours, but in a few months, or perhaps weeks, the fun and games up here will be finished. You know it. And I am not worth any kind of investment. I am broke and happy, that's why I sit up here and drink."

Rolf had nothing to say and stared into the void, his face distorted by something stronger than annoyance.

"If you think Cambodia is so corrupt, why don't you go back to Russia?"

The giant laughed bitterly.

"To Russia? You will make me cry, if you force me to think about my country. Our rivers are poisoned and dried up, inflation is as high as the Kremlin walls, and life on the street is as brutal as a weekend in a Siberian gulag. We are being ruled by evil *bratschnicks*, who want to take away our freedom, our culture and our right to drink excessively. We are being watched around the clock, blackmailed and threatened and we are at war everywhere. Just like it has always been. Mother Russia. The newscasters lie that the world will end soon. The president lies that it won't end. I like being here. For the Khmer, the end of the world will not come as a surprise. One golf course more or less will not make a difference."

Rolf interrupted the Russian. "There's a Cambodian investor in Kep who wants to construct a golf course up here. Perhaps he has the necessary contacts in the government to get permission to build in a national park."

"And that would be Tep?"

"Ah, Maier, so well informed. Then you must know that the resident foreigners in Kep are being asked to come in on the project. In some instances that request looks like an order."

Rolf nodded. "Yes, Pete is on board."

The Russian laughed. "Children, children. Everyone wants to have a go. The French, the Scandinavians. Last week, three Japanese showed up here, industrial spies, came from Saigon in a four-wheel drive and had a look at the area. Sweat shop on the beach, resort on the mountain. Everyone thinks you can put a golden cow onto this cliff. But the French already tried that."

"And who exactly is Tep? Or rather, what is he? I met him a few days ago in the Heart of Darkness."

Mikhail grinned, "Well, then you know everything there is to know. You don't look stupid, Maier, even if you fall off your bike without reason."

It was getting cold. Vichat carried his radio transceiver into the ranger building. But the young man stopped for a second and looked at Maier, "Tep no good. Tep Khmer Rouge. Tep, he fight here, he live here. Maybe he think Bokor belong to him."

The ranger disappeared into his room. Mikhail stared after him, his eyes full of longing.

"He's got a great behind, that Vichat. But he prefers to listen to the warble of his girl instead of throwing himself into my open arms."

Mikhail leaned back like a fat diva and looked into the night sky, theatrical, self-important and mocking at once, "The world is not fair. Not even in Cambodia."

"And Inspector Viengsra works for Tep?"

Rolf and Mikhail laughed.

Mikhail had found his glass and filled it, then drained it in one long swig.

"The dog lover? Has he shown you any property papers which he happened to have with him, when he passed you on his bike? There's only one thing to say. The relationship between Viengsra and Tep is the same as between the dog and the inspector – symbiotically bestial."

"And how dangerous is the policeman?"

The Russian laughed dryly. "It always depends who is swinging the hammer. It's all connected to gravity. And our dog lover is affected by it as much as anyone. Most of the time, he sleeps. Sometimes he does evil things for his boss. Kill the dog and he is finished."

Maier felt sick. But only a little.

"And what does Tep have to do with the execution of that young man, Sambat?"

"You will find out Maier, of that I have no doubt."

MOSQUITO

Maier was getting drunk. That seemed to be the best strategy in Kep. He needed a break. The case needed air. The Russian on the mountain had made him suspicious. Something didn't fit the program. Maier wasn't even sure whether the man was really Russian or truly gay. It could all be an elaborate act. Despite his doubts, or perhaps because of them, he liked Mikhail.

Back on the beach, his fifth Vodka Orange done with, he'd asked Les to show him to a hammock. Now he hung in an alcohol bubble between two posts under a straw shade on the flat roof of the Last Filling Station and listened to the surf, drifting off. The crab boats slowly moved up and down the coast. He could hear them putter back and forth, but he was too lazy to lift his head and look out across the sea. The surf made him sleepy. Soon the mosquitoes would come and eat him.

Rolf, the good-looking and self-confident coffee heir, a man who had everything going for him in life, was trapped in a web of trouble that Maier couldn't decode. Not yet. The detective was sure that his young compatriot wanted to get out. As soon as Maier could make a more informed judgment on Rolf's entanglement, he would provoke a situation, which would present Müller-Overbeck with an opportunity to slip away. If the younger man did not take him up on his offer, he would report to his mother, the Hamburg ice queen. He wasn't here to solve local mafia crimes. Still, the girl Kaley wouldn't leave his increasingly cloudy thoughts. In his drink-addled mind, Maier laid out everything he knew about her – her story, her smell, her weightlessness, her hips, the promise he had given and the moment in the ballroom of the casino. Then he left them right there, laid out, and dozed off, dark thoughts on his mind.

"Yeah, yeah, mate, you have no choice. But the apple is not nearly as sour as you make it out to be."

The scratchy voice of Pete the Englishman woke Maier.

"I didn't come here to invest in some crazy esoteric scheme with the entire expatriate community. Our business is doing well, better than it did when you ran it by yourself. Without me, you'd still be saving for the next set of equipment."

The two owners of Reef Pirate Divers sat directly beneath the entrance to the Last Filling Station, and therefore directly beneath Maier. The sunset melted in epic brushstrokes across the evening sky and the mosquitoes were getting ready to attack. Maier did not dare to move for fear of being discovered. Defenceless, he let the insects descend.

"Let's pull in your countryman first. He looks like he's got money. But he's not stupid. We just have to find his weak point."

"It's bad enough I am involved in all this shit." The Brit laughed venomously. "It says in our contract that I have the right to sell Reef Pirate Divers. But I have no intention of pulling you across the table. We sell the shop, invest in the casino or the golf course, or the dinosaur park, if you like. You know, there are at least two guys in Phnom Penh who want to buy the dive shop; two guys who have the necessary cash."

"I don't want any more deals with Tep. He is dangerous. He probably killed Sambat."

The two men fell silent. Only the buzzing of thousands of insects was audible.

Pete began to talk at Rolf once again.

"You can't prove that. And anyway, we are in Cambodia. This is not our country. We are guests here. All we can do is adapt to local circumstances, invest our money wisely and hope that the locals will also profit. Not just Tep, but hundreds, perhaps thousands of workers he will have to hire."

"You know that more people will die. Sambat was just the beginning. I don't understand why Tep would get rid of a guy who has nothing to do with Bokor in such a cruel and crazy way. Sambat worked with orphans."

Pete did not answer.

"I've had enough. I want to get out and I will take Kaley with me."

The Englishman hissed back angrily, "Then you lose all your dough, mate. And you know that you can't take her out of here. Kaley belongs to Kep. You're not the only one she's connected to. It's ridiculous that she's living with you, mate. Kaley belongs to all of us. I told you that the day after the accident. If you're sleeping with her, you know the score. She just lies there like a wooden board." Pete coughed and lit a cigarette. "So here's some advice. It fucking rained."

"You're a bastard."

"Rolf, there's so much money in all this. The entire business community of Kep will participate in the rebuilding of the casino. And everyone here knows about Kaley. Even Kaley believes that she is the reincarnation of the Kangaok Meas. That's the reason you could hush up the accident. Otherwise you'd be in jail or on the run. And I don't think she'd even go with you. Most importantly, Tep is also convinced she's the Kangaok Meas, otherwise he would have killed her a long time ago."

Maier had an overwhelming urge to scratch himself.

Rolf had got to his feet below him.

"Faith is just something we hang on to, despite the fact

that we know it's an illusion. I believe in the Kangaok Meas. Kaley is like a golden peacock. But there has to be a way to free a person from this ridiculous superstition, this darkness of tradition. And from Tep. The old man is not a ghost, but an ex-general who has lost his moral compass and dreams of the times when he could go round bashing people's heads in with a hammer."

"Well, wish me a quick death, Rolf, if you believe in all this esoteric mumbo-jumbo."

RAIN

"I need something against insect bites. Vodka Orange, please."

The Vietnamese girl silently served Maier his drink.

Les rolled the next joint, quickly and with four fingers.

"I'm surprised you lasted as long up there."

"I fell asleep. I started drinking too early today."

"That happens."

"Normally it happens to other people."

The American laughed, "I fell asleep on the roof last year, buddy. Just like you. I got dengue fever. It shook me three weeks straight. Without my girl, I wouldn't have made it. Besides the girl, there's no cure for it. That's why the Brits call it break-bone fever."

"Black Dog" blasted from the speakers. Maier didn't really like rock music, but the sounds suited in the Last Filling Station. Anything was better than disco. And Les was a nice guy. But it was time to get answers and nice people were always the first toehold in the answer game.

"Did it rain after you slept with Kaley, Les?"

For a moment the American didn't say anything at all. Maier began to worry that he'd overstretched his direct approach. Les probably had a gun or a club under his counter.

"Yes."

The owner of the Last Filling Station looked anything but happy after spilling his confession.

"Tell me the story, Les."

121

"It's a long story and you don't want to hear it, Maier. Not if you plan to invest around here."

"I am not going to invest in Kep, Les."

The old war vet growled.

"So what the hell are you doing here?"

"I am a private detective. I am trying to solve a case involving a German client. In order to get closer to solving it, I need to know about the accident and I need to know the story of the rain. You are the only person in Kep I can ask. You are involved in all this here, just like everyone else, and you are also the one who has the least to lose if the community ever goes pop. And that is very likely, and very soon too."

"Might be your head that goes pop, Maier."

"Les, the first time I came into your bar, you could see I was not just another hapless westerner about to drop a million into a hole in Southeast Asia. And you asked me whether I was OK. I mean, what a question to ask."

"Maier, I got nothing against you, buddy. But you got no idea what kind of a swamp you are sliding into here. The people in Kep are cursed – the Khmer, the Vietnamese and the *barang*. All of them. It don't matter what you are looking for here, all you'll find is Cambodian curse."

"And you don't find that scary, Les?"

The American brushed his thumb-less hand across the faded tattoos on his left arm.

"I have seen whole valleys go up in flames, turned to steam by the payloads of B-52s. For my country, I poured napalm over children and I pushed men out of helicopters. In Khe Shan, we were attacked by Vietcong who had loaded syringes taped to their arms, syringes filled with heroin. Every time I walked out of the compound after a battle and found a dead soldier, I had myself a shot. It was always Grade A quality. The war made me both killer and victim. I saw ghosts. Before death stalks the paddies, a young woman appears. Everyone, every child, who's served at the front will tell you this. I see the same ghosts and accept the same laws of nature that people here have faith in. Kep's my final destination – as the name of my modest establishment should tell to you."

Maier looked Les straight in the eyes. "Then you lose nothing if you tell me what is going on here."

Les looked uncertain and began to roll another joint.

"What kind of music do you listen to, Maier?"

The detective shrugged in his vest.

"You have found my weak point, Les."

"People who don't like music are strange, Maier. What did you do in your last life?"

"As I told you, I was a journalist, first in East Germany, then, after the fall of the Wall, in West Germany."

The American's eyes widened with surprise. "You're a commie?"

Maier laughed and tried to steer the conversation into more profitable waters.

"I was a journalist for six years in communist Germany. I was born there and grew up there. I was a war correspondent working for an agency in the reunited Germany for eight years. I have seen a few ghosts too, in my time."

The American digested the news and changed the subject. "Kaley was married to Tep's oldest son. He was a real piece of work, worse than the second son, whom you know from the Heart. This guy, Hen, he was a cop in Kep. He stole from tourists and set a small bungalow operation on fire that wouldn't pay him his bribes. He also had something to do with the bomb at the hotel in Sihanoukville which killed a foreigner. He opened a small brothel behind the Angkor Hotel and brought some girls in from Saigon. Kaley had Hen's child eight years ago, a daughter. A beautiful girl called Poch. Hen used to beat Kaley. At that time there weren't that many foreigners in town. But we all knew what was going on. Kaley was the most beautiful woman in Kep. She still is today, but then, she looked totally irresistible. It hurt to watch her being mistreated. But no one did a thing. Perhaps we were all sadistic swine, because we could not have her for ourselves. Of course, the entire expatriate community was scared of Hen and his father. Two years ago, Poch borrowed a hammer from the neighbours and beat her father to death in his sleep. Shortly after, Kaley and the kid stood in front of my door. What could I do? I took them both in. I slept with her and it rained. A few days later, she went back to Tep."

Les sighed. His eyes had glazed over with sadness and loss.

"Tep took his revenge. He installed Kaley in the brothel and invited the men from the plantations. It always rained afterwards and local people believe that anyone who sleeps with Kaley is cursed and will die a violent death."

"What do you think?" Maier asked and lifted his empty glass.

Moments later, an ice-cold Vodka Orange stood in front of him. Drinking was part of the job – Maier repeated this troubling thought like a mantra and held on to the bar.

"I don't think I got much time left. That's why I didn't throw you out."

"And what happened to the daughter?"

Les held up his hands in defence. "You will have to ask Rolf that. And now go home, I've had enough of you."

Maier left some dollar bills on the counter and drifted into the night. He'd not been this smashed in a long time.

ENLIGHTENMENT

Though Maier had spent years in Southeast Asia, he'd mostly stayed away from the taxi girls. He wasn't averse to the looks of Asian women, and he'd communed with a few. But for Maier, sex had to be an explosive exchange, a kind of celebration of body and soul. If the woman wasn't hot for it, then neither was Maier.

Taxi girls weren't hot for it. At least not hot for sex.

And when the occasional hotel receptionist or flight attendant had sought to slip between Maier's sheets, usually she had done so in the hope of being able to hang on to him. Sex was weapon and tool in Asia, especially as long as so many women couldn't emancipate themselves. Equality for women in Asia was a future as desirable as it seemed utopian to Maier. How often had he looked at a Cambodian woman's behind and then taken the young lady from Bremen or Santa Barbara who'd been drinking at the next table home with him? As a war correspondent he'd never had to worry about finding partners for the long nights on the frontlines of the world. A pretty and lonely NGO worker or reporter could be found even in the world's darkest recesses. For a private eye, having a love life was more complicated. Maier rarely told people the truth about what he did. But at the age of forty-five, his remarkable eyes had never let him down yet. Eyes like magical flashbulbs.

Lying in Maier's hotel room, Carissa slowly turned in bed so he could admire her in his own time. Her hips gleamed with sweat and Maier watched a large drop of moisture slide down a smooth thigh, before it was trapped in the hollow of her knee.

"You should meet Raksmei, Sambat's sister. She's no shrimp. Half *barang* and half Khmer, a ravishing-looking woman. If you ever look into her eyes properly, you'll never share a bed with me again. That said, she's too young for you."

Sex and death stuck close to one another. The little death and the big death. Carissa had heard of the underwater execution and travelled down from the capital in search of the story.

"The NGO is called Hope-Child and Raksmei founded the orphanage and pulled in the foreign donors. Her brother Sambat used to help her, but for the past year, he has been hunting down paedophiles and kidnapping their victims right from under their noses. You know, some of these sex tourists that come here – as well as many well-connected locals – are after kids. Sambat had very good connections in the media who protected him. Even had a couple of Swiss guys busted, with the help of journalists. They had this mutually beneficial relationship and as he was half-*barang*, he thought he'd be reasonably safe. Raksmei thinks that his murder has something to do with Bokor."

Maier slowly slid his hand down Carissa's spine. Despite the conversation, he found it hard to keep his fingers off her. He liked this woman more than he remembered.

"Why are these two young Khmer so active? You definitely need protection if you are going to kidnap trafficked children from their captors. This sounds so incredible."

"Raksmei and Sambat are orphans. No one knows anything about their parents. That means that the most beautiful woman in Cambodia is alone right now, drowning in sorrow, vulnerable. Why don't you go and see her? She might help you with your case. As you won't let me help you…"

"You can help me any which way you want, Carissa. I am powerless. And I like older women."

The Kiwi journalist pushed a few stray white hairs from her face and laughed.

"When I first met Raksmei, she thought I was an old woman. In Cambodia, only old women have white hair. In her eyes I must have looked sixty."

"You'd pass for fifty any time."

The kick in the ribs hurt.

"Maier, you are a low-down chauvinist."

"Let's celebrate that."

"Help me with my story. You know much more than I do about what's going on here. What's happening up there at the casino?"

Maier held his aching side and contemplated into which cheek of her delectable arse he would sink his fingers and twist. Then he shrugged and feigned innocence.

"I have no idea what is going on at the casino. I was in Bokor but not in the casino. I fell off my bike and broke my head open, as you can see."

Carissa carefully pulled a lock of hair away from his ear.

"I can see a man who got whacked over the head with a blunt object and won't admit it. Maier, you're a right bastard. You pump me all the time and give nothing back."

"I like pumping you, Carissa."

"Until your case is solved, then you run off and work some other exotic locale where you'll also pump a journalist or an NGO secretary who is so lonely that she will go to bed with a down-at-heel private eye and think it's romantic."

Maier had nothing to say. She was right, he also knew women in Kathmandu, Bangkok and Singapore. Women with whom he'd almost stayed. And now, in his room at the Angkor Hotel, with his old flame in his arms, he could imagine staying with her. It *was* all pretty romantic.

"Can you imagine me moving back to Phnom Penh? What would I do? Prove that half the older men in town have committed crimes against humanity?"

Carissa sighed, "No, of course not. We're both used to our freedoms. And after forty, people rarely change. But I have another seven years to go before I am forty, Maier. You're too old for me. Your life has already run its course. Mine is almost still ahead of me."

Maier had only recently started thinking about his age. He had got as far as deciding to avoid wars for the rest of his life. He had decided that he wanted to grow old. But a relationship, or a family, the concept of permanent cohabitation in compromise lay a long way off. Still, he felt hurt by Carissa's sarcasm.

"Don't be macho now and don't start feeling sorry for yourself. You're great in bed and I have to be careful, otherwise I'll fall in love with you a second time. You're a strange man. Just looking into those eyes of yours, which never rest until they see something pleasant or foul, makes me dizzy. But then they move off somewhere else. You're an obsessive. You're like a child in a toy shop, blown away by all that's on display and you go all the way to get it. Life just offers too much to a man like you. And that's why you're so lonely, Maier."

She crawled into his arms. He did not have to look at her to know she smiled sadly.

"There's a Chinese curse…"

"Yeah, Maier, with which you tried to impress me years ago. 'May we live in interesting times.' You're cursed, lover. All that time ago, it was just your way to pull me in, now it's the truth."

A few minutes later, they'd reached another place, free from the tired obligations of verbal communication.

DAWN

He woke up alone. The bed was still warm next to him. The night and the hangover from the day before stuck deep in his bones. What a woman.

She couldn't have gone far. For the second time since his return to Cambodia, Maier was suddenly scared for his old girlfriend. He got up, put on a pair of shorts and went downstairs. It was just getting light. The guard lay snoring in his hammock. The sun would remain hidden behind the Elephant Mountains for a while yet and it was refreshingly cool. The early morning looked innocent; a few birds rushed over his head along the almost deserted shore road, an old woman stood by the roadside and, still half asleep, wrapped her *krama* around her head before she set off for the crab market, laden down with plastic buckets. Even at a considerable distance, he could make out the red hair of the Englishman. Carissa sat on the beach with Pete.

Not that Kep had a real beach, but he could see the two clearly on the sandy strip below the road. Pete gesticulated wildly, but at this distance Maier could not make out what he was saying.

"Good morning, Maier. I am just trying to explain to your old lover here, that her investigations could kill her, if she insists on digging around down here."

For once, the detective shared the same opinion as the wrecked-looking dive operator.

"You look like you had a wild night, Pete."

"I always have wild nights, mate. At least since I've lived in Cambodia."

He lit a red Ara and blew smoke-rings into the perfect morning air.

"I don't understand you people. The country is beautiful. The people are polite and a bit retarded. The women are hot and always within reach. Genocide has its good sides too. Come on, Maier. Germany is wealthy today because we flattened you in World War Two. And we flattened you because you killed too many people. It's the same here. In twenty years, Cambodia will be back on its legs. And if we make the right decisions now, we will be able to contribute to the rebuilding of a nation. We will be the new colonial masters, independent of state power or ideology. We take what we can, wherever we can. That's called globalisation. The published truth about a few not totally legal investments will not stop or even slow the development of this country."

By now, Maier had made up his mind that he didn't care for the Englishman. Apart from his shady business associations, he carried too much baggage from back home, too many tabloid hang-ups vis-à-vis his European neighbours. And he carried it like a medal around his neck.

"Pete, I think you are a bit behind the times. Germany and Great Britain have been at peace for some years now."

Pete sighed. "You're idealists. The world is bad. We have to make the best of it."

Maier laughed. "Your world is bad, Pete. Our world is OK."

He knew this was all just posturing, his old girlfriend would not be put off by the Englishman. She would follow her story to its bitter end. Any journalist in her situation would want to know why Sambat had been killed.

Pete got up and wiped the sand off his pants. He looked stressed.

"Maier, mate, don't come back to me later and tell me that I didn't warn you. I'm assuming that your investor story is bullshit and that you're some kind of journo as well."

Maier looked across to Carissa but her face was turned and hidden under her white hair. All of a sudden, he was angry. Angry at Carissa, who'd risk her life for a story about a few old murders. Angry at Pete who'd risk anyone's life for a few dollars. The probable result was the same and went with the locality: killing and burying were still acceptable solutions to all sorts of problems in this broken land. And many foreigners took to the local traditions like fish took to water. Maier no longer felt like holding back.

"I am not a journalist, Pete. But I might become your worst nightmare yet. If anything happens to Carissa, I will personally order the tiger shark back and make sure he gets fed."

The English pirate jerked his head in surprise and met Maier's stare with expressionless eyes. Not a good sign. Most people were scared of Maier when he threatened, as he threatened rarely. There was no hope for this man.

"Yeah, Maier, mate, now I'm almost impressed by you. Wow. So I'll say it again. The future of Kep won't be defined by you two ageing angels. Even yours truly here will have just a tiny hand in what's going to happen."

Without another word, the red-haired pirate got up and walked along the shore towards the market. Carissa hadn't moved. Now she turned to Maier. She had tears in her eyes.

"Who the fuck do you think you are, Maier? No one hears a thing from you for four years and then suddenly you show up and throw everything into disorder. You fuck your old girlfriend for a few nights and pull every scrap of information she has from her, only to solve your enormously important case. You're here for a few hours and people start dying like flies. But you give nothing yourself and make grand speeches how you will take your revenge on that little wanker, if he burns a hole into your mattress. Mate, wake up."

Maier waited until she'd calmed down.

"Ok, Carissa, I will tell you everything I know, but you have to promise me not to go to see Mikhail in Bokor. I was wrong. I think it is a trap."

"Maier, I'm not going to promise you anything. I know Mikhail, he's eccentric, but he's not a murderer. And he knows more about the people here than you do."

The sun had risen above the Elephant Mountains. It was starting to get hot. Carissa looked beautiful. But Maier could not bring himself to apologise for his emotional agnosticism.

"Ok, wait one more day and we'll go together. I have been invited for dinner by Tep."

"On the island?"

"On his island. Pete will take me across later."

Carissa looked at Maier for a long time. She looked like a white goddess in the bright morning sunlight, a divine entity who'd just appeared on earth to find a prince. It was probably already too late for Maier. He wasn't prince material.

"Maier, you might not come back from there. Pete is close to Tep, very close. And if he assumes that you are some kind of snoop or investigative journalist and passes that impression on to Tep, then that nasty old general will get rid of you."

"A few days ago, I deposited a large chunk of money in a bank to which Tep has connections. Enough money for a house down here. I am sure he knows about it and will try to convince me to come in with him on his schemes. The true reason why I am here is to get Rolf out of Cambodia. But he will not leave without his girl. I am trying to find out what is forcing him to stay and what Kaley has to do with Tep. And the only way to find that out is to accept the invitation."

Carissa thought for a while.

"What happens when the case is done? You will just disappear again?"

Maier swallowed hard. Maier had no idea what Maier wanted.

"I don't know what will happen. I won't stay in Phnom Penh."

He didn't say anything for a moment.

"Perhaps you might tag along to Hamburg?"

The goddess from New Zealand said nothing and stared across the placid water. Maier rearranged his beard and tried to rearrange his thoughts.

"Perhaps," she said, finally.

Maier felt queasy. He had reached a place he was not familiar with. He smiled. Finally, a real challenge, something totally new.

"Don't get happy yet, old man. First we have to solve the case," she mumbled and fell into his arms. A few hundred metres away, he watched Pete turn around and stare back at them.

DOWN BELOW

Rolf Müller-Overbeck lay in the hammock he had probably slept in. He looked wasted and hadn't washed in a while. His long hair was greasy and some food had got caught in his days-old stubble. In fact, he looked almost dead.

The dive shop was deserted. Neither Pete nor Samnang, nor any of the other employees could be seen.

"Holidays?"

Rolf barely moved, and waved him away with tired arms.

"There's a story doing the rounds in Phnom Penh that someone got eaten by a shark down here. I suppose my customers from Frankfurt told everyone in their guest house horror stories. We have only cancellations for the next few weeks. I've sent our workers home."

Maier sat on the wooden stairs to the office of Reef Pirates.

"And where is Kaley?"

"Kaley is gone."

Maier looked past the dive-shop owner out to sea. Koh Tonsay was almost completely obscured by fog. The sky had turned dark grey again and the air was incredibly humid. A singular morning had given way to a depressing day.

"I've had enough, I can tell you that, Maier. If I could see a way out of Kep, I'd jump into a taxi right now and go directly to the airport in Phnom Penh."

"So what's stopping you?"

"I can't sell my share in the business at the moment. And I

can't leave without offering Kaley an opportunity to leave as well."

"Has she stopped turning up for work?"

"No, she's just gone. Back to her barber shop behind the hotel. Since then it has rained twice. I can't bring myself to go up there. But I'm far enough in my thinking now that I no longer care about the money. I have to leave. I'm getting sucked into this morass here so deeply that I'm drowning."

The young German looked at Maier with large paranoid eyes, partially visible under his matted hair.

"I still have a life ahead of me, I think. But if I stay here... I really thought that we could do something for people. But anything we try to set up here comes down to exploiting those who need protecting most. I almost agree with Mikhail now. Maybe all the foreigners should leave, so the country can make up its own mind where it wants to go."

Maier had a question on the tip of his tongue, but he couldn't formulate it. The young German was completely overwhelmed by his present circumstances. Without the help of others, he'd never make it out alive.

"I am not sure that would help. I think the Cambodians are perfectly capable of screwing themselves up, even without the help of foreigners."

The detective was sure that the foreigners who had invested in Kep were only alive because they were of use to the general. Maier had the feeling that all the locals he'd spoken to, whether Khmer or foreign, suffered from a common psychosis that was connected to Kaley. Something was afoot that had nothing to do with real estate.

"What happened to Kaley's daughter, by the way?" Maier remembered.

A strange, strangulated noise emanated from Rolf's mouth. After a while he said with a cold, tired voice, "It's like this in Kep, Maier: if you buy land and become part of the community, you're privy to information which outsiders do not have access to. Cambodia has many secrets. The first foreigners who came here all speak Khmer and they know the area, the people and even the ghosts. You understand?"

"I will most likely buy one of the ruins in Kep, Rolf. I have just been waiting for my money."

"You are buying from Tep?"

"I am answering a dinner invitation on his island tonight."

Rolf turned back and forth in his hammock to make sure no one else was in hearing distance.

"I wouldn't do that, Maier. That could be a really dangerous trip. I'm not sure you understand, but it's your soul that becomes corrupted here. You're forced to make realisations that don't exist in Hamburg, at least not in the Hamburg I grew up in. Here you cross a threshold. In this sense, Kep is probably the most exclusive beach resort in the world. Where else would you be able to witness an underwater execution? I warned you."

"Not to go to the island or not to buy land?"

"I told you a few days ago that Kep is changing from ghost town to pimp town. I was not entirely right. I think the ghosts still have the upper hand. The Khmer say that people who were killed but not cremated never come to rest. Every Khmer has seen ghosts. Some people even believe that some people are not people at all, but are really ghosts. And that they can bring great sorrow and suffering to others."

Rolf really got going now.

"It's amazing that we abandon part of our rational western thinking, our Eurocentric view of the world, after a few months in this country, amazing how quickly that happens. It's a process that erodes the space between reality and illusion. Opinions are just like clothes."

Maier laughed drily. But he was not sure what was going on. Too many pieces of the puzzle were missing. The scene in the ballroom flashed through his head, again.

"Ghosts, you might be right, Rolf. I saw some when I was here in '93."

The young German turned away.

"If you buy land, let's talk about ghosts again. And if you want to buy the dive shop, let me know. Until then, take care of yourself."

L'AMOUR

Maier had an hour to kill until Tep's boat would pick him up. Enough time to get a haircut. He passed the Angkor Hotel and walked up the hill to the two small huts.

Mee and Ow sat in the shade of a mango tree and were doing their make-up. Both of them wore gloves that reached all the way up to their elbows, to keep the tropical sun off their skins. They looked briefly at Maier, with the curiosity usually reserved for a passing dog. It was too early for professional enthusiasm.

The huts stood a hundred metres above the Angkor Hotel on a lightly forested hillside. They looked about ready to be torn down. The bamboo walls had fist-sized holes and the sheet metal roofs had rusted through in places. General Tep hadn't invested much in the less than salubrious village whorehouse.

Maier passed the women, nodding briefly at them and entered the second hut. Two barber chairs, torn red leather, stood in front of a dirty mirror beneath a long counter. The counter and the mirror stood in the forest floor. The walls were covered with faded posters of Cambodian boy bands and starlets. No sign of a barber.

At the far end of the hut he could see a beaded curtain. Maier heard voices. As he was about to cross the threshold into the hut, he could hear Mee and Ow curse behind him. It sounded like curses.

For a moment, the detective hesitated. He carried no weapon and he had no business here. But he separated the bead strings and carefully stuck his head into the small, dark room beyond.

As he parted the curtain, the light that fell through flickered across her skin. Kaley lay naked on a wide bunk. Maier thought he could hear her hiss like a snake. Four unadorned walls and a small, rickety side table scarred with cigarette burns, the only other piece of furniture in the room, made up the picture. A bunch of hundred dollar bills lay crumpled on the table. A spent syringe and a packet of blue tablets lay next to the money. He could smell expensive aftershave, cheap alcohol, sweat and death – a disconcerting combination of odours. Maier felt a little dizzy. There were moments in life when he wanted to throw up without being drunk or sick.

This was what they called "all the way down".

The old Frenchman had heard the Vietnamese girls outside and was just buttoning up his trousers. His gold chain shone on his hairless chest. His white shirt was soaked with sweat, the grey hair hung off his head like a long-used dishcloth.

A phone rang.

"Monsieur Maier, in Cambodia, thank God, there are fewer rules to observe than in France, but in a brothel, everyone must queue. As a newcomer you might not be aware of this. That's why I am not put out enough, after you have brought my enjoyable Saturday afternoon to an abrupt end, to have you killed."

The phone continued to ring. It had started to rain. Kaley moved slowly on the bed and looked up at Maier.

Maupai pulled a mobile phone, a rare luxury in Cambodia, from his pocket. The Frenchman had been shooting up. Maier noticed that blood had soaked through the right sleeve of Maupai's shirt.

"Allo?"

Kaley made no effort to cover up with the torn blanket that lay on the bunk next to her. She smiled at Maier sensuously. At least that's how it looked. But he was not quite sure what he was facing on the bunk. The tension in the small windowless room was unbearable. The rain started hammering onto the roof with greater force.

Maupai was still on the phone as he fell onto the bunk next to the girl. Despite the twilight in the room, Maier could see that the Frenchman had lost it. He no longer looked like a retired film star.

"Bad news, Maupai?"

The Frenchman dropped his phone.

" Ma femme...elle est morte. Joséphine is dead. She died at Calmette Hospital in Phnom Penh this afternoon."

Maupai began to scratch himself nervously. He could not look into Maier's face.

"The doctors always talked about fresh air. They just wanted to get rid of us," he whispered.

Maier shook his head. He found it hard to have pity for the Frenchman.

"While you are in here, having sex with your neighbour's friend, your wife dies? Maupai, you have problems."

The former bank director hadn't heard him. He was miles away, his eyes drifting towards something beyond the beaded curtain.

Outside, the Vietnamese girls were giggling. One hot, one cold. Where could you go in such a situation? What did it mean, to have arrived in this hut, at this juncture in your life? Weighty stuff zapped through Maier's head. His eyes wandered to the most beautiful woman he had ever seen, who seemed to wrap herself around her own golden brown body. Now she lay curled like a python. He could hear her sigh. Somewhere, water dripped into the room.

After an embarrassing eternity, the Frenchman got up. He stood like an automaton and did up the buttons of his shirt, slowly, pedantically, one by one, looking straight ahead into the big nothing.

"Maier, do you have a gun?"

"No, I do not. And you do not need one, Maupai. Can you not hear it is raining? Is that not your rain, your own personal rain of death? Save yourself the gun and enjoy the few remaining days you have, before the curse catches up with you."

"And I will die a terrible, violent death. Oh, Joséphine, I will not be able to tell you of my adventures. I only did it to save our marriage. Now there's just the wait, for the end."

"Maupai, get lost."

The Frenchman turned and looked at the woman on the bunk, as if he'd just stepped into the room.

Kaley answered his gaze with a dark smile. As the Frenchman began to return the smile, his face twisted into a grotesque mask – trying to process the terror that was waiting for him outside.

"I will leave you alone now. See you on the other side. You will have to make your sacrifice as well, Monsieur Maier. Just like young Rolf. Just like all of us. The Kangaok Meas demands that we destroy ourselves, before we are reborn as gods," he whispered as his voice grew hoarser.

Maier smiled along with them. Now all three of them were smiling and the world was fine. A world populated by primates who'd lost control.

Kaley stretched slowly and looked at the two men as if she had nothing to do with the room or its male visitors, as if the two intruders were alien, incomprehensible phenomena, propelled into her life by some dark, malignant force.

Maupai left without another word.

Maier turned and sat next to Kaley on the bunk. He had nothing to say and no reason to stay. Kaley would not give him any answers to his questions.

And still he asked. "Why did you not stay with Rolf?"

"I need money."

"Rolf has money."

"I work for my papa. He is an important man, a powerful man."

"I know, I will have dinner with him tonight."

"I know."

"I have not found your sister yet."

Kaley leaned forward and pulled Maier's shoulder. Her smile was open, perfect, warm. Her breasts shook ever so slightly. Sweat ran off her golden brown shoulders. She looked like an angel in reverse.

"I know. And you find her. I am sure. Do you want me help you, Maier?"

"I do not think this will help finding your sister."

Kaley sighed. "Maybe the Kangaok Meas is just story."

"Perhaps. But I am no longer sure who you are."

"I am Kampuchea," she hissed and wrapped herself around him.

He wanted to tell her that he'd seen her in the casino. He wanted to tell her what he'd seen. He remembered her look to the ceiling. She had to know that he'd been there. But there was no point in saying anything. He could not tell someone who lived on the world's margins and tried to hang on, someone about whom he knew next to nothing – he could not tell someone like that about good and evil, about what it might mean to be human. He only had the right to do that if he looked into the abyss at the end of the world himself. Maier was not sure whether he was qualified enough for spiritual insights. He almost felt like he was back in school. In a school where students studied darkness and its habitués.

"Maier, drink. Les says you are friend."

Maier grabbed the whiskey bottle which she had pulled from underneath the bunk and took a long swig. Red Label. He almost wretched it back up, the cheap booze was so bad. He quickly took another swig.

"Les my friend. He like the others, but he my friend."

"And Rolf?"

She said nothing for a while. The rain had almost stopped. The drumming on the roof had turned to an irregular tapping. It sounded like the bag in the casino. He had to get out.

"Rolf so far away. He scared of Kaley."

She looked at him sadly.

"He is probably not the only one," Maier said drily, but she did not understand him.

"He not understand."

Maier leaned back into a moist bamboo wall and buttoned up his shirt. He could feel the cheap booze stick in his beard, like glue. He took another swig. He wanted to get out. He needed to get out. He wanted to stay. Everything began to turn. He wanted this woman, but he had to solve the case.

Maier didn't fight, he merely dropped. His hands began to shake. Cold sweat ran across his face. He sank into himself. Kaley would catch him and carry him across the fire into a new life and a new Cambodia.

The woman began to sing.

Pete shook him awake.

"Maier, welcome to Club Kep. Wake up, mate, we're already late. You're expected for dinner."

Maier had a furious headache. He was alone in the room with Pete. Kaley had disappeared. Maier stood up and stumbled about uncertainly. He looked down his front. Had he slept with her? What kind of drink had that been? He tried to focus in silence and pulled his clothes straight.

The English pirate laughed hoarsely. "She just lies there like she's dead, no? Just like I told you."

Maier rolled his eyes and asked, "Can you not imagine that such an experience is different for everyone?"

"No, Maier, I can't."

The world looked better outside. Maupai was nowhere to be seen. The two Vietnamese girls had disappeared as well. Maier stumbled after the Englishman down the hill to the beach. The sun had just set above Koh Tonsay and Samnang was waiting, motor running.

L'ÎLE DES AMBASSADEURS

Maier enjoyed the trip. No rain clouds and no dolphins. No tourists from Frankfurt. Samnang passed the eastern shore of the island in a wide arc. Coconut palms lined the picture-postcard beach.

The young Khmer captain stared across the water without expression. Maier did not find this reassuring, but the sunset hung like a Turner painting and lent the day plenty of painful *Endzeitstimmung*. He was sailing into the beginning of the end of something.

The redhead from England was also quiet and smoked one Ara after another.

As a journalist, Maier had always known why he worked in dangerous situations. He had a mission, a job, to go to hell, to visit places where no one would go voluntarily, to collect information and impressions and to carry them back into the world to remind the people back home how easy their lives were. It had also been a way to get to know the new reunited Germany, by working with other Germans who were always on the road. Maier had loved the friendships and the cut-throat competition of war reporting. He'd met the same remarkable people over and over – in Rwanda, in Bosnia, in Cambodia, in Afghanistan. Everyone spinning the wheel, until they'd used up their survival points. After some years a sad routine became apparent. One friend after another died. A few got out of the game because their partners couldn't take it any longer. Maier had stayed on. Until Battambang.

But nothing had really changed. Maier was back in Cambodia, back in the country of his dead friend, Hort. He was sitting on a boat transporting him into a tropical *Heart of Darkness*, surrounded by people who didn't know why he was here, but who wanted to kill him anyhow.

His client circle back home had shrunk and become more exclusive and he no longer needed to look as closely at political conditions as in his last life. He no longer needed to work as transparently as a journalist either, and this was one aspect of his new profession that Maier liked. As a journalist one was often tied to a truth, usually not one's own. All that mattered for a detective was to close one's case successfully. This didn't have to have anything to do with truth, not one's own and not that of others either.

But detectives and journalists followed common threads – snooping around, unearthing information and asking questions, the search for informants, and, in conflict countries, the ever-present danger of being killed for asking one question too many.

Maier would have to be very careful tonight. He could only hope that the former Khmer Rouge general had made the effort to check his financial background.

They had already turned to the south side of Koh Tonsay. Samnang slowed the engine and lifted the propeller out of the shallow water. A white, solitary bungalow stood two hundred metres ahead, a little set back from the beach amidst a coconut plantation. Tep liked things private.

"This is it. The Villa Ambassade."

Three girls ran along a narrow wooden pier. A speedboat was moored to the rickety structure and bounced gently up and down in the waves. Pete had climbed to the front of the boat and dropped the small anchor into the water. The boy that Maier had already seen in action in the Heart appeared behind the three girls.

As he stood up, Maier could hardly believe his eyes. The girls were around twelve or thirteen and wore identical black pyjama suits, complimented by crude flipflops cut from spent car tyres – the uniform of the Khmer Rouge. Their hair was cut short, they wore red *krama* around their necks and carried Kalashnikovs. What a show of force. Welcome to my genocide. Samnang stayed in the boat and Maier could feel that Pete had tensed up. But it was too late for second thoughts. They'd arrived at the place he'd wanted to visit all along. He ignored the pier and jumped into the shallow water. The Englishman followed and lit an Ara.

The youngest and meanest girl got off the pier, stepped right to the water's edge and pointed the gun at Pete's chest.

"No smoking," she barked.

There was no arguing with the weapon or the girl, but Pete wasn't sure how to get rid of the cigarette. The girl looked like she would shoot him if he dropped it into the water.

"That's how you give up smoking," he mumbled and gave his Ara to Samnang.

"In a minute she'll tell us that smoking is decadent."

Maier didn't feel much like joking. He already had the feeling that he was a prisoner. He followed the boy to the villa. The girls marched slowly after them. Not a word of greeting.

"Be really careful what you say here. Tep is very eccentric. Especially when he's at home. Just keep focused on the business."

"Is he trying to bring back the Seventies? Does he have many of these killer girls?"

"Many."

Maier shook his head.

The Khmer Rouge had long stopped functioning as a guerrilla force. No one in Cambodia dressed and walked like these girls today. Once again, his thoughts drifted back to what he had seen through the hole in the floor of the casino.

Their host was waiting for them on the wooden veranda of his villa. The veranda faced the jungle. The man obviously didn't think much of sunsets. Today the old Khmer was in uniform. His short hair had been cropped shorter and stood in stubbles on his square head. Tep wore the uniform of a Khmer Rouge general.

The old soldier nodded without a word and waved Maier to a rattan chair. He didn't offer his hand. There were only two chairs on the veranda. The boy and the three girls in black lined up behind Tep. Pete had disappeared.

A large tattered flag graced the wall of the bungalow. Maier was pretty sure that the three yellow Angkor towers set against the red background had once served as the colours of Democratic Kampuchea, the short-lived Cambodia of the Red Khmer.

Kaley stepped out onto the veranda, with two glasses of wine balanced on a plastic tray. She too was dressed in black. She had put her hair up under a black Mao cap and didn't know him. She handed him one of the glasses without a word. The flag and the outfits, all this iconography of failure, reminded Maier of skinhead gatherings in Germany, but these people looked more serious and spooky.

Tep was watching him attentively. Maier watched back. He had the feeling that he wasn't being appraised by the old man alone. You could easily get paranoid in the presence of Khmer Rouge, but he felt he was being observed by someone else. The door which led into the villa was covered by a curtain. Maier thought he could make out someone breathing behind the cloth. It wasn't Pete, of that he was sure. No, this sounded like a much older man.

Maier's brain suddenly did somersaults. Perhaps Pol Pot, Brother Number One, was still alive. Perhaps he had not been poisoned by the Thais in 1998, but had retired to the idyll of Koh Tonsay. Crazy idea. Maier wasn't that important.

"Mr Maier, you are our guest for almost two weeks now and you not come to visit me in my home. And you meet everyone else in Kep. Maybe you like to find friend because you have no friend?"

Maier cleared his throat. "I have been trying to understand the investment."

Tep smiled like a gentle, slightly senile pensioner.

"And how is investment climate in Kep?"

"It seems that all roads, and boats, lead to your doorstep."

Maier was not sure how to address the man. Comrade didn't seem a good choice. And he wasn't going to call him General.

"Yes, they do," the general confirmed. "All roads lead to Tep. But you visit the very small one-way streets in Kep. I hear that you go to Bokor Casino to look."

The eyes of the old man did not go well with his friendly-grandpa style interrogation technique. They drilled right through Maier. He'd have to choose his next words very carefully. "True, I was in Bokor a few days ago. I only saw the casino from the outside. An amazing building."

Tep nodded.

"It so run down. I will change it. Bokor is very special place in Cambodia. I will make resort there, maybe even golf course. What do you think, Mr Maier?"

"I don't understand why you are so keen on tourism, as well as the past?"

Maier realised immediately that he'd made a mistake.

"Which past, Mr Maier?"

There was no turning back. Maier had pushed ahead too far and too quickly.

"Your past, Tep. You are surrounded by children in black uniforms. That's a tradition from a time when foreigners were not welcome here."

The Khmer laughed and shook his head.

"You wrong, Mr Maier. Cambodia always welcome the foreigner, even in Angkor time. Only foreigner who want to make problem, who want to know our business, who maybe want to stop Cambodia become great country again, like Vietnamese, or American, we don't like to see."

Maier didn't say anything. He started wondering whether the three machine guns that were loosely pointing in his direction were slowly homing in. But he didn't look directly at the girls. He had his hands full with Tep.

"You see, Mr Maier, all foreigner who come to Kep and stay more than holiday, I meet. And you understand, in Cambodia today, the government very weak. So, in the province, the local man has to do the best to rebuild the country. We need to rebuild the country, Mr Maier. We have little money. America bomb everything and when we beat the foreign enemy, the Vietnamese, our real enemy, invade. Stay ten years, no problem. Big problem for Khmer. Vietnam make problem for Cambodia long time, take our land, destroy our country. We cannot do business with Vietnamese or American. So I ask, I meet clever man like you and I think, you work for this side or that side? Maybe you here to make problem for Cambodia, take our land or take our woman and child?"

Maier shrugged and answered, "You know all about the activities of the *barang* in Kep and hence you should know that I am here to help Cambodia. Cambodia needs contact with the rest of the world. You cannot do it alone. The world is too small a place for that today."

The old Khmer suddenly leaned forward and grabbed for Maier's right wrist.

"The whole world want to help Cambodia. The UN, the CIA, the newspapers and many people think they can fuck the women and kidnap the children, put people in factories, where they make clothes for *barang* for a few riel. All this just to make economy in your country strong. And then you come and tell us we are murderers. Are you this people, Mr Maier?"

Maier sat motionless and took his time to answer. Tep continued to hold on to his wrist. The breath of the old man was stale and used up.

"I came to you tonight to discuss business. If you want to accuse me of other things, get your information right. A man with your connections should be able to find out whether I am just talking or whether I really have the money to buy a villa or two and restore them."

The general laughed sourly. "That right, Mr Maier. I am honest with you. I cannot find out why you come here. I spend my life in Kep. I come from Kampot Province, where I grow up in a village. But I cannot decide if you want to make problem for my country and steal from Cambodian people, or if you are useful to rebuild Cambodia."

Tep rose and grabbed Maier's left hand as well. The detective wondered whether he'd be asked to dance next.

"Mr Maier, I tell you a story about Cambodian village. You know, local people in Cambodia are very superstitious. One day a group of monk come to my village. The monk is telling the villagers that they can kill all bad spirits in the village, if the villagers give them money and the animals. The villagers happy for help fighting many bad spirits, give the monk their animals and the money, and the monk leave the village. In the evening, a young boy is walking home from his rice field, when meet the group of monk. The monk drinking and eating. They kill all the animals already. They very drunk. The boy run home and tell his mother about the monk. The mother not believe her son and take him to the monk. The monk tell the mother, her son have the bad sprit inside and not his fault what he say. The monk tell the mother to leave the boy. They promising to help the boy. The mother agree and the monk take the boy and torture him for a week. After, the monk leave the boy almost dead near the village and disappear. Is the boy clever or stupid?"

Maier was certain now that a third person was a silent participant in their conversation. In the silence between the general's words, he felt a shadow leaning over him.

"I am poor farmer son when French are here. My uncle die, building the road to Bokor. Like many other Cambodian, he die for the French. Later my brother work as guard in big villa. One day, the son of owner drive his car into a tree and tell his father my brother the driver. The father was friend of King Sihanouk. They arrest my brother and take him to the jail in Kampot. We never see him again. You see, no matter who rule Cambodia, the people without power never can do anything."

"Tep, we face the same situation in Germany. We have a lot in common. I grow up under a socialist government as well."

"You are from East Germany? Why you tell people in Kep you are from Hamburg?"

The old Khmer knew too much. Maier felt dizzy again. No ordinary Khmer Rouge, general or not, would know where Hamburg was. He made a last effort to worm himself out of being a suspect, which meant convicted and executed.

"I live in Hamburg. Until 1989, I worked in East Berlin, as well as in Hungary, Poland, Czechoslovakia and Romania."

The Khmer loosened his iron grip somewhat.

"Did you work for the Staatssicherheitsdienst? Do you know HVA?"

Maier had not expected this question. The HVA, the *Hauptverwaltung Aufklärung*, had been East Germany's secret service, its CIA. Maier had bumped into its agents in Eastern Europe, had even tried to seduce one of them in Breslau once. He shook his head. He hardly felt the needle penetrate his skin. The old Khmer smiled. Maier began to sink.

A voice, a German voice, ancient and thin, like cold clear soup, hissed behind him, "He never worked for the Stasi. A man like him would have been noticed in the Runde Ecke right away. But we can never be one hundred percent sure."

Tep let go of Maier's hands. The detective tried to turn but it was too late. He felt the thin white hand on his shoulder more than he saw it. For a few seconds, Kaley's smile crossed his inner eye, then everything went dark.

PART 2

THE WHITE SPIDER

THIRIT'S WISDOM

You could rely on the Germans, even when it came to death.

They'd phoned Dani Stricker immediately after Thirit, her turtle, had died. Dani wasn't surprised. Her time in Germany was coming to an end. Without Harald, she felt more like a stranger every day, more than she'd felt for the past twenty years.

She hurried through the rainy park to the Mannheim Botanical House.

Harald had brought her here at the beginning. The heavy, humid air reminded Dani of the rainy season back home. She got homesick every time she entered the huge building, but she'd never told Harald. And they'd come back, as often as Harald had found the time, to admire the crocodiles in the entrance hall, and the Mongolian gerbils racing about in their enclosure, or they walked through the butterfly garden, before they drifted across to the reptiles who lived in several rows of glass tanks. Only the large turtles lived outside.

Citizens could support one of these slow creatures and for her twentieth birthday, Harald had registered Dani as the godmother of Thirit, a tortoise from Southeast Asia.

In the years that followed, Thirit had become the closest connection Dani had to home. Once she had mastered some German, she'd taken the tram to the park every month and had told Thirit about her childhood. Thirit had known all of Dani's secrets, had listened to the young Cambodian woman for hours, as she had told her of her unfortunate sister Kaley. Thirit had had to listen to terrible stories, of murdered monks Dani had seen lying on the road in her village, of communes where people only worked and never ate, of friends' parents who had been picked up for 'training' by Angkar one night and had never been seen again. Thirit had never commented or thrown in a critical remark. In Cambodia, a real friend never did that.

The guard of the Botanical House, a young man in a muscle shirt, welcomed Dani. He was utterly taken by her, she noticed. Some western men were fascinated by Asian women and the park employee probably had no idea that she was ten years older than him. For a moment she felt something like longing, but the feeling was quickly swept away by thoughts of the coming weeks.

"Very sorry, Frau Stricker, but Thirit died last night. These animals have a life expectancy of ten to fifteen years. Yours was almost twenty years old."

Dani was not sure how she was to react. The Germans expressed their commiserations like other people, but surely no one expected tears for a turtle.

Dani did not have any.

"Can I see Thirit one more time?"

The young man shrugged his shoulders in embarrassment and looked at the floor.

"Unfortunately one of my colleagues already disposed of the animal. We had hoped that you might want to sponsor another turtle…"

Dani shook her head sadly.

"I am leaving Mannheim in a few days. Thanks for informing me."

She left the man standing there, admiring her, and walked through the doors of the Botanical House.

Her life in Mannheim was over.

But where next?

Her phone rang. She ran to a nearby closed café and stood under the awnings.

"You asked me to call once more. I have found your sister. And the man you are looking for. Everything is going as planned. Do you have any further instructions?"

Dani's heart beat all the way into her skull.

"My sister is alive? You have no doubt?"

"Absolutely sure. There is no doubt. She lives in Kep, on the coast."

Desperate thoughts raced through her mind. She had sworn not to return to her country. She had tried to become a German for twenty years. But it only took a few seconds to change her mind.

"I am coming to Cambodia."

For several seconds, there was no answer.

Finally the man answered calmly, "Don't come here. The situation is complicated and dangerous."

"I want my sister. Where is she?"

"Perhaps you should wait a week or two. But I would really advise you not come."

Dani resented the man's advice. She had to see her sister.

"I am Khmer. I know my country is dangerous. You work for me and I will come to pick up my sister."

The man chuckled, "Ok, don't say I didn't warn you. Send me your flight details by SMS to this number. Be patient. You hired me to get rid of the man. Has that changed?"

"No."

Dani shook the ice-cold rain from her hair. The man had hung up.

SHADOW PLAY

Maier lay on a bunk covered with a straw mat. He couldn't move anything but his eyes. It was almost dark. The room in which he lay smelled of old stone, of moss, of wild animals. A suite in a luxury hotel it wasn't.

Outside, from somewhere unimaginably far away, he could hear birdsong, perhaps a few insects. No people, no engine noises. Maier felt incredible and assumed his mental well-being to be the result of the drug they had given him. Or perhaps his euphoria had something to do with the fact that he was still alive. Wherever he was now, his life couldn't be worth much to anyone but himself.

Shadows moved around him. He tried to turn his head – to no avail. He was paralysed.

"You see, Maier, it's my mission to find out who you are. I will not let you go. You can no longer walk anyway. The general told me that you might want to invest in us, but I am convinced it is too late for that. Things have gone too far. Our relationship is not transparent and unnecessarily complicated. For this reason, I will take you back to 1976, metaphorically speaking, and I will interrogate you before you are disposed of. I am sure you understand. Tried and trusted methods."

Maier could almost see the man, not directly see him, but feel his presence. He spoke German.

Maier was not scared. It was too late for that. It was probably too late for Müller-Overbeck and Kaley as well.

He was alone again. Shadows brushed through space for long seconds. Time had slithered into a black hole. The back of Maier's head hoped that they had given him Flunitrazepam, Ruppies, R2s, Ropys, Flunies or something similar. He couldn't remember a thing but his head was clear.

Had he been permanently damaged? He wasn't worth much if he remained paralysed. He tried to laugh. After a while, the mosquitoes attacked. Maier groaned, he was the perfect meal.

Children's voices. Serious children's voices. No laughing. Light. Shadow. Orders. Maier managed to turn his head. His eyes were swollen, but he could see that he lay under an old mosquito net. Caught in the net of a huge spider. The room in which he lay was bathed in soft late afternoon sunlight, which flooded through an open, stone-framed window, like the blood of a freshly slaughtered buffalo. The walls were constructed from huge carved blocks of stone. He'd been taken to an old temple ruin of the Angkor Empire.

Someone removed the net. Three young girls, their hair cut short, all of them dressed in black uniforms, looked down at him. Their oblique expressions, perfectly synchronised, made him feel like a victim.

"Maier, were you born in Leipzig?"

The voice was old and tired, yet sharp and focused at the same time. Full of cold, bureaucratic routine. The man spoke a peculiar German. Maier thought he could detect a faint Eastern European accent. Whoever was outside his field of vision, in the process of deciding what would happen to him, had conducted thousands of interviews like this.

"Yes."

"Maier, are you working for an intelligence service?"

"No."

The girl nearest to him drove her fist into his face.

Maier cursed.

"Maier, did you study political sciences in Berlin and Leipzig between 1976 and 1982?"

"Yes."

"You worked as a foreign correspondent in the GDR? You travelled abroad?"

"Yes."

"That means you were trusted not to defect, trusted at the highest level?"

"That's true."

"I don't see any reason why the relevant offices would have had so much trust in you."

Maier did not know what to say. The second girl hit him hard on his right thigh. The child was good at her job, with immovable face and trauma rings around her eyes. The pain was terrible, a good sign as far as Maier was concerned. A little more beating and he would be able to walk again. He didn't say anything for a while.

"I was a good journalist."

"Did you work in Cambodia at the time?"

"No."

"You absconded to the West before the Wall came down?"

"I had an offer from dpa to work as a foreign correspondent in Eastern Europe and South Asia."

"Your ideological turn-about presented no problems for you?"

"There was no ideological turn. I was a journalist in the GDR, then in the reunited Germany. And then I stopped."

"Yes, yes, Battambang, '97. A bomb that killed a Cambodian colleague. A man called Hort, through whom you met your girlfriend Carissa Stevenson."

"I don't have a girlfriend. The man was my fixer, my employee. Ms Stevenson is an old colleague."

The third girl stepped up and hit him in the face. Maier's brain had started to crank up properly and he could make a pretty good guess at the next questions. As well as at the attached trap. He saw no way out.

"Carissa Stevenson is not your girlfriend?"

"No."

"Then you have no real interest in whether she is dead or alive?"

"Of course I have an interest, professional as well as motivated by friendship. We have known each other since the UNTAC years. Hort introduced her to me, as you said."

"Didn't you just tell me that you no longer work as a journalist? How can your interest be professional? Are you lying to me, Maier?"

"No."

The first of the three girls had stepped very close to Maier, holding a long acupuncture needle. She gently lifted his right arm and pushed the needle through the palm of his hand.

Maier passed out.

"Maier, were you born in Leipzig?"

"Yes."

"Maier, are you working for an intelligence service?"

"No."

The second girl hit him in the face.

"Are you Christian?"

Maier tried to shake his head.

"That's a shame, Maier. I would always give a second chance to a German Christian. You have another ten days of interrogations ahead of you. Choose your answers carefully and the young ladies will keep the needles away from your testicles."

Slow, scuffled steps receded. Maier hadn't seen his interrogator. The three girls continued to watch him, their faces twisted by nameless resentment. Maier tried to breathe slowly and evenly to get his heartbeat back under control.

Borderline experiences in Cambodia. He coughed with exhaustion and closed his eyes. Perhaps it was better to be tortured with eyes closed. The detective knew he was on the verge of burn-out. Short and sharp panic attacks shot like black pinballs from one corner of his drug-addled brain to another. He heard a cockerel crow outside. He felt like screaming himself, but he was not that far yet. Or perhaps he'd already passed the screaming stage. He let himself slide downwards.

Maier lay on the wide stone terrace of a temple ruin. He knew he was badly injured. Dense jungle reached to the horizon ahead. Dark green, light green and a thousand shades in between for which there were no words. Not a soul down there. He couldn't move. He could only stare at the green hell beneath him, above him, all around him. He managed to lift his right hand. The breeze almost pulled it away. As he looked past his dismembered thumb he could see the blue evening sky.

Maier noticed that the walls of the room he lay in were covered in bas-reliefs. A gigantic battle unfolded around him. He gazed at the scene for some time without understanding. Then he slowly remembered what the thousand year old carvings represented.

Gods and demons pulled at opposite ends of a *naga*, a mythical snake, which had curled around the sacred Mount Mandhara. Through the labour of gods and demons, the ocean of cosmic milk which surrounded the sacred mountain grew more and more stormy and eventually gave up *amrita*, the nectar of immortality.

Heavenly *apsaras* – sacred celestial nymphs with perfect breasts and swaying hips – floated above the scene and gazed down at him with serene expressions.

This old Hindu myth could also be found on the walls of Angkor Wat. But Maier had never seen this version of the masterpiece he was now looking at, despite feeling rotten and depressed. There was nothing left to do but look.

Carissa had gone ahead and rounded a curve in the forest road. He'd just heard her voice, then she'd been swallowed by the jungle. Unarmed and curious. Greedy for the new. Maier ran up the mountain as fast as he could. Animals that no white man had seen lived in the huge trees along the roadside. But Maier could not see animals. He didn't want to see or hear them.

Where was she? His woman?

Carissa lay on the road, sleeping peacefully.

Maier took in every detail of the crime scene. An army of ants had constructed a highway across her naked belly. Her white hair obscured most of her face. He could not read her last scream.

The bullet had entered the skull from behind and emerged below the lower jaw. Carissa would never say another word. Everything, almost everything was blown away. The ants began to consume her eyes. The tiny soldiers danced around her dark unreachable pupils like kohl.

A girl with short frizzy hair washed him. She was older than his earlier tormentors, around twenty perhaps. She was different. She did not smile but she did not look as numb as the black creatures with the needles. She kept her pale blue almond-shaped eyes low. Maier recognised that in another life she would be beautiful. But one couldn't choose. Perhaps in the next life.

"My name is Raksmei. Eat something, Maier."

Maier expected another beating when he didn't answer. He did not want to eat. Not even a Vodka Orange would have helped right now. He could smell shit and old leather. He could hear something hovering, flapping its wings, outside, beyond his reach.

Kaley sat next to him and held his injured hand.

"My name is Raksmei. Eat something."

"I have not found your sister yet."

"That does not matter. You have done your best."

Had his best been all that good?

"Have you come to Cambodia to arrest the German?"

"No."

"The old man is sure you here because of him."

"Who is he?"

"He is very old. He comes and goes. For more than twenty years."

He felt himself drift in shallow water. The current was slow. He could stretch out and drift away, like a message in a bottle. He was embedded in silence, as if submerged in cotton wool, or fresh snow. In the absence of peace of mind, this was pretty good. There was no fresh snow in Cambodia. The water was tropically warm. Something moved in front of him. A white spider, as big as a car, sat on the water's surface. Long white legs bopped up and down, gnarled like ancient tree trunks.

The spider turned towards Maier.

"Maier, do you work for a security service?"

"No."

"Are you Christian?"

"No."

"What do you know about Project Kangaok Meas?"

His legs began to get caught up in the net of the spider. He felt himself slowly sink. People could drown in just thirty centimetres of water. He needed answers.

He was a detective, a journalist, an adventurer, a ladies' man, a lone wolf. All just shells.

Maier screamed into the room, "You smell like a Stasi spook. Why haven't you cut my nose off yet? Why haven't you bugged my cell? Why haven't you asked me whether I work for the CIA? Or the KGB? Or the IRA, the PLO or al-Qaeda? I don't need to look at you to identify you. You smell of old files and the sweat of the dead you have on your conscience."

Exhausted, Maier fell back onto his bunk.

Kaley and Raksmei had disappeared.

The spider sat in the corner of the room and laughed blood.

"What, what, what?"

"If I told you that I know something about the sun and the moon, I would be lying."

"The sun and the moon? You are working for the sun and the moon? Maier, we are not on the same team."

Grey spittle dropped from the lower jaw and spread across the stone floor like something indescribable, searching out Maier's cold flesh.

"The only thing I know is what I will do with you."

Maier started singing to himself. The smell was unbearable, like rotten, atrophied flesh. The three girls, dressed in black bikinis, floated into the room on a long black surfboard, made from old car tyres and wrapped in barbed wire. The scarred, bent back of the spider burst open and thousands of tiny black spiders wearing black rubber shoes flooded the cell. In seconds, floor, walls and ceiling were covered in cold, black energy.

Then they began to crawl up his legs. Maier was caught. Maier was composed. This is what the end looked like, felt like.

"Sometimes the same is different, but mostly it's the same."

The Khmer Rouge had forbidden everything. Shopping, music, gossip, prayer, love and even laughing and crying had been punishable by death or worse. But in the moment of dying, prohibitions did not apply. Maier did not feel like praying, so he laughed. Insanity was the solution. That seemed perfectly reasonable. It was part of being human.

Maier got up and pushed the three girls aside.

What was his small suffering in comparison to the decades-long chaos Cambodia had experienced?

He stepped to the window, and, without turning, without searching for the eye of his tormentor, without bothering with the small spiders that were eating the world, he let go and rose into the clear blue evening sky.

BIG SISTER

Dani Stricker could hardly believe it. She did not recognise a thing. The country looked utterly foreign to her.

The new airport was different to what she had expected. What had she expected? The buildings were practically shining and the arrival hall was as neat and clean as the departure lounge in Frankfurt. Everything smelled new. The immigration officer wore a real uniform, hardly looked at her and, once she'd paid the twenty US dollars for a tourist visa, he stamped her German passport without pulling a face or asking for a bribe.

Her arrival card read "Welcome to Cambodia".

Fear and pleasure, a strange euphoria shot through her. The war, which she carried in the back of her head like the memory of an absent child, was nowhere to be seen. Outside, the taxi drivers hustled around her and carried her bags to a waiting car. For a moment she felt like she knew all Khmer people. After all, they were her people. Then she flushed, acutely aware that she had been away for twenty years. And that almost all the people she had once known were dead. Only her sister, Kaley, remained alive. And that man.

It was hotter and more humid than the Botanical House back in Mannheim. The air smelled sweet and heavy, saturated by the smells of blooming flowers and cheap talcum powder, the way Danny remembered from her childhood. The scene in front of her flickered from foreign to home, from alien to familiar, back and forth, rapidly.

She looked around, perhaps expecting her hired assassin to emerge from the crowd to hand her the head of the man whose death she had wished for all these years. But of course she didn't know the man and she couldn't see anyone who might have fitted the bill.

A family of Scandinavians, with five blonde children, tried to lift several heavy suitcases from their cab. The children screamed excitedly, the parents looked stressed. A tour group, Japanese, living up to the cliché, their necks bent forward, straining against several huge cameras, filed past her into the sun. A huge and pale *barang* in a loud Hawaiian shirt stood near the taxi rank and gesticulated into his telephone. The man had an impossibly red face and briefly looked distractedly in her direction. Who were these people? Who came here voluntarily? And why? Dani had bought a travel guide, but she was still surprised to see so many tourists. Her last impressions of her homeland, her overland escape, on foot, through a ruined and vicious country, were hard to connect with the reality of this new Cambodia.

In early 1979, she had fled her commune, had walked along the heavily mined road leading west, had forced herself not to drink from ponds filled with the corpses, sometimes entire families, who'd been butchered or poisoned. Again and again she had lain hidden in the brush for hours to avoid patrolling Khmer Rouge units. Most of these soldiers had been undisciplined children with murder in their eyes. Again and again she'd thought about her sister whom she had left behind. Her life was worth nothing. Once she'd eaten a dog, a piece of dog that she had found, half cooked by the heat, on the broken tarmac. A man had appeared and tried to kill her with a stone until she gave up the carcass and ran. The man had had a leg missing. He had not been able to follow her. She had passed pagodas that had been turned into pigsties. In Sysophon, she had seen five shorn heads lined up on poles.

The Buddha statues, those that hadn't been smashed to pieces, had cried in their temples. On the way between the small town and the Thai border, she had not managed to eat again, despite the fact that she had a little old rice and dog in her pocket.

The land she had walked across was silent. Throughout her entire month-long journey, she had not heard or seen a single motorised vehicle. Every now and then she had heard a young Khmer Rouge soldier laugh, despite the fact that Angkar had forbidden laughter. But she'd also heard the footsteps of ghosts preceding and following her, all the way to the border.

Countless times, she had passed dead soldiers and civilians. The victims had been young and old, male and female, Buddhist and Muslim, Cambodians and Vietnamese. Cambodia had become a country where cannibalism had become commonplace. She'd noticed that the killers had often cut the livers from their victims and grilled and eaten the organs right next to the corpses. Intestines, swollen by fat black maggots, had burst from slit stomachs. Others had lain in the brush, tied together and beaten to death. Yet others, many more, had lain in open ditches, half buried and half left to the elements. The wild animals had long left this cursed land and migrated into Thailand or Laos. The Cambodians had rotted in their pits, untouched. Dani had walked on, even though she had hardly a will to live left. She had kept thinking about her little sister whom she had abandoned to the Khmer Rouge. What was the point of survival if everything one experienced was the suffering and death of others? There had been no future. The future had been forbidden by Angkar, along with everything else.

She looked her driver in the eyes. He was about her age. He would not meet her curious gaze and turned his head. A shock ran through Dani Stricker. No question, the horror was still here. People remembered in silence. It was embarrassing. It was still there, beneath the glittering surface of the new

Cambodia. It did not fit in with this new life, but it served as a foundation for everything she was trying to absorb right now. For a moment she wished she had Harald with her, but he had died with her old life. She was alone.

Dani took a deep breath and got into the old beaten-up Toyota. How many lives could a person experience in the few short years one lived consciously? She shook her head. That was truly a *barang* question. No wonder her home had become an alien place. She had become so German.

As a young woman, she had once visited Phnom Penh. She remembered a sleepy, clean town with wide boulevards. Not much of that city had made the jump into the twenty-first century. All hell had come out to play on the airport road into town. Cambodia was waking up. After the dark years, the process looked a phenomenal challenge.

The traffic was hair-raising. Hundreds of mopeds, many loaded with families or impossibly large piles of goods, drove on both sides of the road in all directions. No one wore a helmet. Mothers clutched two or three children, riding side-saddle behind their husbands. New temples, new apartment blocks and new businesses sprouted from every street corner. The taxi passed the university. The buildings looked overgrown and run down, but the young students, dressed in pressed white shirts and blue trousers or skirts, were streaming through the entrance gates into the road, laughing and kidding each other like students in other countries. Cambodia screamed *new*. Huge billboards promoting the country's three political parties lined the roadside. Policemen stood in small clusters at busy crossings, machine guns casually slung across their shoulders, and dared each other to stop a vehicle and rob the driver for the coming weekend's drinking money. Some things hadn't changed.

"You want me to take you to a good hotel? I can find a very cheap room for you."

Dani, tired, shook her head.

"I have a reservation at Hotel Renakse. Please take me there. You know, the hotel in front of the Royal Palace."

The driver gazed at her in the rearview mirror with empty eyes. She had not forgotten her mother tongue but the man could tell that she did not belong here.

Dani's mobile phone rang and she dug it out of her handbag.

"Rent a car, a four-wheel drive if possible, and come up to Siem Reap. Take a room and wait for my call. My last call."

"Your last call?"

"Yes, in a few days it will all be done. When you have found your sister, leave the country immediately. No one will follow you beyond Cambodia's borders."

"So far you haven't done anything for the money I paid you."

The man laughed drily and said in English, "That's how it is in this business. The clients want unmentionable things done and at the same time they demand information."

He hung up. Dani Stricker wound down the window, leaned back and stared into the traffic, lost in her thoughts.

THE NEEDLE

He still lay on the bunk when he woke the next morning. The hallucinations of the previous day had receded. He could hear birdsong in the jungle. Maier still existed. He lay in a thousand-year-old temple in the dark heart of Cambodia, alive and mentally intact. But he was no longer in the mood for it. Today would be his last day. A knife, a bullet, an injection, he didn't care which. It just had to be quick.

"Do we know each other?"

The White Spider. Maier recognised the man immediately, despite the fact that he had never seen him before.

Today he was wearing his human shape. The man was at least seventy, as tall as Maier, but twenty kilos or so lighter. He wore khaki jeans, a thin white cotton shirt and a tie. He stood, slightly bent, over the detective. The Omega on his wrist was probably accurate, to the second. He probably had leather wings under his shirt. His face hung back in the shadows, Maier could not make him out clearly.

"Who am I?"

"I have never seen you before. And now that I have seen you, I never want to see you again."

The White Spider smiled thinly. He combed through his thin silver hair. His hands were huge, his fingers long and thin like hairless bones.

He stared down at his prisoner with narrow blue eyes that sparkled in a thin face. He looked like someone who enjoyed

172

a good bottle of wine, who read the right books and who never sat in the sun. Culture had never saved anyone from themselves.

"I can have you killed straight away, without further discussion. Would you not like to cling to the hope that you can talk yourself out of this for a little while longer? Don't you have a will to live, Maier? Are you even a real German?"

His voice was as thin as the fingers on his pale hand. A voice that came to Maier from far away. A voice that knew no resistance and no doubt.

"Why were you sent to Cambodia?"

Maier looked past the man now into the clear sky, towards freedom. Then he pulled back into the cell. Where he belonged. Outside, everything would be different.

The world he had left no longer existed. In his absence, everything had continued turning, without his input, his hopes and his fears. He embraced the darkness now. Here he would make his deal with the devil that stood in front of him now.

"I can see neither life nor hope in your eyes. I don't really know why I am here. I don't know what it is to be German. You are German. Me too. Still, someone should dig a ditch in a rice field and throw you in it, along with your friends. That's where you belong. I belong to the world. Not just Germany, but the world."

The man was silent.

"I assume my kidnapping and imprisonment is down to the paranoia of a few crazy holdovers of long-gone wars. You must think I have stumbled upon some dark secret from your past."

Maier gasped for air. A voice in his head was trying to make him panic and chanted "Shitty cards, shitty cards", over and over.

Maier lay, the man stood. He seemed to contemplate something. Maier tried to relax. Just a little. He could not ask this man to continue torturing him. His capacity to absorb pain was exhausted. Freedom or death made preferable alternatives. Sometimes, the same was different, but mostly, it was just the same. Maier had thought to the end. Losing was better than hesitating.

The White Spider turned towards the window. For him too, there was no way out. The deal was on the table. Perpetrator and victim had united into an organism called brute. The interrogation had ended. All that was left was the clean-up.

Raksmei had appeared next to the White Spider. Maier had the feeling he'd met the girl somewhere before. But her eyes were the same as on the previous day. Pale blue and far away. A Khmer with blue eyes?

He couldn't reach her. She held a syringe in her right hand.

"Tell me why you are here and I may let you live."

Maier could detect a faint expression of hope in the old man's face.

"You know why I am here. You have always known."

He was alone with Raksmei, He could not move. The sun fell through the window the same way it had done the previous day.

A day without Maier.

It had all gone so quickly, this life.

The young woman knelt next to him, tied him off, found a vein and stuck the needle into his arm. Maier smiled and opened his eyes wide enough to let her look inside.

The world was full of shit and gasoline, baby.

HOMECOMING

Dani Stricker had tears in her eyes. She couldn't help it after sitting in a crab shack in Kep all afternoon. She had discarded her assassin's advice. Siem Reap could wait. Once, a long time ago, in another life, she had come here, with her sister. They had run away from the paddy fields for a day to see the ocean. Their parents had never allowed them to go so far from the village. Dani's sister had been very young then, before the Khmer Rouge had changed their lives forever. With the few riel Dani had taken from the family purse, she had bought steamed crab for her sister.

Her cell phone rang.

"Where are you?" the feminine voice with the strong *barang* accent enquired without a word of greeting.

"At home. I have come home. I am in Kep."

She hoped that she didn't sound tearful. She could still taste the lemon sauce which came with the crab on her lips. The man said nothing for a moment.

"You are an idiot," he said finally, "I told you not to come back to Cambodia. I told you I had found your sister. Now you are in Kep and in danger and so is she. The man you want dead is not dead yet."

She didn't like the tone of the man's voice. She was paying him well. Before she could protest, he carried on, "If you have transport, leave immediately. Go back to Phnom Penh and wait for me to get in touch. And I mean immediately. I will call you back when it is safe for you to have a beach holiday. You are jeopardising your sister's life."

The line went dead. Dani was furious. Who did he think he was? Cambodia was her country. No one could be of any danger to her here. No one was even likely to recognise her. She ordered a pot of green tea. She could still return to the capital tomorrow. The man was clearly paranoid. She so missed her sister.

Dani watched the mellow surf lapping against the rocks below the shack. She heard steps approaching beside her and looked up expecting the waitress and her tea. A girl with short hair, dressed in black pajamas approached quickly and grabbed her roughly by the hair. She jerked back in surprise, but it was too late. The girl plunged a needle into Dani Stricker's throat and pushed the plunger.

BILGE WATER AND MEKONG WHISKEY

The water slapped against the side of the wooden boat. The smell of rotten fish was overwhelming. Had Maier had more room to manoeuvre, he would have stuffed bits of cloth or pieces of wood into his nostrils, but he lay less than twenty centimetres below the boat's deck in bilge water. He was trapped.

He'd managed to vomit twice without suffocating or being discovered. Did he want to be discovered?

He could see across the lake through a small hole in the side of the boat. Phnom Krom, the mountain at the western end of the Tonlé Sap, bopped up and down a few kilometres away. Grasses and drifting plastic rubbish floated close by.

The boat was being loaded. Heavy boxes packed with fish crashed onto the deck, which pressed down onto Maier. The wooden boards above his head were bending closer and closer. He wanted to scream, but most of all, he wanted to know more.

Why was he still alive? Had the young woman helped him escape? What was he doing under the deck of a fishing boat? How long had he been unconscious?

A loud, authoritarian voice barked an order. The men who were loading the boat stopped in their toil.

Maier could detect uniforms in the shallow water outside, moving towards the boat. Now he saw one of the men who'd been loading the fish, a typical Khmer fisherman, skinny and brawny, his back, bent from years of hard labour, burnt almost black by the sun. A policeman grabbed the man by the throat and screamed at him. Everywhere Maier could see now, uniforms were closing in. If Cambodian policemen stalked around in dirty water, up to their hips in the sauce, holding their Kalashnikovs above their heads, their uniforms muddy, they had to be under great pressure to produce results. Or they'd been promised a fat reward. They were looking for him.

But who knew that he lay under the planks of a boat on the Tonlé Sap? He barely knew himself. Someone had taken him from the temple to the lake shore and loaded him onto the boat. As much as he tried to stretch, he could not see or hear the young woman who had executed him with her syringe.

The commanding officer now stood directly in front of Maier's spy-hole and scratched his balls. Two of the officer's minions crashed about above Maier and began to bang on the wooden deck. Through the narrow gaps between the planks he could see that the men were trying to figure out how solid the deck was. Sweat and frustration dripped down on him.

A few minutes later they gave up and began to wade towards the next boat. The policeman in front of Maier growled, spat into the dirty water and disappeared.

The boat's engine coughed into life. The screw hit the water and the vessel began to move. Maier could see Cambodia pass through the tiny hole by the side of his head. Unnoticed, he slid through the floating village of Chong Neas, beneath Phnom Krom. An hour later, the boat passed the flooded forests of Kompong Phluk, whose fishermen lived in huts constructed on high poles, which reached far out into the water. But the boat didn't stop. Maier could hear the sound of a transistor radio from afar, a girl singing a mournful tune across the water, before sinking back into the rhythm of the engine and the rush of the water.

In the afternoon, the mosquitoes devoured Maier. He let himself go. What else could he do? He was sure the men on the boat did not know of their stowaway. He was a ghost and he tried to live the moment. After the days in the temple cell, he felt slightly euphoric, despite the insects, the vomit, the water, and his present imprisonment.

As evening came, they reached the mouth of the Stung Sangkar River. Every now and then he saw faint lights on the shore, lined by poor fishing communities. Then the night swallowed the land and only the gurgling water reminded Maier that he was still alive.

He woke up with a start. He was cold. The boat had stopped at a pier, probably in the early hours of the morning. A few weak bulbs flickered above an embankment. He could hear drunken voices.

The boat must have reached Battambang, the largest town on the Stung Sangkar. He began to shake. The sun would soon be up. Battambang had hotels and telephones. He would ring Carissa. His lover was the only person he could trust. But first he had to get out of his water taxi.

The detective lifted his bite-covered arms and pushed hard against the wooden planks above him. The wood bent a little, but there was no moving it. They had laid him below deck and then nailed everything shut. He would freeze to death before sunrise. He had not drunk or eaten anything for at least sixteen hours.

Suddenly he heard steps on the pier above him.

"Maier?"

A woman's voice, quiet and self confident. Khmer.

Maier groaned, "Yes?"

"I will get you out, but it will take some time. I don't want to make a noise. Everybody think you dead."

"I do too," he answered weakly.

BATTAMBANG

After a couple of days, Maier began to walk. But he couldn't run from himself. He slept under a net in a neat, small room located in an unremarkable family home on the edge of town, a bottle of water under his arm.

Every few hours, he woke, bathed in sweat, listening to the panic recede, and cursed the world. He hadn't seen Raksmei since his rescue. Twice a day, the family with whom he stayed invited him to eat. Rice and *prahok*. Maier did not eat much. The boys who lived in the house tried to animate him to play football, but he wouldn't leave the safety of the net.

A few days later, she suddenly stood in his room, a pile of newspapers under her arm. Jeans, white cotton shirt, leather sandals. She had parted the short hair with a garish plastic hair clip. He noticed small golden rings in her ears. She hadn't worn those in the temple.

"I have only bad news for you, Maier."

Maier looked at her silently.

Raksmei appeared to be two people at the same time, changing and shifting from one moment to another. The blue eyes were confusing. There couldn't be many children her age who were half-Khmer and half-*barang*. To Maier, Raksmei seemed to be both self-confident European woman and traditional Cambodian girl from the countryside. The impression was disorientating. Carissa had been right, the girl

180

was special. She reminded Maier of someone. He hoped that his brain was only temporarily muddled by the drugs they had given him. The drugs she had given him.

"Maybe you read article in *Phnom Penh Post* first."

She left a phone and a bottle of Mekong Whiskey and disappeared. Maier didn't feel like bad news.

CAMBODIAN WITH GERMAN PASSPORT KILLED IN KAMPOT

Daniela Stricker, a Cambodian carrying a German passport, was found dead in her hotel room in Kampot. A 42-year old Canadian was arrested near the Green Apsara Guest House while trying to flee on a motorcycle and has made a full confession. The murder weapon, a golf club, was found at the crime scene.

The police in Kampot are looking for a 45-year old German real estate speculator. Police investigations suggest the man left Kampot a day before the crime took place. It is not clear whether the man is a suspect. A week ago, Sambat Chuon, an employee of Hope-Child, a Kampot based NGO, was registered as missing. The local police dismissed any possibility that the disappearance and the murder of the German national could be connected. According to a German Embassy spokesman speaking on condition of anonymity, Mrs Stricker was from the town of Mannheim and had been recently widowed. Suicide has been ruled out.

A passport photo accompanied the brief article. The woman's face was familiar. After staring at the image for a while, he knew. This had to be Kaley's sister. Shit. And the German speculator? Maier didn't have to speculate all that much – he was being set up. He still held the paper in his hand when the young woman returned two hours later.

"Do you see my brother die?"

"No."

"But you are diving near where my brother die, right?"

"Your brother was sunk with stones around his feet. When my dive partner and I reached him, he was already dead and there was nothing we could do for him. The water was full of sharks. I am sorry."

"I sure it all the same story."

Maier swallowed, "Me too."

"You are journalist?"

"No."

She had saved his life. He had to tell her the truth. There was no one else in Cambodia who'd listen to him.

"I am a private detective. I am here to look out for a young German man in Kep. I was hired by his mother. It's Rolf, the owner of Reef Pirate Divers."

Raksmei watched him for a while.

"He disappear. I hear he have problem with partner and go to Phnom Penh to sell business."

She hesitated for a moment.

"You not here to find out what happen in Kep and Bokor and why somebody kill my brother and this lady?"

"No, I did not come for this reason. But we both think all this is connected and I am sure my client is up to his neck in trouble."

Raksmei nodded sadly.

"Raksmei, why did you save my life? And what were you doing in that temple with those people?"

"I look for murder of my brother. I want to know what happen to all the children who disappear from Kampot in last two years."

"And?"

"The people who stay in old Khmer temple near Siem Reap, they trade with property on the coast. From Koh Kong to Sihanoukville and to Kep. But I think this is front for something different. Do you know Kangaok Meas Project?"

"The old man in the temple asked me the same question. A woman in Kep told me a story about Kangaok Meas, an old Cambodian story."

"The story of golden peacock and Kaley?"

"Yes."

"Kaley is Khmer Rouge. She with Tep, old Khmer Rouge General, who use her to get *barang* business partner. Maybe she mad. I not know her much."

"She asked me to find her sister. I think the German woman killed is her sister. I am pretty sure."

Raksmei looked at Maier doubtfully.

"I think Tep kill her family long time ago. He call her Kaley. She Tep slave, I think."

"That is possible, but it is too simple, Raksmei. All the men who slept with her in Kep allegedly fall under a curse. They say if it rains after a man has spent a night with Kaley, he will die a violent, agonising death. All the locals and westerners in Kep believe this."

"Old story from old Cambodia. Do you believe in ghosts, Maier?"

Maier hesitated to answer. In this country one lost touch with reality even quicker than one's life. "Since I lay on that bunk in the temple, I believe in anything. Perhaps the horrors of the past left something here in Cambodia. So many unimaginable crimes have been committed in this country. It's hard to see how things could be as they were before. Some of the horror sticks."

"I never see ghost, Maier. But the Khmer, they live with ghost every day. But my brother and this lady not kill by ghost."

"No."

Maier read the article once more.

"I will go and visit the man who is in jail in Kampot. The man accused of Dani Stricker's murder."

"Maier, the Cambodian government say you missing. Everybody looking for you. Tep know many police. He not stop until he find you, dead or alive."

"And you too."

"Yes, me too. You want to know why I save you? Alone I can do nothing. I save you because I think you crazy to come to Cambodia to solve crime. Maybe you so crazy you help me. I want to know what happen with my brother and what happen in the temple with the young girls."

Raksmei sat down on the cool tiled floor and appeared to be ordering her thoughts.

"I run orphanage in Kampot. A few month ago, my brother find out that some of the girl we report missing are on Bokor mountain. He go up there one time but he not tell me what he see. Tep want to find the money to buy casino and make all new. I think this connected to Kangaok Meas Project."

"Could I make an international phone call?"

"Good to hear from you, Maier," Sundermann said. "We were getting a bit worried. Two days ago, Frau Müller-Overbeck paid us a visit. She was very upset when she told us that her son had disappeared. I don't want any details now, but I assume you are on his trail."

"Her son is in Phnom Penh. He is trying to sell his business. That's all I can say right now."

"She will pay a fat bonus if you bring him back to Hamburg."

"Dead or alive?"

"It's that serious, Maier?"

"The people who are close to this young man are dying like flies. He is deeply involved in a crooked real estate deal with occult overtones."

"That sounds like Cambodia, Maier."

"And the police are looking for me at this point. No one knows why I am here, though, or who I really am, so there's no need to worry. I need another week to solve the case and get the young man out of here."

"Don't become a fly, Maier. You're one of the best. If it gets too hairy, then slink across the border into Thailand and we will send Altwasser as a replacement. I will pass your news on to Frau Müller-Overbeck. Don't bother with the report. It's all under control this end."

"It is already very hairy. I will be in touch."

"Alive, please, Maier. If he dies, there will be a lot of trouble and no bonus."

Sundermann wasn't a bad boss. Maier had all the freedom he wanted to do his research. He was expected to work independently and discreetly. And he was expected to produce results.

"I have one week left, then I need to take the young man back to Germany," Maier said.

"You go to Phnom Penh and find this man."

"He refuses to leave Cambodia without his girl."

"Girl?"

"Kaley, the girl in the story of the Kangaok Meas."

Raksmei slowly shook her head.

"Not possible. I think she belong to General Tep. No one can help. My NGO cannot help. She too old."

Kaley's desperate request to find her sister had sounded genuine. But Maier was beginning to think that the mysterious beauty was either mad or did indeed work for the general.

"Somehow Kaley is at the centre of all this though. I saw her in the temple."

Raksmei shook her head.

"Not possible, Maier. Kaley is in Kep."

"She sat next to me on my bunk and asked me where her sister was."

"I think you dream, Maier."

"And the White Spider? The old German?"

Raksmei took her time to answer.

"A *barang* who speak Khmer and Vietnamese. Speak very well. A friend of General Tep. He here long time. He live and speak like Asian man. No like Khmer Rouge man. But maybe he here in Khmer Rouge time. I don't know."

"Are you scared of this man?"

"I don't know. He always friendly to me. But everyone scare the White Spider. Everyone shaking when he come into the room. He not like people speak bad with him, disagree with him. He never shout. Always speak very quiet."

"Do you think Tep is scared of the man?"

Raksmei shook her head.

"Tep is old friend. They like brother and brother. I never see Khmer and *barang* good friend like this. But all the girl in the temple very fear from him."

"How many girls live in the temple? Do you know?"

"Maybe twenty. They come and go in big black car. They all look and talk same same."

Raksmei stared into empty space, lost in thought.

'Did the Khmer Rouge not manipulate children to get them to brand their own parents as traitors or anti-communists?"

"I know, Maier. They do that before, long time before. Young Khmer people like me not know much about Khmer Rouge time. My friend in Kampot, they don't know who is Pol Pot. We not want to remember and the parents not want to talk about these times. But I know, the soldiers who come to Phnom Penh in 1975, many of the children, young boys and girls."

"Do you know who your parents are?"

Again Raksmei took her time to answer.

"No. Somebody tell me my father is *barang*. My brother, he say same same. Papa is *barang*. But maybe mama is *barang*. I don't know. I think I am born in 1980."

"At that time, there were not many *barang* in Cambodia?"

Raksmei nodded.

"No *barang*. The Khmer Rouge throw out all the foreigner or kill them. But maybe there is some exception."

Maier realised he was hurting the girl with his questions and changed the subject.

"How did you get into the temple?"

"I know General Tep long time, since I am little girl. He help me and my brother. We grow up with old lady in Kampot. I call her aunty but she not aunty. She die eight years before. After that I live with my brother in her old house. Tep, he give money and food. I remember him long time."

"I had not imagined Tep to be a generous man."

Raksmei laughed, but Maier could sense that the girl was angry.

"One time he try to chat me up. When I start Hope-Child he give some money. After my brother gone, I give up NGO and offer to Tep I can work for him. He accept."

"And why does he tell you about his dark secrets?"

"In Cambodia, people like this, man like this. They not think that a woman they know long time can make problem for them."

Maier laughed drily.

"That's not a Cambodia phenomenon. It's like that everywhere."

But Maier still had doubts. A large piece of the puzzle was still missing.

"I have to go to Kampot."

Raksmei brushed her short hair across her forehead and smiled. She pulled a small wad of dollar bills and his passport from her pocket.

"I find in your room in the temple. Tonight I take you to Phnom Penh. From there you go alone."

After she'd left, Maier opened the bottle of whiskey.

FREEZER

Maier pressed ten dollars into the hand of the man on duty. The lucky recipient pulled a stretcher from the ice box and disappeared. The mortuary in Calmette, Phnom Penh's barely functioning government hospital, was silent, dirty and cold. The hospital was a place to die in. A last way-station. The doctors bargained hard for every dollar. The medical equipment, such as it was, did not work and cockroaches ruled the grey building with impunity, day and night. During the UNTAC days, the hospital had gained the moniker "Calamity". Patients and their families lay on mats in the corridors. In the yard, the sick slept under mosquito nets on the bare ground. Nurses demanded hard cash for every shot of morphine. No one who was admitted was expected to recover, but Calmette was the best hospital in the country. The place where they stored foreign corpses. Maier hesitated for a second before he pulled the cloth back.

The journey from Battambang to the capital had been wonderful. He travelled through Raksmei's country, a country whose stories he had absorbed for many years, and had written about in his articles. He felt very much alive. Raksmei had warned him that the roads and trains between Battambang and Phnom Penh would be watched. Maier preferred to remain dead for now. This had called for a journey on the Funny Train.

The French had brought the railroads to Cambodia, but since the end of the war, only one train a day commuted between the capital and Battambang and, after decades of neglect, the tracks were in pitiful condition. The three-hundred-kilometre journey took around twenty hours. Usually the train was so packed that every available bit of roof space of the gutted and rusty carriages was occupied.

Maier had suffered through the trip in the Nineties, during the UNTAC presence in Cambodia. In those days, the journey had been free for passengers prepared to ride in the first two carriages. This hadn't been a charitable gesture by the railway authorities. The front of the train had been regularly blown up by landmines that Khmer Rouge units had dropped onto the tracks during the night.

As the roads around Battambang were unnavigable during the rainy season and virtually useless the rest of the year, local people constructed their own trains – from old tractor axles, water pumps and a home-made wooden platform – the Funny Trains.

These unlikely and unsafe vehicles transported up to ten passengers at a time and moved down the tracks significantly faster than the regular train. When two Funny Trains met, one could be quickly dismantled, deposited next to the rails, until the tracks were free once more.

The young man who operated the unusual vehicle didn't say a word, which was fine with Maier. The detective spent the day in silence, a water bottle in his hand, dressed in a torn shirt and the pants of a Cambodian farmer, a *krama* around his head. He tried to process the events of the previous days. He didn't do too well. His thoughts turned back to his mission again and again. He knew Kaley's sister had been killed but he had no idea why. This German Khmer had not seen her sister for years, decades even. He had to see for himself. He thought of Hort. Right now, the necessity of knowing felt like a yoke around his neck.

Village children ran along with them, waving and screaming at the top of their lungs, then Maier was left to his thoughts again. The driver stopped in Pursat and bought a bag of fried frogs. All that was left of the French-era train station was a single wall, against which the male passengers of passing trains urinated. Just like Battambang.

Maier ate nothing.

The Funny Train reached Phnom Penh Airport after dark. Maier jumped off, paid the driver and took a taxi into town. Every bone in his body seemed to have moved during the bumpy ride. He rented a cheap room in a guest house at Boeung Kok where he'd left money and a couple of phones. Then he waited for dawn.

Maier had seen, photographed and examined many corpses. Death made the human body unfamiliar. Whatever had made the person who'd left the body behind was no longer there.

There's wasn't much left of her head. Whoever had swung the golf club had wanted not just to kill. Daniela Stricker's face was totally disfigured. The lower jaw was missing. The back of her skull had also been bashed in. As if the murderer had wanted to obscure the identity of his victim.

After a while, he forced himself to search her torn clothes.

Her hands and arms were punctured by small round holes, which had become infected. She had been tortured, most likely by the three little girls. He turned the woman around. He could see livor mortis on her hip and along her back. The discolouring of her skin suggested she'd been moved a few hours after her death. He took another close look at her head. No doubt about it, Ms Stricker had been tortured, shot, moved from the scene of the crime, and then been beaten with a golf club. The police had covered up the true murder.

Maier would have to travel to Kampot to talk to the man in jail there. He heard voices approaching the door of the mortuary. The detective pushed the dead woman back into her cooling slot.

The employee burst in and gesticulated wildly. Maier didn't lose a second, pressed another twenty dollars in the man's hand and followed him through the only door, up a set of stairs and into a small office. Seconds later he saw the boy, Tep's son, his baseball cap turned backwards as usual, pass the door, followed by three young girls. The girls wore jeans and T-shirts today. They wore their hair short and their expressions left no doubt that they'd come from the temple Maier had been held at. The boy carried a revolver.

The hospital employee behind Maier shook like a leaf and started mumbling to himself. The small room they were in had one window. Maier told the man to close the window behind him, and escaped into the bright morning sun.

Who had known that he'd be at Calmette Hospital today? Was the appearance of the boy and his three angels a coincidence or had he been betrayed?

The detective tied his *krama* around his head and marched, his head bowed, through the entrance gate of the hospital and disappeared in the crowds on Monivong Boulevard.

ROLF

The German's handsome looks had all but faded. Maier almost didn't recognise the young coffee heir, who lay sprawled in an armchair in the back of Restaurant *Edelweiß*. Rolf Müller-Overbeck didn't react as Maier threw himself onto a sofa opposite and pulled off his *krama*.

"Hello, Rolf."

"Hello, Maier. Thought you'd been fed to the fish in front of Koh Tonsay by now. Almost feel like I'm meeting an old friend, after not seeing him for many years. Time flies."

The young German dropped the filter of a burnt-out cigarette into an overflowing ashtray and stared blankly at Maier. His clothes were dirty. His shirt was ripped across his right shoulder. He looked almost as desperate as the legless beggars who moved up and down Sisowath Quay.

"You don't seem to be particularly happy about my survival."

Rolf shrugged.

"It's all over, Maier. My business has been stolen and my woman has disappeared, probably kidnapped, probably not to be saved. Your appearance doesn't make much different in the larger scheme of things."

"Perhaps I can help you."

The younger man laughed bitterly. "Help me? Everybody wants to help me. Help me to buy land, help me to start a business, an honest business, help to cheat the locals, to pull them across the table and to rape them. I don't know why you turned up in Kep, but since you did, things have been going downhill. And now you want to help me?"

"What happened?"

Rolf pulled another cigarette from his crumpled shirt and began fiddling with a cheap plastic lighter.

"Why should I tell you anything? You make it all worse."

"After what you have just told me, it cannot get much worse. I can assure you that I have nothing to do with the problems in Kep."

Maier knew that he didn't sound very convincing. Rolf said nothing.

A smiling waitress arrived with two cans of beer.

"Vodka Orange," Maier ordered and handed one of the cans back to the young woman.

"Last week we found out that the land documents most of the *barang* in Kep hold are fakes. Tep. cheated us and then offered generously to transfer our investments to the casino. Otherwise it would all be gone and we could leave Kep. And if that was not acceptable, the general's little killer girls would chase us away. As expected, my partner Pete signed the new contract with Tep. Without asking me."

"And where is Kaley?"

"Disappeared. Inspector Viengsra came and took her. After I refused to invest in the casino, I received a letter. I found it under my door at the dive shop office."

The younger German pulled a piece of paper from his breast pocket.

Maier scanned the page, which had been torn from a child's exercise book. If Rolf wanted to see Kaley again, it read in broken English, he'd have to pay fifty thousand US dollars. The deadline for the drop had already passed.

"I don't have fifty thousand US dollars. Anyway, this doesn't mean anything. Who knows what would have happened if I'd paid.

Maier looked into Rolf's eyes. The coffee heir was all the way down. The moment had come to push forward, directly into his heart.

"What happened to Kaley's daughter?"

Rolf brushed the long hair from his gaunt face and looked at Maier with a hostile expression.

"You're telling me that you have nothing to do with what's going on in Kep and you ask me so personal a question?"

"Why is the question personal?"

"Because I killed Poch, Kaley's daughter."

Maier went for a mild smile. He knew he'd driven Rolf into a corner, exactly where he wanted him. The pressure to confess, to communicate, to share his suffering had to be overwhelming.

"You don't look like someone who kills small children. What happened?"

"Yes, I'm a child killer and everyone in Kep knew that and knows that and they keep their mouths shut because Tep makes them. I am the child killer of Kep. That's the secret of our little community."

Maier said nothing. He was waiting for more.

"I was driving our jeep between Kampot and Kep. Pete sat next to me. Suddenly, a black shadow ran across the road and it went bang."

The young German finished his beer and waved the can in the direction of the waitress.

"We stopped. A small girl was lying in front of the car in the middle of the road. She was alive for a few more minutes, but she didn't say anything. Just this little bundle of suffering and death. Her name was Poch. She was Kaley's daughter."

"She wore black pyjamas?"

Rolf nodded distractedly.

"She had short hair?"

"Yes, just like her girlfriends who stood by the side of the road a few minutes later. I can remember exactly what they looked like. They were angry, angry as I've never seen anyone. They had murder in their eyes. I almost had the feeling that it wasn't directed at me, but at their little friend. As if Poch had been running away from them. But that didn't make sense. And then her mother came."

Rolf swallowed hard.

"You see, Maier, I can't leave Kaley behind. And now it looks like I can't take her with me. As I said, everything is broken. Just read the paper."

"Are you sure that Kaley would leave the country with you?"

Rolf wouldn't make eye contact with Maier. He stared silently across Sisowath Quay.

"I'm not sure."

The younger man was about to break into tears. Instead he lit his cigarette and hid behind a cloud of smoke. He pushed the current edition of the *Cambodia Daily* across the table at Maier and stabbed his finger angrily at the main feature.

"Kaley is only the tip of the iceberg that's drifting around Kep. She never asked me to take her with me. But who, in her situation, would say no?"

Maier understood that the young man had no clear idea of the priorities of his girlfriend. If she still had priorities.

"You remember what Vichat, the park ranger in Bokor, told us about his colleague who'd disappeared, and the girls he'd seen in the ruins?"

ACTIVIST FOUND DEAD AT HOME

Preah Sim, well-known human rights activist and director of the Cambodian Human Rights Society, was found yesterday in his room on Street 278. Sim was 28 years old. Neighbours confirmed to a correspondent from the Cambodian Daily that three young women had visited the activist in the afternoon.

The homicide department of the Phnom Penh police force initially insisted on suicide, but a demonstration by hundreds of workers of the garment industry in front of the Rue Pasteur police station and pressure from the opposition Sam Rainsy Party forced the authorities to reconsider the case. Prime Minister Hun Sen, at a CPP party function in Stung Treng, regretted the death and promised a swift resolution to the case.

"If you have money you can do anything here. It goes all the way to the top. You can cover up murder and accidents as if they'd never happened. But someone somewhere always gets caught up in this. Do you understand what's happening here? And why you can't help me?"

Maier read the article again.

"You have money in Germany. Ask your family. Your mother would send you the money straight away."

Rolf rose angrily, "What do you know about my mother, about my life, Maier?"

"I am a private detective from Hamburg. Your mother hired me–"

"To spy on my life, because she thinks I can't do it alone. Or because she can't bring herself to sell the family business to a stranger. Unbelievable. You're a bastard, Maier."

The younger German had gone pale with anger. He was on a roll, his voice heavy with sarcasm and malice

"So Detective Maier already knows that a German woman has been killed near Bokor, and that he is one of the suspects. All your own fault, Maier. Or my mother's, who won't let go of her son."

"But you won't manage to get out of here by yourself. I can help you to find Kaley."

Rolf laughed.

"You are wanted for the murder of a German tourist and now you want to save my girlfriend. Maier, don't cross my path again."

The young man threw a few bills on the table and disappeared in the throng on Sisowath Quay. Rolf was well informed. But not well enough to know who the dead German tourist was. Maier stayed behind, alone, enveloped in dark thoughts.

CAMBODIA DAILY

The young journalist watched Maier nervously across a table of the Boat Noodle Restaurant. A few of the surrounding tables were occupied by employees – Khmer and *barang* – of the NGOs who had their offices in the adjacent buildings.

He could see that the young man was not comfortable, though he'd chosen the restaurant. Maier was in a hurry and journalists were badly paid in Cambodia. The detective pushed a hundred-dollar bill across the table at Sorthea Sam. The young writer stared at the money and asked in French, "What do you expect for this money? That's more than I earn in a month. I don't think that I have information that is worth one hundred dollar to you."

Maier guessed that the man was very frightened. Otherwise he would have taken the money straight away.

"I have a few questions in relation to the article on the death of the human rights activist. The story you wrote."

"A crazy, dangerous story that will never be resolved," the journalist answered in a shaky voice, and finally, without looking at Maier, slipped the money in his breast pocket.

"Who were the three girls who visited the victim on the day of the murder? Why were the children even mentioned?"

Sorthea Sam looked across his shoulder.

"You say you are a detective from Germany? Not a journalist?"

"No."

"And you are here to watch a German who might be involved in this?"

Maier ordered a coffee and nodded. The young Khmer ordered tea and a glass of water. Sorthea Sam lit a red Ara and sat quite still, smoking in silence. Finally, the young man began to talk.

"Eyewitness accounts. Preah Sim lived in an apartment block not far from the palace. We spoke to the neighbours. The police did not. Four families in the same building confirmed that they saw the three girls arriving and go into Preah Sim's room. They came out shortly afterwards, moments before Preah Sim emerged, bleeding heavily. A black SUV, tinted windows, no plates, dropped the kids off and collected them again. The police published a photograph of a young man who allegedly stabbed Preah Sim. The suspect is in prison and the case is closed."

"And the girls?"

The young journalist mulled over his answer for a moment.

"I only mentioned the girls because I had a strange visitor a few weeks ago. A young man came to see me. He was half Khmer and half *barang*. His name was Sambat and he was working for an NGO in Kampot that was looking after orphaned children. I had heard of Sambat before he visited me, from a colleague with whom he had followed and exposed a Swiss paedophile. Otherwise I would never have believed the story he told me."

Maier stirred his coffee and tried to look as unconcerned as possible.

"Sambat told me that he had seen these girls do military training at Bokor, the hill station on the coast. I thought, this guy is mad, but Sambat was a serious man. I snooped around a bit after that and found out that a former Khmer Rouge general is trying to buy the casino. I even sent someone to Bokor, but there was no trace of the girls. My informant only met a drunken Russian. But then one of the park rangers told him about the girls. The story is so bizarre that I checked back with a few contacts I have in government here. When I mentioned the name of this general a couple of times, I was told to let the matter drop. At the same time I found out that the son of this general had shot some nouveau riche kid in the Heart of Darkness bar in front of a hundred witnesses. That killing was suppressed as well."

The Khmer laughed bitterly.

"I never wrote the story. I never heard from Sambat again, except for the news that he'd disappeared. When Preah Sim was killed and the neighbours talked about the girls, I remembered Sambat. Do you know what happened to him?

"He is dead."

Sorthea Sam looked at Maier in disbelief.

"Dead?"

"He was killed in Kep two weeks ago. The corpse was fed to the sharks, so that they could declare him missing. No body, no murder."

The journalist looked scared.

"How do you know?"

"I was there."

"Where?"

"At the crime scene. I was scuba-diving off the Kep coast and watched how sharks ripped the young man apart. He'd been sunk alive, with stones around his feet."

The Khmer nervously shrugged his shoulders and lit a cigarette.

"Another reason not to follow this story any further. That could become very unhealthy for me. And for you too."

Maier sank back into his chair and relaxed. He also felt like a cigarette but he repressed the urge. He'd hated himself as a smoker too much to start smoking again.

"So what is your theory? Is there anything in it?"

"My theory is absurd, monsieur."

"I would like to hear it any way."

"Money. It's all about money. Everything in Cambodia is about money. There's never enough and the Cambodian government is doing everything it can to shovel international aid into its own pockets, to sell the land to foreign investors and deny our people any opportunity to live a decent life. There are more than enough orphaned girls in Cambodia. It's a brilliant idea. If I had not stumbled across it, I would not have connected Sambat with Preah Sim. But like this..."

Maier smiled softly. He was on the right track.

"Will you pick up the murders again now, with what I have told you?"

The young Khmer shook his head.

"No body, no story. I believe you, but I assume I can't quote you. And the case of Preah Sim is still hot and it is unlikely that they will let the young man who is sitting for it go. He has a good alibi, but his family was forced to stand as witness against him. The man was betrayed by his own father. What does that take? You can imagine what kind of pressure my newspaper will be under if I continue my investigations."

Maier finished his coffee and waited. He had the feeling that the journalist had something more for him.

"I have a small consolation for you – there was another murder three months ago and three girls were seen near the scene of the crime. That one had nothing to do with politics. The wife of a minister had her husband's second wife disfigured with acid. The girl died of shock in hospital. A young man was arrested and sentenced shortly after. They never touched the wife of the minister. I reported the case and interviewed a few of the witnesses. One mentioned the girls. It didn't mean anything at the time. Now we are talking about at least four dead."

Maier thanked the writer and thought of the fifth victim – Daniela Stricker, Kaley's sister.

KAMPOT

An hour later, Maier raced his Kawasaki dirtbike through the suburbs of the capital, on his way to Kampot. The road south had improved since the UNTAC days, but the traffic was still life-threatening. He needed to reach Daniela's alleged killer alive, but he knew that time was running short.

Cambodia knew no driving licences, nor was there a minimum age for drivers, and most private vehicles had no number plates. No one was insured. Every few kilometres, Maier passed an accident. Every time, a small crowd gathered and people stood staring at a mangled motorbike or its dead or dying driver. No one tried to help. No one called an ambulance. Ambulances and doctors were for the rich, who, in the event of an emergency, would have themselves taken to Phnom Penh Airport and medivacced to Bangkok. If there was enough time. Less fortunate members of the population died, in the event of a serious accident, right by the roadside. Just like today. Just like every day. Despite the traffic, Maier reached the small river town before sundown and drove directly to the prison.

Kampot was a sleepy community, held together by a few blocks of French colonial and Chinese buildings from the early twentieth century, which spread around a large Art Deco-style market hall. Many of the old buildings were in need of restoration. Especially the old jail.

The prison was in the centre of town, on the banks of a stagnant, dirty pond. Coconut palm trees and high grasses grew around the compound. The prison wall was topped with rusty barbed wire that had once been electrified, decorated by torn pieces of prison clothing. An old watchtower leaned away from the wall across the street as if trying to escape its responsibility.

Maier parked his bike in front of a café on the other side of the pond and walked through the open prison gate. A group of soldiers sat around a rickety plastic table and played cards. They didn't notice him pass.

The main building looked like a French small-town apartment block from the Fifties – four stories, rectangular and drab, thought up by bureaucrats. The two other buildings that served as accommodation for the guards had survived from the colonial era and were about to collapse.

Maier walked through the main entrance into the cool semi-darkness of the almost empty reception hall. A naked bulb flickered uncertainly in the ceiling. A soldier sat in a dirty green shirt and faded shorts at an empty table and played with his mobile phone. The building was deadly quiet. There couldn't be many inmates.

"*Soksabai.*"

The guard raised his eyes, an expression of well-worn boredom on his blank face.

Maier offered his hand and looked the man directly in the eyes, smiling broadly. The guard put his phone down carefully and accepted the handshake and the enclosed ten dollars with a gentle, impenetrable. smile.

As in any proper prison, a large keyring hung from a rusty nail on the wall behind the desk. The guard slipped the money into his pocket, grabbed the keys and waved for Maier to follow. He wore no shoes and Maier followed the patter of his bare feet along a pitch-dark corridor. The cells on the ground floor were all empty. Suddenly the guard stopped and felt along the wall for a switch. In the light of a solitary bulb, Maier followed him up a naked stairway to the first floor. The layout was the same. Maier followed the soldier along a corridor until they reached the third cell. The guard switched the cell light on and unlocked the heavy steel door.

An unimpressive man in his forties sat, obviously confused, on the edge of a bunk.

Maier nodded to the man and turned to the guard, but the soldier had already disappeared. He'd left the door open.

The man didn't move and stared into empty space, like a deer that had been caught in a car's headlights. He was unshaven and had black rings under his eyes. He didn't look dangerous. Another victim.

The damp cell had no windows. The bunk was the only piece of furniture. The half-finished plate of rice and *prahok* on the floor had been taken over by cockroaches. The room stank, as it does when misery gains the upper hand. The man must have sat in darkness all day.

"Good afternoon, my name is Ernst. I am a representative of the International Red Cross. I have been sent to see how you are being treated."

The man looked at him in disbelief.

"What time is it?"

"Two o'clock in the afternoon," Maier lied. "I am here to ask you how you are being treated. Do you understand my question?"

"Is this a joke?"

Maier shook his head with a serious expression in his eyes and showed the man an ID card of the Red Cross.

"Your name is Renfield? Wayne Renfield?"

The prisoner was still watching him doubtfully. Maier felt his fear. This man was scared of being killed. He nodded carefully.

"Are you the only prisoner here?"

The man shook.

"I think so. There was an old man on this floor a while back, but he died. Every now and then they put some motorcycle thieves in here, so they don't get lynched by irate villagers."

"How long have you been here?"

Renfield suddenly fell to his knees and looked up at Maier.

"Can you get me out of here? I'm sitting here waiting for someone to come and kill me. I am innocent. It couldn't have been me. I was already sitting here before the woman got murdered. I've never killed anyone. I was only here for the kids. They gave me one year..."

Maier didn't care much for the men who came to Cambodia to abuse children. It brought out his vigilante side. He tried to push evil thoughts aside. But not altogether. The children who'd tortured him in the temple cell had been on his mind all day.

"I can help you, Mr Renfield. But you have to trust me. You have to tell me why you are here. I am sure this is a typically local misunderstanding, and that we can resolve it, if you did not commit the murder of which you are accused."

Maier sat down on the bunk next to the man and offered him his hand. The handshake of the Canadian was coated in fear.

"What was your name again?"

"Ernst, Robert Ernst. The Red Cross in Phnom Penh sent me, after we read an article about you in the *Phnom Penh Post*."

Renfield was skinny and tall and had a chin like Kirk Douglas. His cheeks were grey and his white fingers shook nervously. He had chewed his nails down to the tips of his fingers. He wore torn, stinking socks, baggy and stained khaki pants and a stone-washed denim shirt. He wiped his hand continuously through his greasy long hair that dropped across his shoulders. Not a pretty picture.

But Maier was not here to hand out Christmas presents. So they would come to kill this man.

"You told me you were already incarcerated here before the murder?"

"That's what I tried to explain to the cops in Phnom Penh. This English guy with bright red hair, who said his name was

Pete, came to see me a week ago and told me I was free to go. He told me Tep had bailed me out and that I owed him a favour. No problem, I thought. Either I fuck off out of the country right away or I pay my debts. The English guy left the keys to a motorbike and disappeared. He left the cell door open, it was unbelievable. I simply walked out. I got on the bike and drove off towards Kep to go and thank Tep. No one tried to stop me."

Maier looked into the eyes of the prisoner and tried to smile with a neutral, officious expression.

"And what happened next?"

The Canadian jerked around. "You don't believe me either, do you? This is just another trap. You'll tell me I'm free to go and then I get shot in the back on the way out."

With a calming gesture, Maier tried to wave the man's paranoia away.

"I am not in a position to free you, Mr Renfield. I merely want a statement from you so that we can help you from Phnom Penh. Now that I have your statement, I am sure you will be released soon."

Maier laughed politely. "Of course, I cannot just take you with me."

"I understand, I understand," the prisoner mumbled eagerly and tried to relax.

"So you never saw the woman you allegedly murdered?"

"Never saw her. Never met her. Have no idea who she might be."

Renfield swallowed. Perhaps he realised that the truth was not doing him any favours.

"You understand? You must understand. I didn't knock her off. I was right here in jail and after the English guy had given me the bike keys I left. That sounds mad, but that's how it was. And the soldiers who guard this dump said nothing to their colleagues; otherwise they would have lost face."

There was nothing more to find out.

"Mr Ernst, how does it look? Will I ever see the prairies of Alberta again? Will I get out of here alive, or am I sitting in a trap, waiting to be sacrificed for something I didn't do?"

Maier looked at the man for a moment. The truth was secondary today. It was time to go.

"Mr Renfield, I will tell your embassy and the police in Phnom Penh that I am of the opinion that you are not the killer of Mrs Stricker. The Red Cross has no sympathy for you in regards to your actual crimes, the abuse of children, and we will pass this on to the Cambodian authorities. I assume you will be able to serve the rest of your sentence in Phnom Penh, while the murder of the woman is likely to be resolved later this week. Have a nice day."

Maier got up and shook the Canadian's hand once more. Still moist and full of dread. Renfield knew how quick the end could come in Cambodia. That's why he'd told the truth. This paedophile had not killed nor disfigured Daniela Stricker.

Maier left the man in his cell and felt his way back to the stairway.

Downstairs, the guard had returned his attention to his mobile phone. He nodded to Maier and smiled gently. The detective escaped into the humid afternoon.

THE LAST FILLING STATION

Maier spent the night in a small guest house in Kampot. The next day he stayed in his room, had his food delivered to his door, slept and dreamt empty dreams.

When it got dark, he got on the bike and drove to Kep.

"I need a gun. It cannot be difficult to buy a gun in Cambodia, surely?"

Maier had waited until just after midnight before he'd dropped into the Last Filling Station. Les had shown no surprise as the detective had entered his bar.

"The red snoop is back," was all he'd said.

The old American nodded at the Vietnamese girl and seconds later a .22 calibre revolver and a box of cartridges lay on the bar counter in front of Maier.

"This little thing is not registered, buddy. And it's small so you won't go through the wall behind you when you pull the trigger. I don't want to see it again. Get rid of it when you're done. You owe me a hundred and fifty US dollars."

Maier loaded the weapon.

"Turn up the music for a minute, Les."

The detective stepped outside and walked down to the beach. A loud rock song blasted from the bar and shattered the humid silence. *I am the world's forgotten boy, the one who searches and destroys.*

Maier stepped up to a palm tree, kept five metres distance and pulled the trigger. The bullet burst the tree bark. He waited until the song had finished.

"You don't trust anybody?"

"Kaley's sister was not killed by the Canadian who is sitting in jail in Kampot. At the time of the murder, that man was already a prisoner. Pete let him go and he was picked up again immediately. The woman was tortured and shot in Bokor. The work with the golf club was meant to hide this."

The American nervously brushed his hand across a tattooed arm as if trying to cure an itch. For a moment, the old war veteran looked as if he was going to despair. Maier was sure he could trust this man. Les called for the Vietnamese girl. The small silent woman appeared from the kitchen, carrying two more guns. Les spoke a few words of Vietnamese to her and gave her a keyring. The girl gesticulated angrily. But the American shook his head gently and took the weapons from her hands.

Maier realised only now that Raksmei had been sitting at one of the darkened tables at the back of the bar since he'd arrived.

"I wait for you long time, Maier."

He nodded at the girl and smiled. She looked incredible in a pair of old and very tight jeans and a pink, buttoned-up shirt. Her blue eyes were lined with black kohl. Her short frizzy hair stood in all directions and had been dyed a soft red. She looked ready for a wild Saturday night in Phnom Penh, but it was Wednesday and she sat in the only bar in Kep.

"The whole world wants a piece of Maier. Tep's people were waiting for me in Phnom Penh."

Maier had planned to ask Les whether the old soldier could take him to Bokor without being noticed, but it would have to wait.

"What you do with the gun, Maier? Shoot the ghost?"

Maier laughed. "I would not dare pay a second visit to Tep's without a gun."

"You go back island?"

"Yes, tomorrow morning. Alone."

Raksmei nodded seriously.

"No problem, Maier. I not come with you. If Tep catch me, I am dead. I not think he like that I help you run away."

Maier nodded thankfully.

Raksmei finished a glass of water and stood up.

"You take me to Kampot? You not stay in Kep tonight? Pete is at the dive shop and son of Tep come here today looking for us. And he ask for you in Kampot."

The American nodded in agreement.

"Yeah, the English guy dropped by with a lawyer from Phnom Penh and showed me copies of my land ownership papers. He told me that all the papers I had were fake. He's been doing the rounds for days, with all the *barang* who bought land in Kep. Usually the same story. Either we invest the money in the casino and pay rent for the properties we bought or we can get out. The Scandinavians already left. A few of the French have too. Maupai is still here. He came in yesterday, drunk, and told me that the casino would be saved through the cooperation of the local expatriate community. If you believe that, he will rule Bokor like the Sun King one day and Indochina will make a comeback. He's basically gone insane since the death of his wife."

"What happened to Kaley?"

"Inspector Viengsra charged her with prostitution and took her away. Shortly after, Tep's son chased Rolf out of Kep. As far as I know, our young German hero is in Phnom Penh."

Les laughed without joy.

"That was a few days ago. Since then no one's seen Kaley in Kep. But Tep is still here. Sometimes he's over at his island, sometimes up at the brothel and sometimes at his beach resort."

Maier gave the American his best smile and said goodbye.

"I will be in touch."

"If you need anything else, buddy, let me know." He paused for a moment, then added, "You are alright, Maier, aren't you?"

"I am alright. Please organise me a boat that I can take to the island tomorrow."

Two minutes later, Maier raced without lights along the coast road to Kampot, his revolver in a pocket of his vest. Raksmei sat behind him, her arms slung around his waist, her right hand on his weapon.

Maier had made all his decisions in the hospital in Phnom Penh.

"If you ever look into her eyes properly, you'll never share a bed with me again."

When he stopped a few minutes later at the offices of Hope-Child, the girl behind him had fallen asleep. He switched off his engine and shook her awake.

"Maier, come in, your hotel might no longer be safe."

"It is almost certainly safe. I checked in under a false name."

In the light of a pale half moon, Raksmei stepped towards him and threw her arms around the detective. Maier looked at her eyes. What a terrible and beautiful place this country was. For a moment he looked past her, tried to feel Carissa in the darkness of the tropical night, but she was not there.

Raksmei climbed back on his bike and they drove to his guest house.

Carissa's words followed him like a warning.

"Don't get happy yet, old man. First we have to solve the case."

He finally took Raksmei where he could see her and opened his eyes for a second time, wide enough to let her look in. She stared back, from a place Maier could only guess at. Her skin was like the surface of a placid ocean, from a world in which placid oceans existed. When he slid his hand down her back, from her shoulders to the bottom of her spine, she shuddered slightly. As if the surface of the water rippled. She showed no fear, nor obvious joy, but enough silent lust to pull him down into the water.

••••

They lay next to each other in his room, silent and sweating.

Hours later, after her breathing had calmed, he stood next to her, revolver in hand and stared down at the beautiful sleeping shape of the girl. Her face had a very serious expression. So familiar.

It was time to go.

Maier got dressed quietly, reloaded the gun, and collected Raksmei's clothes. No one would follow him this time. As he stood outside the door in the dark corridor he waited for a moment and typed a message into his mobile phone. The reception along the coast was not great and Maier hoped that his brief instructions made it to Kep.

He locked the room and threw Raksmei's clothes behind the reception.

It had started to rain.

Maier pushed his motorbike to the old bridge, the only one which led across Prek Kampong Bay, before he started the engine and slowly drove towards Bokor. When he reached the edge of the jungle, he ditched the bike and started walking. He never saw nor heard the three youthful black shadows peeling out of the fog behind him and closing in.

HELL IS EASY

Maier felt great and assumed his mental well-being to be the result of the drug he had been given. Everything in his head repeated itself over and over, at unfathomable speeds. He knew that he'd been lying on his bunk for ten thousand years. He could feel himself lying there ten minutes ago. Or perhaps his euphoria could have something to do with the fact that he was still alive. Wherever he was now, his life couldn't be worth much to anyone but himself.

Outside, somewhere unimaginably far away, he could hear birdsong, perhaps a few insects. No people, no engine noises. Familiar, but he couldn't put his finger on it.

After some time, he managed to move his head.

The White Spider sat in front of him. Alone. The man was so old, a single kick would end it all. But Maier could not even move his little toe. He could not even see far enough along his body to check whether he still had his toes.

"I assume that you feel reality has become more flexible. In a few days you will be able to find your way around the inside of your head again. You will then be able to sort your visions from your life."

Maier watched the man silently. He did not want to try to speak yet.

"You are in a monastery near Bokor. You have been with us for a week, and you have been doing well. Some other guests would have gone insane by now, or expired. But we haven't amputated anything yet. No one knows that you are here and no one is out there looking for you. You have been reported missing to the authorities, but this is nothing out of the ordinary. People go missing in Cambodia all the time. And you are wanted in connection with the death of a German tourist, I have heard. The police found a gun with your prints on it that has been counter checked with the German authorities."

Maier tried to focus on the man's wristwatch. Walls had appeared in his head, which made it impossible to form judgments. He needed to make judgments on what the man had just told him. But he couldn't.

"What do you want with me?"

Maier was surprised, the question had simply slipped out of him.

The old man heard him and leant forward.

"I like precise answers, it comes with my background. You, on the other hand, ask precise questions. I am not used to that."

For a moment, he seemed to be searching for words.

"I have not been asked anything for a very long time."

"What is your background?"

"My background is in vermin removal. I realised as young man that this was my calling and I never got away from it again. I have had different experiences in life and have done different jobs, but I always felt most comfortable in my first job. I am sure you understand. Through the vagaries and coincidences of life, I have become a mirror of the twentieth century. A mirror for the blind. Look closely, without blinking. Concentrate."

Maier's head was clear. He could see the man in front of him, but he had not caught up with himself yet. Some large chunk of his life, his personality, appeared like a brief dream which, following his return to consciousness, threatened to disappear down a black hole. That might have had its good sides, but he could not put his finger on anything positive. He wasn't even sure whether he was still truly Maier, whether he had ever been truly Maier, or whether he might be Maier again at some point in the future. He had lost his desire and ability to make judgments. He was happy.

"I will tell you my story very slowly, Maier. I am a Catholic. I believe in hell. I am familiar with it. My hell can only be days away. That's how it is when you grow old. After a long and productive life, one can't help becoming a little cynical. You used to be a journalist, now you are a detective. You grew up in a totalitarian country, but now you live in apparent freedom. You have seen a lot during your travels. That's why you can and will write down my story."

The White Spider nodded at him, a celebratory expression in his pale blue eyes.

"Yes, I am appointing you as my biographer. I will pay you for your services, every day. With your life. Your work will enable you to continue living. You will be my Scheherazade. I will show you things only a few people have seen. And if you manage to bring my story to paper, you will earn the right to live, until our next session."

Maier tried to nod, but his head wouldn't move.

"And if you do a good job you will soon understand again who you are and how to read the truth."

Maier had nothing to say.

"But you must choose, Maier, between life and death. And if you choose life, it will be my life. My story."

The old man had got up and staggered towards Maier. A young, beautiful woman with short frizzy hair and inscrutable blue almond-shaped eyes had appeared next to him. A European? Maier could not be sure.

He had seen her somewhere before. Maier thought about her so hard that his head almost exploded, but he could not recall the name of the young woman or where he might have met her. Her name had disappeared into the black hole.

She wore black pyjamas and stood in bare feet. She held two syringes in her hands. The left syringe was filled with blue liquid. The right one was clear. She did not smile and looked right through him.

"You are my biographer, Maier, and I will make you the witness of my life's work. What do you think, helping an old friend, a countryman, far away from home, to take leave of the world? What do you think of your assignment? Isn't my offer irresistible?"

The White Spider had bent over Maier and watched him attentively. Maier knew that the most important moment in his life lay in his own green eyes right now. In his eyes, which he'd used all his life to seduce women and to pull the truth from people. Perhaps his life had all been one long preparation for this moment. For a few seconds, he opened his eyes to let the old man look in.

The White Spider nodded sympathetically and the girl put the syringe with the clear liquid aside. Seconds later he felt the needle in his arm and fell into the sky.

"Do not worry. Everything is simple and straightforward in hell. You don't need a translator and there are no questions to ask. Just make sure you don't blink, Maier."

THE TWENTIETH CENTURY

Maier woke in the morning, wheelchair-bound. He sat on a wide stone platform, just above the cliff from which the coastline was visible. He heard voices somewhere but he couldn't see anyone. He breathed in and out deeply. It seemed the best way to find out whether he was still hallucinating or whether he had returned to some reality. Shit, he'd been caught a second time.

The forest had crept across the stones for centuries and had spread so much that one had to step right up to the temple wall to get an idea of the building's dimensions.

Maier could move his arms and turned the wheelchair around. Lizards and squirrels chased along the hot stones and invisible birds sang from the trees. It didn't look like hell. But Maier had never been sure whether he'd recognise hell if he happened to end up in it. He remembered the old German's offer. How long had he been here? Suddenly, the mental floodgates broke, and a thousand questions rushed like an avalanche through Maier's head. What had happened? How much of what he took for reality was hallucination? He needed answers.

He remembered the girl who had given him the injection. Then it was all gone again and he sat in a wheelchair and admired the view and the jungle.

Maier heard voices behind him and turned his wheelchair once more.

"Ah, good morning, Maier."

The White Spider spoke English today, out of respect for his companion – a tiny Japanese man who looked like a butterfly collector. The man was in his mid-fifties and wore a green saggy cotton hat, short khaki jeans and a shirt with a thousand pockets. He wore three cameras around his neck. Only the large net and the jar full of chloroform were missing.

A girl, dressed in black, followed the man, carrying a heavy camera tripod.

The Japanese nodded amiably at Maier.

"Are you also a guest of the Khmer Rouge? Everyone always says how unpredictable and dangerous these people are, but this is my second trip."

Maier must have had questions written on his face, because the little man continued.

"I am here to stock up on my collection of objects from the Angkor period. And the White Spider is a reliable supplier."

Maier wasn't surprised. He knew that smugglers, bandits and former Khmer Rouge soldiers had long sold the finest carvings and statues to private collectors from around the world. Just recently, Maier had heard of a catalogue of objects that still resided in temples. Collectors could place orders, the items were stolen, hauled across the porous Cambodian-Thai border and sold. Cambodia did not have the money or the political will to fight the thieves and vandals. For this reason, many smaller pieces had been taken to the national museum in Phnom Penh. What was left would disappear in the coming years. The Khmer Rouge had advanced from murderers to co-conspirators and suppliers to the bourgeoisie.

The Japanese man had lit a red Ara and theatrically blew smoke through his nostrils.

"We have a saying in Japan, '*Kiken nashi niha, yorokobi mo nai*'. It means as much as 'Without danger, there is no happiness'."

Maier was not sure whether he really agreed with anything the art collector said. The pleasure of being close to the White

Spider was a dubious one and didn't stand in any kind of relation to the risk one took. But the Japanese hadn't understood that yet.

The White Spider smiled at Maier and said, "Your assignment starts today, Maier. My assistants will provide you with a laptop. You should start taking notes immediately. The quality of your documentation will dictate the quality of your life."

The Japanese visitor had walked along the platform to the edge of the cliff and began to take pictures. Every so often he turned and snapped the small group around Maier.

"You see, Maier, in our business, discretion is everything. This man is not discreet. He. is a good customer, but this time he has brought cash. And as you can see, he is clearly a security risk. What do you think, Maier?"

"Why don't you take his camera? You are the boss around here."

"That's right," the old German laughed and waved for the collector's assistant. The girl waited until the art collector looked at the world through his view finder, before she smashed the tripod into the back of his head. The Japanese man dropped to the ground like a sack of flour. Two more girls, dressed identically, emerged from the temple, took the man's cameras and threw them into the forest below. Then, all three dragged him away like roadkill. The collector could no longer move and cried softly.

"It is essential to kill with enthusiasm. I learned that in Croatia a long long time ago. If you don't have enthusiasm for your line of work, then change job. Killing is not an occupation for dispassionate people."

He added, with an almost cheeky gleam in his pale eyes, "Neither is living."

The girl who had given Maier the last injection put a laptop computer onto his lap and pushed his wheelchair after the White Spider.

"I am Raksmei, Maier. You can't remember me but you will. I have given you drugs. I will help you," she whispered behind him. Maier did not react. But he was sure that this girl was the sister of Sambat, the boy who'd been executed in Kep. When had he last seen her? How had she managed to get inside?

A second girl helped lift Maier over the threshold of the temple.

The Japanese lay on a rusty hospital stretcher in an almost dark, damp hall. A few candles, stuck to the base of a pillar on which a statue of Buddha or Ganesh might have once stood, threw an eerie, unpredictable light into the room. Maier could smell blood and garbage.

"We prepare our girls for all eventualities. Everyone has to be ready for combat at any time. Ready without hesitation, without thinking, without having to look into the eyes of their commander, without sentimentality, they will be able to successfully go through with the job at hand, so to speak. The readiness to overcome incredible odds and challenges is an old Khmer Rouge tradition, especially when it comes to health care. And our art collector will make the perfect cadaver to bring our students closer to surgery."

The White Spider snapped his fingers and the girls tied the Japanese to the stretcher. Raksmei had a syringe ready, but the old man shook his head.

"Unfortunately we cannot afford to waste medication indiscriminately. We have to do without during training."

The old German nodded to the youngest girl, who rolled a small steel table to the stretcher. The Japanese had woken up and, with a confused expression, looked around the dark hall. When the girl approached him, he screamed so loud that Maier thought his head might burst. Without hesitation, the girl grabbed a bone saw off the steel table and began to amputate the art collector's right leg. Screaming still, the Japanese shat himself and passed out. Urine and blood mixed below the stretcher.

In an instant Maier understood where he was, what he was and what would be expected of him.

"Yes, Maier, everything is becoming clear now. Now you are ready to accompany me on my last journey. Now you are my biographer."

THE BIOGRAPHER

Maier was empty and tired. The continuous hallucinations had worn him down. The murder he'd witnessed had numbed him. He had written the first entry in his biography.

The White Spider oversees two girls attempting to amputate a man's leg in a temple hall near Bokor Palace. There are no qualified medical personnel present. In order to simulate war-like conditions, no medication is administered to the patient during the operation. The patient, a Japanese national, dies during the procedure, presumably from shock.

It was hard to write more than a few lines about the butchering in the temple hall. It was hard to write anything.

Now he sat, still in a wheelchair, in the shadow of the old casino and watched twenty girls, still in their teens, as they were being drilled in close combat by Tep and his son.

It was agreeably cool on the plateau and the pale morning sun barely managed to pierce the clouds of fog which hung between the crumbling buildings of the French hill station. The training was as brutal as the operation had been on the previous day, and Maier was sure that some the girls would not survive their apprenticeship. Again and again, Tep, dressed in a tracksuit like a football coach, made the girls attack each other with bamboo sticks, while his son pulled one or another girl out of the mêlée and let her smoke *Ya-ba* on the casino steps. The

222

cheap amphetamine had its desired effect. After three or four pills, the girls were so highly motivated that they picked up a machete without hesitation.

Inspector Viengsra sat on the balustrade surrounding the property. He smoked one Ara after another and watched the drama. The policeman had long passed the point of being able to participate in physical training.

The White Spider appeared next to Maier and looked down at him, smiling broadly. The old German wore a freshly-pressed, spotless white shirt, and a large black floppy hat, under which his pale blue eyes roamed like fog lights.

"I see you are taking notes. That's great. Everything should be noted, even our mistakes. No one is perfect."

Maier was not sure whether the old man referred to the death of the Japanese man or the training of the girls. If he continued writing for his captor he would be as guilty of the crimes he documented as the actual killers. Every sentence he put to paper was part report, part confession. That of the White Spider, as well as his own. The moment had come to make a fundamental decision. As if the White Spider had read Maier's thoughts, the old man turned and snapped his fingers.

Raksmei pushed a second wheelchair next to Maier.

"Oh, no."

Carissa sat next to him and smiled unhappily. Her face was as white as her hair. In the pale morning light she looked so very beautiful and broken. He looked at her in silence.

"You were right, Maier, I should not have followed you. You don't bring any luck to girls. But it's good to see you."

"I'm not exactly having the time of my life either. For now, think yourself lucky you've still got legs. I told you this was one investigation you should have left your fingers off."

The White Spider stepped between the two.

"In order to motivate you properly, I have invited your girlfriend to join us for a while. Unfortunately, Ms Stevenson seems to have similar problems with her legs as you did and cannot walk at present. Whether we will operate on the lady in the next few days depends on your literary abilities. You understand me, Maier?"

Maier nodded numbly and began to write.

Extreme hand-to-hand combat. The apprentices are fighting with sticks and machetes in front of the Bokor casino. Amphetamines are used deliberately and excessively to motivate the fighters. The results are remarkable. At least one of the girl fighters is unable to continue and tries to cut her throat with her own knife.

A girl had brought a chair and the old German sat down next to Maier.

"What is your name?"

The White Spider did not answer for some time. Finally he cleared his throat and looked at the detective with something akin to fatherly pride.

"I keep forgetting that you are my biographer. Your detective career is over. I have to get used to that. Keep writing, keep writing.

Maier managed to smile at the man with forced benevolence.

"My name is Lorenz, Hilmar Lorenz. I was probably born in Düsseldorf in 1925. I grew up in an orphanage. From there I joined the *Hitlerjugend* and then the SS.

In 1943, I worked in Croatia, Bosnia and Herzegovina. That's where I found my calling. I worked as a point man between the SS and the Ustashe. I worked in the camps. Tens of thousands, Maier, tens of thousands of people marched past me to their deaths. I was part of a gigantic machine. When we began to take heavy casualties on the Eastern front, I knew that Hitler and the German dream had failed. A year later, in September

1944, Tito urged some Croatian and Bosnian troops to change sides and join the Partisans. I still remember that morning clearly. I acted immediately. Out of necessity and conviction, I might add. I like being on the winning side. As I had a lot of intelligence information, the Partisans did not kill me. In order to prove my worthiness, I was ordered to lead the communists, disguised in Ustashe uniforms, into my own Ustashe camp. I became a Trojan Horse. The Partisans and I killed everyone. We killed my friends and colleagues, fellow fighters, even the prisoners. Everyone. That's what saved me. I was accepted, I was on Tito's side. I performed an ideological U-turn and realised that ideology is secondary. It's not about the 'Why', it's all about the 'How'."

Maier took notes and tried to remember what he could of southern Europe during World War II. The Ustashe had been the most feared fascist militia in the Balkans and had been every bit as brutal as the Khmer Rouge. Lorenz was not too far off the mark – it hardly mattered whether totalitarian systems were left- or right wing. The Germans and Dachau, the Khmer Rouge and the Killing Fields, the Americans and Vietnam. Death knew no ideology. One could become a war criminal in any culture.

Maier continued to write.

Lorenz proved to be flexible, ruthless and cunning enough to integrate himself into the communist power clique. In 1945, Hilmar Lorenz, under the assumed name of Yvan Nazor, organised a series of massacres along the Austria-Slovenian border. Thousands of Ustashe units as well as countless Wehrmacht soldiers perished in these efforts. Following the foundation of Yugoslavia, he became a member of the internal security services.

"I only got to meet Tito after the war ended. I was not the only *SS-Standardjunker* who made a career in a communist country. In Vietnam, scores of my old SS colleagues fought for the communists against the French. That didn't surprise me. I was a child of totalitarianism and hence I was sent to Cambodia as a Yugoslavian diplomat in 1973. Tito knew that he had the right man in the right place. For me it was like a third spring."

The girls had completed their training for the day, and Tep, followed by his son, approached Maier. The general looked at Maier as if he were inspecting a flat tyre on his SUV and grinned, "Not long now, Maier."

When the Khmer Rouge marched victoriously into Phnom Penh on April 17th 1975 and took power, Hilmar Lorenz was Yugoslavia's diplomatic representative to Cambodia. In the following months, Lorenz took part in a number of secret meetings of the Cambodian communist party's central committee. Often, he was the only European present. In 1976, Yugoslavia donated nine million dollars towards rebuilding the shattered nation. Lorenz stayed in Cambodia until 1979, aside from a few short trips to Belgrade, and would only be recalled after the Vietnamese invasion.

"I don't understand what you are doing here today. Surely there are other, more vicious regimes about, which would go to great lengths to utilise your services and expertise?"

The White Spider appeared to play through all possible answers to Maier's question. Finally, he bent forward and began to admonish his prisoner.

"Please do try and keep the irony from the voice of the biographer. Otherwise I will have it removed with a knife. A man like you would not be able to survive such a loss. It's very simple, Maier. I have grown old. My experience and services were very much in demand in 1975. I was probably as old then as you are now. In the new Cambodia, I am not needed, officially. But I came back for nostalgic reasons and the country can use any kind of help with its reconstruction. I am a consultant. I think that's the going term nowadays."

Following the disintegration of Yugoslavia, Lorenz visited the German embassy in Belgrade. With the help of partly forged documents, he managed to prove that he had a right to German citizenship. Neither his past in the Waffen-SS, nor his work as a Yugoslav intelligence agent was uncovered during the application process, and since 1991, Lorenz has been a German citizen again.

"I was a pensioner, a damn pensioner, like millions of others. Germany has grown old and careful. But I was in no mood to die in a small apartment in Darmstadt. I returned to Cambodia with UNTAC, just like you, though not as a journalist, but as an investor. I used the money I got from the sale of my apartment and bought land in Phnom Penh. And one day, during a visit to Kep, I bumped into Tep, my old friend Tep, with whom I had crisscrossed his country thirty years before to take stock of the revolution. He was almost destitute and I bought him a piece of land on the coast. A thanks and a token of remembrance, for the good times. We both made a fortune when land prices shot into the sky a few years later. Enough money to get mad ideas."

The old German's mobile phone rang. He said nothing on answering the call. After a while he slowly got up and walked towards the black SUV that stood waiting next to the casino. Raksmei, the young woman whom Maier had thought to be European, the little sister with the needles, helped the White Spider to his vehicle.

Before the German got into the car, he called for Viengsra, the policeman who'd fallen asleep next to his dog. Lorenz shook his head in resignation, carefully climbed onto the backseat, closed the door and lowered the window. He grinned at Maier, as if he'd just had a brilliant idea, and shouted, "When tourists come to visit the casino, we retreat to the pagoda. We have had some problems with a Russian who lives up here. But you are welcome to stay. Your legs should almost be usable again. Tep's son will keep you company and will assist you in getting rid of this useless policeman. I am relying on you, Maier."

The moment had come as quickly as Maier had expected. While he didn't like the policeman, he had no desire to kill him. This was the final journey Lorenz had mentioned. A journey into the human off-side. Maier did not want to follow the old German.

"And don't wait too long. A man awake and in fear of his life is more dangerous than a man who is sleeping. Until tomorrow."

The White Spider retreated into the darkness of the car and the dark window slid up silently. As the SUV pulled off, the window lowered once more.

"That was just a joke, Maier. We still need the policeman. I wish you an enjoyable evening. Keep writing. I want a story, not a notebook. Write with style and flair if you want to save your girlfriend's legs."

THE HANGMAN'S BOUDOIR

"Were you ever married?"

Lorenz smiled happily. The young fighting girls had cleared some of the overgrown garden behind the casino. Carissa, Maier and the White Spider sat in wheelchairs in the morning sun. The view across the Gulf of Thailand was gorgeous, the ridges of islands in the distance half submerged in clouds, the water placid and calm.

"Now, Maier, now we are getting closer to each other. Your critical, well-structured thinking is coming into play. Perhaps this is your true calling. Perhaps you lived your entire life in preparation for this moment. Now you are asking the questions that a good biographer would think of. You are beginning to dig for the morsels of information that lie buried between the lines of the official version – exactly the things that make a man what he is. You are writing my testament."

Maier had turned his notes into prose during the night. He was no poet, but he weighed every word. The fear that the little shrimps would amputate Carissa's legs if he did not produce sat deep in his bones. To avoid this scenario, he needed to write like a Nobel winner.

Maier's most difficult assignment had only just started.

"I was married twice. I met my first wife in Croatia in 1942. She worked in a women's camp, in which I was employed as representative of the Reich. I was very young, still almost a teenager. Her father was a German, her mother from Croatia. I could never have married her back in Germany. She was ten years older than me. We were married by the camp commander. As I said, I was young. And I had no urge, like many of my colleagues, to rape the female inmates. They were too sick, and anyway, that kind of thing stood everything on its head. My mission and my ideological convictions stood in the way. We were trying to get rid of these people. A few months into the marriage, I was told that my wife was protecting one of the inmates.

"She had married me in order to save her friend, perhaps her lover, perhaps a dissident. My wife even told me in which part of the camp her friend was housed. She never really thought about what kind of a man she had married. Isn't that strange? I did not bother finding out who her friend was."

The White Spider sat facing Maier, eyes glazed over, drifting away through the memories of his youth. Maier said nothing. He had opened a dark door in the White Spider's head. He hoped he would not drown in the flood of memories that was pouring out.

He was the biographer of death.

"Though she was older than me, she had a much lower rank. The next day I went to visit the camp commander. I told him the truth. At the same time I informed the SS in Zagreb. The commander would not have agreed to my suggestions without pressure from the outside. As I said, I was still young."

Maier took notes, in direct speech. He would rewrite the text later.

Somehow.

The White Spider leaned forward and brushed his old thin hand through Carissa's white hair. The journalist recoiled from the pale, skinny fingers and looked past him, her gaze fixed.

"Yes, Maier, women. I learned early. If you really want to achieve something in life you will have to do without some things, some circumstances and even relationships, which we take for granted, which we feel we have a right to, simply because we are alive. But it's not like that. Man has no right. He takes it. Think of what will happen to the world if we let everybody reproduce, on and on and on. The lack of natural resources, our environmental vandalism, climate change, the little wars in the developing world: all results of our irrational attitude towards reproduction. One day this will bring us down. I don't care much. I won't be around to see it. But think about it. In China, the government tries to control population growth by passing laws. It doesn't work, because the system is so corrupt, but in principle, the Chinese are on the mark."

"What was your first wife's name?"

The White Spider looked at Maier directly. The question had brought him back from his philosophical meanderings.

"Take notes, Maier, this was one of the key events in my life. I remember exactly how I stepped into my office that morning, after talking to the commander. The day is so clear in my memory, as if it had all happened yesterday. It was a bloody cold day. Sixty inmates had frozen to death the previous night. My wife was a guard in a place called Stara Gradiška, the women's camp of Jasenovac. Her brother worked with her. He was really a nice man. But he had no ideology. He was an opportunist. A typical Croatian. I ordered two other Croatian guards into the office, very reliable men. Then I had her brother called. His name was Miroslav. I told him that my wife had been cheating me. Of course, he tried to defend his sister. He knew exactly what it was all about. My two helpers garrotted him right in front of my desk. My secretary passed out."

The old German had got so excited he was out of breath and now coughed quietly into a white handkerchief.

"Take notes, Maier," he repeated. "I am in the mood to have the odd toe removed from your girlfriend's foot. My girls never get enough practice. The visit of the Japanese collector was a rare opportunity to simulate the conditions of a field hospital in a combat situation."

Maier began to write in silence. He did not dare to look across at Carissa. Lorenz looked at the detective, his eyes filled with expectation. Maier swallowed.

"You did not tell me your first wife's name."

"That's correct, Maier. That's how it goes when you tell stories. I am getting there. Just a little bit more."

Maier nodded and briefly glanced past the old German, at life. It was a long way away and he did not belong there. He had taken his place, close to the cold flame of the old white devil.

"I filled in an execution order for the entire block my wife had mentioned. About three hundred women and children. I had the camp commander sign it. The document contained very precise instructions as to how the inmates were to be killed. My wife was ordered to get them to dig their own graves. It was her job to kill them, with a shovel to the back of the head, one by one. After the thirty-eighth execution, Nada shot herself in the head."

Maier and the White Spider sat, united by the indescribable. Maier looked at his captor and fell through black eyes into the depths of a bottomless ocean. Lorenz grabbed his wrist and smiled gently. "I killed my second wife myself, Maier."

ALL'S FAIR IN LOVE AND WAR

Maier and Carissa had spent a second night on the roof of the casino. The boy had cradled his AK like a baby and had fallen asleep on the stairs in front of them. Four of the girls took turns guarding them during the night. They hadn't spoken or slept much. Just before dawn, Carissa had moved in his arms.

"Maier, we need to get out of here. I feel sick all the time."

"I'm not exactly doing great either. Just be glad for the moment you still have your legs. Today we can walk again. Lorenz knows that everything here is going down the drain. He talks about dying all the time. Perhaps he has enough and wants to provoke an end, even if, or precisely because this would destroy his plans in Cambodia."

Carissa got up and fished a crumpled joint from her trouser pocket.

"By the way, Rolf went crazy in Kep the other day. He had a fight with Pete at the crab market and then broke into Tep's resort. I don't know if he stole anything. After that he disappeared. Kaley was taken away by the policeman. I actually expected to see her up here in Bokor."

Maier had caught up.

"They pumped me full of drugs and took me from the island to a temple north of Angkor, hidden deep in the jungle. The stuff they gave me really crushed my mind. I didn't know what was happening, or where I was. I even thought you'd been killed on the road to Bokor. But I escaped, found out that

233

Kaley's sister, a German, had come to Cambodia, presumably searching for her sister, and got killed by Tep. I just missed him at Calmette where I went to make sure it really was Kaley's sister, but then got caught again coming back here."

Maier's memory was back – he could remember that Raksmei had guided him through his toxic dreams, but he wasn't sure what had happened in his mind and what hadn't. He didn't have the energy to look closely at the past days, to separate hallucination from fact. He had caught up and found his centre once more, but the recent past appeared as several narratives that were coagulating into a new reality, its only objective survival.

"Did they interrogate you?"

She wouldn't make eye contact with Maier.

"Yes," she mumbled.

A gust of wind brushed across the casino roof and Carissa took a deep drag on her joint. Maier shook his head. Carissa brushed her hand through his short hair.

"I think that Mikhail is involved in all this. But when I came to visit, he wouldn't tell me a thing. On the way back to Kampot, Tep stopped me on the forest road and took me to the pagoda on the plateau. I spent last week in a hole there. They didn't kill me, because the old German thinks that you will cooperate better if I'm alive."

The fog lifted as the sun rose. Below them, the Gulf of Thailand stretched towards Malaysia. Phu Quoc, Koh Tonsay and a few smaller islands were clearly visible. Fishing boats moved up and down in front of Rabbit Island.

The boy had gone downstairs. Maier couldn't see anyone around the casino. The old buildings of the hill station, the post office, the church, the mayor's office, the old water tower, surrounded by rough rock formations and tall grasses – the entire community looked like a place from which man had been banished a long time ago.

Maier tried to imagine what the hill station might have looked like during Sihanouk's reign in the Sixties. The roads had been surfaced and lit by gas lights. The staff had worn pressed white uniforms and had spoken enough French to supply the guests with the illusion of savoir vivre at the end of the world. The cocktails had flowed night after night and the king had seduced countless women, specially flown in for the monarch. There had even been a toy train up here. The rich could be absurd anywhere.

There wasn't much left. Bokor was now a shadow world and the presence of the handful of rangers, who hardly dared to leave their station, was too weak to put a stop to the darkness. As Vichat had said, Bokor was ruled by ghosts.

"Today, we get down to business. I am sure that Kaley is here. I am ready for anything. I will not let them torture us again."

Maier turned to Carissa.

"By the way, do you know what role Raksmei plays in all this?"

Carissa shook her head and squashed her joint on the red fungus which covered the rooftop.

"I don't know. It looks like she's the old man's assistant. But she hasn't been up here long. I have no idea which side she's on. I thought I knew that girl. And I think many of the girls that are being trained here come from the orphanage she ran in Kampot. A terrible thought. But I don't understand what they are doing here. What are they being trained for? Are Tep and the old man planning a second revolution?"

Carissa looked burnt out. Her white hair stood in all directions and the black rings under her eyes lent her a ghostlike quality, hardly softened by the morning light.

"I have an idea. Have a look at the papers when we are back in Phnom Penh, for unsolved political or otherwise remarkable murders. I mean professional assassinations. I would be surprised if witnesses did not see young girls near the scene of the crime."

Carissa nodded in silence.

"I have the feeling that we got involved in something that's a little too heavy for us. What do you think, Maier?"

Maier returned her gaze and said, with all the optimism he could muster, "Today we find Kaley and disappear."

Raksmei stepped onto the casino's rooftop, two syringes in her hands. The boy stood behind her, gun pointed at Maier. Behind the boy, two girls in black, remote-controlled eyes fixed on their prisoners, stood on the stairway.

Raksmei stepped up to Maier and said in halting English, "A car is waiting for you downstairs. Be quick and you will get there before this shot takes effect and your legs give out."

He had no choice. The boy would shoot him if he tried to run and the shrimps would skin him before he'd reached the stairs. Raksmei's expression didn't change as she pushed the needle into Maier's arm. He felt dirty.

The old police station lay a kilometre below the ranger station. The boy raced the SUV as quickly as possible along the potholed road.

There was no sign of Mikhail, but Maier could see Vichat standing on the terrace of the ranger station. Ten minutes later, the boy hit the brakes in front of the overgrown building. A sign on the wall next to the broken door read *Police Municipale*. Like the other buildings scattered across the plateau, the former station was a ruin.

The White Spider was waiting in the shade of a mango tree, carrying his oversized hat in his thin nervous hands. Lorenz wore a worn, snow-white linen suit.

Two wheelchairs stood at the ready. The boy and Inspector Viengsra lifted Maier and Carissa into their chairs. The boy placed the computer on his lap and pushed him into the building. The White Spider followed him slowly.

"You are doing well, Maier. You are finding your feet. But you keep things a little short. Please do unfold your talents a little more, put a little more oomph in it, a little flair. And do ask me whatever you like, if there is something you don't understand."

Les Snakearm Leroux sat in a chair in the office of the former station. The cells and toilets that Maier could see were empty and smashed up. Just like Les. The American pilot was not sitting. He had been tied to the chair.

Lorenz waved for the boy.

"Leave us alone today. These two here can't move and for me, it's a lot more exciting to be surrounded by three people who would like to kill me. Raksmei will help if there's a problem."

The boy and the inspector looked at the old man in disbelief, but he waved a tired hand and his henchman disappeared. Seconds later the car started outside. Lorenz waited theatrically, until the engine noise had faded.

"As you know, Lesley Leroux is the owner of a bar in Kep. Having been told that we caught you here, he came up on the plateau and walked into the arms of our girls. Unfortunately, it turned out that Les had done a spell as a prisoner of war some years back and we were not able to find out who had informed the old man. Now, he is no able longer to tell us."

Maier couldn't look away. The American had some serious head-wounds and they had sawed off his left thumb. He had been bandaged but he was still bleeding like a recently butchered animal. He was alive.

"Did Leroux work for you, Maier?"

The biographer shook his head.

The White Spider sat down heavily on a rickety stool, the only option other than the chair Les had been tied to. The weak sunlight fell through the window onto his gaunt face, which appeared to dissolve into thousands of tiny wrinkles.

Maier stared into empty space, fascinated, and chewed his tongue. The amphetamines massaged his brain and urged him to jump up. This time Raksmei's shot had been anything but paralysing. Now he felt wide awake, and sitting opposite his adversary, irrationally happy. He didn't dare look at Carissa for fear of giving himself away too early.

All's fair in love and war.

He would choke the old bastard to death.

"You're alright, Maier, aren't you?"

The American had raised his battered head. Maier looked Les in the eye and nodded.

"It's over, Les."

"That's good. I've had enough. This countryman of yours is worse than the Vietcong,"

"You are OK now, Les."

Lorenz had gotten up and stepped impatiently in front of the American.

"Maier, you are here to write my story, not to help this decadent drunk to die."

For a moment, Maier really saw him as a spider, a tough old tarantula, working her last net.

"Tell me the end of your story. What are you doing here?"

The old man looked at Maier with pity in his pale eyes. Maier thought the man looked at him as if he were an about-to-be crushed cockroach or a poisoned rat – something that was dying.

"You are right, of course. I appear like a dinosaur to you. Irony is rising up inside you. But you are wrong about me. I am not that old-fashioned, Maier. It's all about the money today. Dollars, euros, yen. Ideologies, racial theories, national pride, honour itself, these are all outmoded concepts that belong to the time of my youth. Those were simple years when people in Europe knew less. Today, they know everything, everything but values. They know too much. The West swims in an ocean of useless information – gossip, rumours, lies. I have made peace with all that. I will not die in Germany or for Germany. But I will tell you why I returned to Cambodia. Please take notes."

Maier contemplated killing the man with his laptop. Instead he opened his file.

"I am all ears, Herr Lorenz."

The old man grinned.

"In contrast to our American friend here, who has eaten his."

Now he laughed like a small boy.

Carissa hissed impatiently in her wheelchair next to Maier.

"For the past two years, we have been offering an exclusive service. All in line with the priorities of the new century. For a substantial amount of money you can hire us, to get rid of your political enemy, your competitor, your lover, your lover's lover or husband's lover or members of your family. Anyone. You can read about it in the papers. I am surprised, Ms Stevenson, that no one from your professional circle has cottoned on to us yet. We have had to shut up a few local journalists already. Our ladies work in Vietnam, Thailand, Laos and of course Cambodia for clients with the right money. As soon as we find the right teachers to train our staff in language skills, we will go global."

"You will teach these girls English with a stick?"

The old man, full of pride, ignored the detective's sarcasm.

"You see, Maier, Cambodia has an oversupply of young girls. There are no jobs. Even prostitution does not offer every pretty girl an opportunity. The war killed too many men and yet women don't get any opportunities. Tep, my old friend, wants to sell Bokor. That's looking good, we just need a bit more money. Thanks to his efforts in Kep, not a great deal more. Then we can throw out the rangers and train more girls. We will soon have to leave our temple hideaway. The tourists are coming. That's why we will be restoring the casino, building a swimming pool, a golf course and a heliport, all the stuff Bokor needs in the twenty-first century. As an alibi for the real business at hand. Don't you agree it's a solid plan?"

"And where do the girls come from?"

Lorenz sat heavily.

"From orphanages, from mothers who can't feed their children. Cambodia is a country of unlimited possibilities."

Hilmar Lorenz returned from Germany to Cambodia in the early Nineties and, with the help of former Khmer Rouge officers, started setting up an assassination service with global ambitions – the Kangaok Meas Project.

Lorenz's guardians are educated according to the inhuman and extreme values of the Khmer Rouge. Members of his organisation have allegedly committed more than fifty murders in Phnom Penh, Siem Reap and Sihanoukville in the past two years. The organisation is also active in neighbouring countries.

Raksmei held two syringes in her hands and stood behind the White Spider.

Maier closed the laptop.

The girl pushed the first needle into the old man's back.

Lorenz turned and tried to grab the girl but the sedative worked quickly and he slumped forward on his chair.

Raksmei walked around the tall bent-over figure and pushed him upright. Lorenz looked up at her in surprise.

"Raksmei?"

Maier and Carissa had both stood up. Raksmei grabbed hold of the old German's arm, pulled the sleeve of his white shirt up and gave him a second shot, without bothering to tie him off first.

"For Sambat, my brother."

She gently smiled at the old man and brushed his silver hair straight.

"Raksmei, you know who I am?" Lorenz asked with an uncertain tone in his voice. It didn't suit him.

She did not answer.

"How long has he got?"

"He can talk thirty minutes. Then one hour quiet. Then dead."

Carissa untied Les from his chair. The American was conscious.

"Is it over, Maier?"

"It is all over. We will say goodbye to Bokor now."

Without turning around, Carissa and Raksmei grabbed Les and led him outside, into the sun.

Lorenz's eyes followed his daughter in silence.

"I was a good man. A friend of the people. When the Vietnamese invaded in '79, I could have hidden in my embassy. I would have been safe there. But I fled with Tep. I knew that my career in Yugoslavia was finished. I knew I would risk my life. But I could not let Tep down. He was a good soldier and he took our mission seriously. He was my friend."

Maier sat back into his wheelchair. Slowly, ever so slowly, he was beginning to relax. For the first time in a week, he wasn't in mortal danger and he knew what was going on. The White Spider was drooling. Paralysis was slowly setting in. He was watching a man die.

"After Phnom Penh had fallen, we came down here and slept in a cooperative. In the morning we planned to head west to the Cardamom Mountains, as good a place as any to disappear for a while. Just before we left, Tep caught a woman roasting some animal over an open fire. Angkar had forbidden any such act. Tep was as loyal to Angkar as I am to him. That's how it is in war, Maier. Even while we were being chased by the enemy, he took a hammer and killed the woman. Her husband worked in a field nearby with his daughter. Tep walked up to the man. I stood on the edge of the field and saw exactly what he did. He said something about Angkar to the little girl and hit her father. The man fell to the ground. He gave the little girl the hammer. These are the moments, Maier, on the edge of everything, when we get close to the gods. I had some moments like that in Croatia."

The voice of the old man was getting weaker. His eyes had glazed over.

Outside, in front of the police station, Maier could hear the flapping of leathery wings.

"I'm almost gone, Maier. Not even my daughter wants to watch me die. No one will bury me. Tep will not let you get away, but even that no longer matters now. The Kangaok Meas Project is running. My last engagement. You see, the girl who killed her father in the rice-field, her name was Kaley. Tep took her with us. He gave her to me as a present and thus saved her life. I took her the same afternoon. She could not have been much older than twelve. Raksmei and Sambat are my children. My children with Kaley. She was the reason why I came back to this small, primitive, insignificant country. Her sister also came back from Germany to find Kaley. Tep got rid of her."

The White Spider gasped for air. Then he calmed and let the toxin work its way to his core.

"And as you may know, Maier, Tep married Kaley off to his oldest son, who was killed by Kaley's youngest daughter, Poch. With a hammer, I might add. When Tep tried to train the girl as one of our assassins, she ran in front of the jeep of that young German guy. The little girl lived like Kaley, following only her own laws. Just like Raksmei, who just killed her father. Everything repeats itself again and again, like in the old story about the Kangaok Meas, which these uneducated half-people keep alive with their superstitions."

"Does Raksmei know who her parents are?"

The old man coughed up some blood and shook his head.

"No. Tep insisted that Raksmei and Sambat should grow up as orphans. The Khmer Rouge often separated children from their parents. Later, when Raksmei had grown up a bit, shortly after I came back to Cambodia, he tried to seduce her. She must have been the same age as Kaley, when she gave birth to my children. It almost broke our friendship. Now I wonder why I was so cross."

The White Spider laughed.

"But she is not stupid, this daughter of mine. She was never scared of me. When she was brought to the temple a few weeks ago, I was sorely tempted to tell her the truth. But I would have had to tell her everything, including the fact that I was responsible for the death of her brother. Tep was sure she'd be reliable and she knew something about drugs."

The voice of the old man seemed to drift away from him for a moment. His lips barely moved.

"But in her heart, she always knew. Do you really think a woman like Raksmei can kill her own father without recognising him? I am proud of my daughter."

"Does Kaley know that she is Raksmei's mother?

The old German laughed, just.

"She knows nothing. After the birth, Tep took the kids away from her and had them sent back to Kampot with the Khmer Rouge. She thinks her children are dead. Do you understand why I returned to Cambodia as soon as possible? I wanted to make sure my children had a chance."

"And then you killed your son? What chance did he have?"

"A misunderstanding. War is never simple. As soon as the first shot is fired… Sambat was here and watched the Kangaok Meas ceremony."

"What ceremony?"

"Maier, Tep found out that my son was here and Viengsra killed him and threw him in the sea."

Maier looked at the dying man without pity.

"He did not kill him. He drowned your son alive. He tied stones to his feet and drowned him."

For the first time, Maier could detect particles of pain in the eyes of the old man. He didn't have much time left.

"And where is Kaley now?"

"Maier, you did not understand me. The Kangaok Meas is a concept of the Immaterial, a manifestation of the sensuous, a golden peacock, reborn in each generation. And in this life, Kaley belongs to Kep, to Bokor. She is the whore of Cambodia and all who sleep with her will experience a violent end. That's what the locals believe. More importantly, that's what Kaley believes."

What had Rolf said? There had to be a way to free people from the darkness of tradition, even from superstition.

Maier was less idealistic. People, whether highly educated or illiterate, always stayed the same. The killing technique changed, but the thought was the same.

The White Spider coughed blood and slid deeper into his chair.

"When I slept with Kaley, she was still a child. You must understand. We were at war. There was nothing to eat. And Tep and I saved her. At that time, we could not see that she was the Kangaok Meas. We only realised that later."

Lorenz fought for breath.

"Lift me up, Maier. Don't let me die like a rat. Please do me one last favour and call my daughter back in."

Maier shook his head.

The White Spider stared up at him, his gaunt long face wracked by pain and anger.

"How many people have you poisoned, Hilmar Lorenz?"

Maier wanted to kick him but one did not kick dead people.

The White Spider's phone rang. Without turning, Maier left the former police station.

DEATH IN THE TEA PLANTATION

"The butchers will be here in a few minutes and they will be looking for us."

"I know a trail, past the old jail and into the jungle. It's difficult to follow us there."

Les sat against the wall, almost passed out.

"Will he be able to make it?"

Raksmei looked at Maier. She nodded.

Les groaned. The young woman had a syringe in her hand. The White Spider's daughter looked breathtaking and deadly. Suddenly Maier felt like a human being again. A human being pumped to the gills with amphetamine.

"That's my last one. He will make it with this shot."

Raksmei tied off the American's arm. A dog started barking. Carissa and Raksmei helped the battered war veteran to his feet.

The trail led downhill. After a few minutes they crossed two narrow streams and Les managed to walk without help.

Below the police station, the path got steeper. Les walked silently and, despite his injuries, overtook the other three.

After an hour they reached the bottom of a valley. An overgrown, barely visible building lay off to the left of the trail.

"The old prison."

Raksmei made no effort to stop and followed Les along the narrow trail that led between tall grasses.

"The trail will divide a bit further. The left path leads back to the Black Villa, the right trail drops down into the jungle. We go right. The road is bound to be guarded."

Carissa and Raksmei crashed into Maier, thrown to the floor by the power of the explosion, and pressed them into the soil. Just ahead, a round hole had been ripped from the trail. Raksmei had blood on her face but she started to get up. Someone was screaming behind them. The hunters were on their way.

Maier knew that they had only seconds. They had to leave.

"Carissa, take Raksmei into the jungle. I will see you in Kampot. Rent a car to go to the border. I will distract the dogs and meet you tomorrow."

Carissa was unhurt. She grabbed the young Khmer woman's arm.

"If there are more mines on this trail, we are fucked."

But there was no time to ponder. Tep's men were barely a hundred metres behind them.

"Let's go."

The two women ran down the hill. There was no sign of Les. The bushes were dripping with blood. The American could not have survived. Before Maier could take a step, the boy and Viengsra stood behind him.

The inspector smiled like a toothless child and spoke first. "Monsieur Maier, my dog found you."

The boy had his finger on the trigger and grinned.

The two men led Maier across to the overgrown prison.

"We mine the trail this morning. Otherwise you escape. Someone wait for the girl at Black Villa already. General Tep very angry. You kill his friend."

Maier stumbled ahead of the two men. Suddenly the boy grabbed him by the shoulder and pushed him into dense undergrowth, past the abandoned building. A trail opened and they stood in front of the main entrance of the old French jail, its door flanked by two handsome pillars. Maier fell up the slippery stairs.

"We wait for Tep. He want to see you die. He want to take you life, Monsieur Maier."

The boy pushed Maier inside the building. The roof had partly fallen in but a few of the cells beyond the entrance hall looked intact.

The first thing Maier saw was a red head which jumped up and down behind a barred window.

"Maier, you're still alive? I never would have thought."

The boy opened the only functioning cell door and pushed Maier inside.

Pete was pale and looked bewildered. He was unshaven and his gaunt cheeks had become more hollow. His voice was so hoarse that Maier had problems understanding him.

"Yeah, Maier, I haven't eaten for days. These fuckers simply forgot about me. Maier, do you have anything to eat?"

The steel door slammed shut behind Maier.

"My liver?"

The English man didn't smile.

"Maier, I've seen it before. You can't eat anything for days after, if you see something like that."

"They'll take your liver too, Pete."

The cell was empty. Small trees sprouted from the broken moss-covered walls. In a few years the roots would crack the wall open and the building would collapse. Not soon enough.

Pete staggered around in circles, shaking with panic. Maier looked around. The roof had holes, but it was more than four metres away. There was no getting up there.

"Have you got a fag?"

"I don't smoke."

Pete looked at him with unfathomable anger, before he began circling the cell again. The round smooth face of the

policeman appeared at the cell window. Inspector Viengsra
was chewing betel. He lost a thread of red spit and smiled.

"The White Spider show Tep and his son how to skin people."

The man was so simple, one had to be scared. But Maier
didn't want to give up. One hour.

"I hope I not watch. Sometime they go too far, too far,
Monsieur Maier."

"Watch?" Maier asked, not expecting an answer, and stepped
up to the window to laugh in the inspector's face.

"They will roast you and your dog as well, Inspector. The
White Spider is dead and we got away. You have failed. It will
all be your fault when we are dead. You will see how Cambodia
gets rid of people who fail."

For a moment, genuine worry spread across the moon-
shaped face of the policeman as he looked down at the
prisoners. Then he laughed carelessly.

"I help him grill. He need my help. Tep not eat three liver,
for sure."

Suddenly the boy called out in front of the prison.

"Viengsra?"

Someone fired a shot.

The policeman's crying eyes blinked in panic and he pulled
his weapon. Pete ran to the cell window and tried to look past
the inspector. Viengsra started to shoot, wildly. After a few
seconds only the click of the empty gun was audible.

"Shit, the boy is dead."

Pete stepped away from the window.

"Tep wouldn't kill his own son, would he?"

Two more shots rang through the entrance hall of the prison.

The power of the bullets threw Inspector Viengsra to the cell
window.

The cell door opened and the next bullet caught Pete in the
forehead.

Maier remained standing in the middle of the room.

"Yes, young man, wrong time, wrong place."

The Russian grinned, bowed theatrically and raised his weapons.

"I thought all the while you were involved in something up here. Should I shoot you straight away?"

Maier had put up his hands.

"What are you doing here, you damn *gopnik*? Correct answer please, your life hangs by the proverbial thread, a thread so delicate even the king of Cambodia has never seen it."

"I am a private detective. From Hamburg. I work for a family in Hamburg, to bring their son back to Germany. Rolf is the son."

Mikhail laughed, pushed his grey locks out of his face and carefully lowered his weapons.

"Good answer, Maier. I know all this already. And good thing too you got rid of the old Nazi. But things like that, they make waves. And I don't like waves. That's why I live up here."

Maier knew it was pointless to ask the Russian what he was doing in Bokor. One could not ask a man like that questions.

"I am looking for the Kangaok Meas."

"Usually everyone runs away when that name is mentioned. Rolf will never get the girl. But he will try. People are like that. They believe in things they know not to exist. As a Russian, I sympathise. But you, you man, you have the East in your eyes. That's why you will manage to solve your case, detective."

The dog of the policeman had pushed into the cell and sniffed at Maiers legs.

"It's better we disappear. This place will be swarming with black shrimps soon."

"The road is blocked. The trail through the forest might be mined."

"I know that, Maier. I found Les outside. Poor man. Survived three wars and then died up here in the great nothing."

Mikhail shot the dog.

THE ROOF OF THE WORLD

The roof of the casino was the last place where Tep would search for Maier. Mikhail had led him back to the old hotel on a different trail, past the old water tower and through tall grasses. By afternoon, the Bokor Palace had become a hive of activity. SUVs, all of them black and without number plates, arrived one after another and dropped off groups of girls. Lexus was the preferred brand for the killers. Mikhail and Maier had entered through the basement and climbed one of the broken stairways to the top of the building. Now they were watching the scene below from one of the crumbling towers at the front side of the building.

The Russian stared down grimly at the preparations for the great summit of the Kangaok Meas Project. Maier knew that Mikhail had almost shot him. He was in the way.

Shortly after dark, Tep arrived with his son, the White Spider and Viengsra. Now the three corpses lay lined up on straw mats in front of the casino.

For a while the old general stood in front of the remains of the people closest to him, lost in thought. It wasn't his best day. Maier counted twelve girls who stood to attention behind Tep. After an hour, he turned away and walked into the building. The girls carried the corpses around the casino building to the edge of the Bokor plateau and doused them in kerosene. The loud hiss of the flames reached all the way to the rooftop. Two of the girls heaped wood onto the corpses, while a third used a stick to push hands and feet that stuck out of the fire back into the flames. After an hour, nothing remained but three dark spots and a few bones on the ground. One of the girls began to shovel the ash and bones over the side of the cliff. Maier almost smiled. That was how war criminals ended – some of them. But the death of the White Spider was hardly a victory. Men like Lorenz would never become extinct.

A huge, rusty water tank stood in the centre of the roof. The round steel container offered the only protection from the evening's cold wind. Mikhail spread a dirty *krama* on the shadow side of the tank and pulled a tin of corned beef, two baguettes, mangos and a bottle of vodka from his bag.

As far as Maier could remember, he had consumed nothing but rice and *prahok* during his incarceration. He had already noticed that his trousers did not seem as tight as they had been. Nothing got rid of excess fat quicker than torture. He grabbed one of the mangos and devoured it like a starved animal, squeezing the yellow flesh from the skin into his mouth.

The Russian was in good spirits.

"The story of the Kangaok Meas is centuries old. The reincarnation in the story, the continuation of evil, from one generation to the next, originates with the brand of Hinduism that some of the kings of Angkor followed. Brahmin priests were very influential at the Khmer court and they spread the belief in the continuation of the soul. On top of that you have the archaic animist belief system of the Khmer and the cruel history of the last decades. We are in Cambodia, dear, not in Vladivostok or Germany. This place is haunted. I know this country."

Maier shook his head. He was a detective, not an exorcist. Mikhail slapped his shoulder and grinned with yellow teeth.

"Maier, everyone will believe what they want. I've had so many extreme experiences in my life, that I have no options left but to remain open to everything. I am a collector. That's a respectable profession. I collect situations."

The Russian took a swig of vodka from the bottle and handed it to Maier. The alcohol woke him up. He was beginning to feel in tune with himself once more.

"Why did you not shoot me?"

"Maier, young man, I am not a mass murderer. Three thugs were enough for me. And I need your help tonight. Vichat and the other rangers will not come near the casino at night. They are very scared of the shrimps."

"I love vodka. Did you know that?"

"Yes, dear, I remember talking about drinking at length after you'd fallen off your motorbike."

"Was that you?"

Mikhail brushed a huge hand through his greasy grey hair and appeared to evaluate what the detective had said.

"My dear Maier, you ask as many questions as one would expect from a detective."

"That's what the White Spider said as well."

The Russian laughed until his face had gone the way of a tomato.

"Then you know that you have to be careful in Cambodia if you look over another man's shoulders."

He winked at Maier and coughed.

"So be careful."

Maier had dozed off when the Russian shook him by the shoulder.

"Maier, the shrimps are searching the casino. They will be up here in a minute."

The fat Russian had already packed the baguette and vodka and was in the process of climbing into the water tank. Maier jumped up and followed him.

A few seconds later, they could hear voices in the stairway.

The shrimps were not alone. Tep had stepped onto the roof and spoke French.

"Tonight we have the last initiation of the Kangaok Meas in the casino. A little earlier than planned, but this damn detective from Germany make many problem for us. Many big problem. Today he kill my son."

"I am sorry to hear that. Have you caught Monsieur Maier?"

Maier recognised the voice of the other man immediately. He sat next to Mikhail in knee-deep rancid water and tried to hold his breath. The two men stood directly in front of the water tank now, while the shrimps searched the roof. The Russian had pulled a gun and pointed it directly at the thin rusty wall of the tank.

"I get him. Tomorrow we have money to buy casino. Tonight we blow it up. I catch the German OK. I watch all roads to Phnom Penh. Nothing to stop us now. In two years we open resort and golf course. No problem."

The Frenchman had walked a few steps away.

"Can't you lend me one of your girls, Tep?"

The general hissed angrily, "You never have enough, Maupai. You are strong man. We are same age and you want girl more than me. More than Khmer Rouge general. This kill you one day. I tell you, keep fingers away from Kangaok Meas and my staff."

The voices receded, but Mikhail waved to Maier to remain seated. For a while they heard nothing. Suddenly someone began to scratch the underside of the tank they were in. After endless seconds, one of the girls shouted an order and everyone trooped back down the stairway.

Mikhail and Maier rose from the cold, dirty water and climbed back onto the roof terrace.

"What did they say?"

Maier translated the conversation between Tep and the Frenchman.

The Russian took a long swig of vodka and grinned. "You see, young man, I am not the only one warning about Kaley."

The girls had used duct tape to fasten a packet of explosives and a timer to the underside of the water tank. Mikhail ripped the packet off and examined it.

"Maier, this little packet is going to do much damage to the building. They must have installed something similar in the basement. That's where I have to go."

The collector of situations had taken the package apart and stuffed half the explosive into his pocket. Then he reattached the rest exactly as the girls had left it.

He got up, his face beetroot once more, and checked his revolver.

"It's best you stay here. This bomb here has been defused. But they won't notice if they come back and check. I come and get you when the Kangaok Meas appears. Tonight, I will show you that Rolf must up give this woman."

Maier didn't think he'd have another chance to ask the Russian anything.

"What are you doing here, Mikhail?"

"Maier, they will never build a golf course here. I am sure. I am the king of Bokor. This is my home. No need to know more about me."

"I would like to know in whose interest you are working."

The Russian hesitated, then he pulled a torch from his pocket and handed it to Maier.

"You will need it tonight, dear. And here's some good advice from a man who's been everywhere: if you find yourself in a minefield, as sometimes happens in Cambodia, then follow the sticks in the ground, otherwise you will end up like Les. Don't forget that. Follow the sticks."

The giant disappeared down the stairs without another word.

Maier was alone. Almost alone.

"Oh, Maier."

Maier turned around, but the voice had not come from the stairway. Kaley stood in front of him. She wore a green sarong and the black shirt she'd worn when he'd first met her, in what now seemed to be another life. She had put up her hair with the help of two chopsticks, which emphasised her beautiful face, interrupted in its perfection only by her bright shining scar. A timeless, unreal beauty. She smiled uncertainly and held up the palms of her hands. Maier remembered the words of the inspector. Death was a woman.

"Hello, Kaley."

There was only one way onto the roof of the casino. Kaley had not come that way. The woman smiled past Maier.

"You look beautiful, Kaley."

She pulled her sarong straight. The expression of modesty that crossed her face was so remote that Maier could barely breathe. She was fearsome. Suddenly she took a step forward and embraced Maier, clawing at his back with her hands.

"Oh, Maier."

Maier took her in his arms, though he had no desire to be near her. She smelled of the red fungus that had grown all over the casino walls.

Kaley did not want to let go.

"Kaley, tell me what happened."

When she finally disentangled herself she climbed on to the balustrade of casino roof, sat down and let her feet dangle towards the ground.

"You catch me if I fall, Maier?"

"Of course."

Without another word, she slipped forward, but Maier had already grabbed her under the arms. He almost expected her to dissolve into thin air, but she fell back into his arms. She was light, but not as light as one would expect a ghost to be.

"Maier, the people not leave me alone."

"What kind of people?"

"The people who take me from the rice-field. They do terrible thing. I see many time. The Kangaok Meas in Bokor is no good."

She lay in his arms like a drunk.

"Do you know what you are, Kaley?"

The young woman laughed unhappily.

"I am dead, you alive."

"So you know who I am?"

She looked into his eyes for the first time.

"You are Maier."

She lowered her gaze.

"How long has the Kangaok Meas been coming here, Kaley?"

Kaley shook her head.

"Long time. Many years."

"Is the Kangaok Meas scared?"

"I am reborn. I am dead, you alive."

"Can I help you somehow, Kaley?"

The Khmer began to cry.

"You promise you find my sister, Maier."

He did not answer her. He couldn't. Not now. Not after all the death that had manifested around this woman. Kaley began to dance across the roof.

"Can you dance, Maier?"

"Not well."

"Good for me."

She touched him lightly on the shoulders and led him to the centre of the rooftop. Grey clouds rushed across the edge of the plateau. The old water tower looked like it was ready to march away, in the face of all the horror. Maier thought he could hear an orchestra play faintly, somewhere far away, as the fog slowly slid across the casino like creeping death and Kaley waltzed him effortlessly across the roof of the world. Had the vodka been drugged?

A few seconds later it was pitch dark.

FAITES VOS JEUX

"Gentlemen, we gather tonight to celebrate the last Kangaòk Meas ceremony in Bokor Palace. Before we proceed I like to tell you, everyone who know about our project is one hundred percent with us. You have doubt in our business, now is time to go."

Tep's voice echoed through the casino's ballroom, as a dozen or so investors sat down in a row of rattan chairs. The general was in uniform tonight. A revolver hung from his belt. Even in mourning, the old communist looked ready for battle. A few of the men carried briefcases. The room was lit by huge candles usually used in temples. Maier recognised most of the men in the warm twilight of the room – all of them foreigners who had bought property in Kep.

Two girls, dressed in black, stood behind a small bar and mixed cocktails. A straw mat lay in the centre of the otherwise empty hall. Music emanated from an unseen source. Maier knew the song, a mournful tune usually played during Cambodian cremations. Kaley had led Maier into the room in which he'd been beaten unconscious on his first visit. Now they lay next to each other beside two holes in the floor and stared down into the ballroom.

"Do you know that I have been here before, Kaley?" Maier whispered.

Kaley nodded.

"Do you know who attacked me when I was lying on the floor?"

Kaley shook her head.

"I not remember. It not important. Today you not worry. I hide you if someone coming."

The ballroom had settled into silence. Now and then the ice cubes in the guests' glasses tinkled through the great nothing.

Something began to move in the semi-darkness at the end of the ballroom. Tep clapped his hands together.

"With your payments, we buy the casino, stop the rangers and build most exclusive resort in Southeast Asia. We pay a high price to do this. Enemy force kill my son and Inspector Viengsra today. For this reason, very difficult for me to celebrate. But finances for project now sure. Our agency, Kangaok Meas Project, now working. My staff travel all the region for mission. Every day we more rich."

The general's speech was followed by polite applause.

Kaley stepped into the light, followed by twenty girls with hair cropped short, dressed in black pyjamas and rubber sandals. The Kangaok Meas looked unbelievably beautiful and cruel. Kaley wore a dress made from fine gold chains over a black thong. She wore her hair down, almost reaching her broad hips. Her body had a golden sheen. The scene below him looked both ridiculous and terrible to Maier, like a sequence in a Hollywood movie with a huge budget badly spent.

Maier pulled his head out of his observation hole and wouldn't have been surprised if she'd still been lying next to him, but she was gone. Rather, she'd appeared below. But how had she managed to change so fast?

The investors held their breath as the Kangaok Meas swayed past them. She shot a quick glance to the ceiling before she stood next to Tep. Tonight the long scar, accentuated by the white strand of hair, gave her a demonic aura, and split her face in two in the twilight of the ballroom.

Maier made no efforts to hide. The Kangaok Meas locked her glassy eyes with his, then she turned wordlessly towards the general.

The girls had lined up in two rows, silently facing each other.

The old general barely looked at Kaley and continued, his voice heavy with emotion. "Tonight I dedicate for my son. Also, my very good old friend, Herr Lorenz, is killed today. I will catch killer. For me difficult to lose old friend. More difficult to lose two, son and one good friend. This is story of Cambodia."

Tep clapped his hands again and Kaley began to walk up and down the rows of girls. Her face was shiny and cold.

She was grinding her jaws. She must have taken something for this performance. Passing the girls three times, she pointed at two of the identically-dressed, prospective assassins.

The two girls stepped forward, while the rest of the group spread across the ballroom.

Maupai talked excitedly with another Frenchman next to him, but Maier couldn't follow the conversation.

Kaley started to walk from one guest to the next to collect their briefcases. Tep took each case and lined them up in a long row on the bar.

Kaley waved to the two girls who immediately started to approach each other. A low round of applause rose from the investors. For a moment the two girls circled, their eyes full of thirst for killing. One of the girls lashed out. The second girl took the hit to the face without trying to dodge her opponent. Instead she went with the blow and then, like mercury, slid towards her attacker. The first girl looked up but it was already too late. A small piece of metal flashed in the hand of the attacker. A split second later, she pushed the nail into her adversary's eye socket. The loser fell to the floor screaming. Kaley stepped between the two fighters.

But for the screams of the injured girl, the ballroom was absolutely silent. Tep waved for two other girls who pulled the loser onto the straw mat in the centre of the room and began to kick her.

Kaley stood on the edge of the mat and slowly pulled off her slip. Like a dark angel, she stepped closer to the injured girl and bent downwards, her back turned to the investors.

Two of the men had already jumped up and were dropping their trousers as quickly as possible. Maier began to understand what would happen now. He could hear the beating of leathery wings outside the building. He did not want to watch any longer and he had no idea how to stop what he was seeing.

This was like war.

Kaley grabbed hold of the head of the injured girl and slowly, theatrically, pulled the nail from her eye. The girl screamed. Blood spurted across Kaley's breasts, but the Kangaok Meas hardly noticed. She was now crouched on all fours above her victim. The first investor had almost reached and was about to make a grab for her legs. At the last moment, he was pushed aside by a second man.

"I have earned this. I am the most important investor, *n'est-ce pas?*"

Maupai grabbed the Kangaok Meas by the hips and tried to climb the undead woman.

Kaley held the bloody nail in her hand and turned briefly to the Frenchman, smiling broadly, before she plunged the metal into her victim's remaining eye. The head of the Frenchman exploded the very same moment and he fell on top of her like an old sack.

Rolf stepped out of the shadows, two revolvers in his hands and stared wild-eyed at Kaley.

Tep waved for his girls who began to close in on the young German from all directions, but Kaley ordered them to retreat. She rose slowly and approached Rolf, smiling faintly. Her breasts and belly were smeared with blood. Without a word, she knelt down in front of him and began to open the belt of his trousers. Rolf began to shake and raised the two guns. The tension in the room was unbearable.

Maier had no idea how to get his client out of this tight spot. He jumped up, ready to run downstairs and storm the show, but what would be the point. He would be totally outgunned down there.

"Not yet," he said to himself and lay back down.

Rolf stared down at Kaley, crying, his two revolvers centimetres from her head.

The ballroom exploded.

Maier was thrown against the wall of the room he lay in. In seconds the space filled with dust which wafted up from the ballroom. Maier fought his way back to the hole but there was nothing to see. It was pitch dark below him.

Somewhere a smaller explosion went off and a wall collapsed. More dust. He crawled down the main stairs to the entrance, half-blind, and made it outside. It was pouring with rain. The casino's basement was on fire and thick cement dust poured out of the building's windows. The floor of the ballroom had collapsed and had swall-owed all those who'd been present. The detective sunk helplessly into the wet grass in front of the building.

A car started behind Maier. One of the SUVs shot forward. Maier could see Tep in the weak light of the driver's cabin. The old general held on to the wheel, bleeding heavily and stared blindly into the darkness. Kaley emerged from the burning building and marched down the stairs. She looked untouched. In her hands, she carried the briefcases full of money. For a moment she stopped in the light of the car's headlights in front of Maier and looked at him, in apparent confusion.

"You find my sister, Maier."

Seconds later she was gone. The general revved the engine and the car slithered away into the darkness. Maier sat alone, in front of the burning casino, knowing he would never be able to fulfil his promise.

••••

After a long while, Maier mounted the steps to the hotel. The ballroom was a smoking bomb crater. He stared into the darkness, but he couldn't see a thing. His torch did not reach to the bottom. He would have to go down there.

He left the casino and circled the building until he found the back entrance to the basement. The same entrance through which he'd escaped on his first visit. Maier climbed downwards.

The water was still knee deep but the basement floor was littered with large chunks of the ceiling. Someone moaned ahead of Maier and the detective stopped and tried to listen into the darkness.

"Rolf, Rolf, are you down here?"

Shadows moved around him. Someone coughed a few metres ahead. Maier walked on, deeper into the bowels of the building. Then he saw Rolf in the light of his weak flickering torch. The young German lay on a piece of beautifully tiled ballroom floor with which he'd fallen. But he wasn't alone. The girls lay around him in the stinking water as if waiting for something. Of course they were dead, but that didn't mean much in Cambodia.

He grabbed hold of the coffee heir and pulled him in the direction of the stairs. The girls made no efforts to stop him, but they followed Maier with their eyes through the dark water towards the exit. Death was a lady. Rolf was conscious. Maier could not see any gratuitous injuries on the young man. The rain had faded.

The detective stumbled from car to car until he found one with the keys in the ignition. He loaded Rolf onto the back seat and raced off without looking back, towards the coast, away from the cursed Bokor Palace, away from the dead shrimps, away from this damn case.

ENDGAME

"What happened, Maier?"

The detective shook his head in exhaustion and pointed at the car. Carissa had pounced on him as soon as he'd reached the guest house in Kampot.

She looked indescribable, all in red. Before he could say anything, she handed him a Vodka Orange and a half-smoked joint. Maier could not have imagined a better breakfast.

In a few rushed sentences he told his old flame what had happened during the night. Carissa looked on with concern.

"Raksmei wants to stay here, wants to take over the orphanage again. Do you think Tep will come back to take his revenge? After all she played a double game to avenge her brother."

Maier shrugged his shoulders.

"I don't think that she is in danger. Tep escaped, but he is badly injured. I doubt he will seek revenge. He has known Raksmei too long. She is his best friend's daughter and he may not know that she crossed her father."

Carissa looked at Maier in disbelief.

"The White Spider was in Cambodia in the Seventies. He worked as a Yugoslavian diplomat while the revolution was in full swing here. He fled with Tep when the Vietnamese invaded. On the way to Thailand, they killed a family near Kep and abducted and raped the youngest daughter, Kaley. After the war, Kaley had two children with the old German. Tep took the children and hid

264

them in Kampot. More recently, the White Spider returned to
Cambodia to be closer to these children. But when he got here,
he had this idea of starting an assassination service. He made
Kaley a kind of chairperson of the whole project."

"And what happened after the casino blew up?"

Maier shrugged. "Even before the casino went up, things
were very strange. I think I had a flashback from the drugs
that Raksmei had given me in the temple. After Mikhail had
disappeared, I spent the early evening with Kaley on the
rooftop. She was like a ghost."

Carissa shot Maier a look full of pity before turning her head.

"I am serious. A few minutes after the casino went up, Kaley
emerged from the burning building, not a scratch on her, got into
a car with Tep and bags full of money and drove off. Everyone
else in there, except for Rolf, died. I cannot explain it."

Maier noticed that Carissa looked embarrassed by his lack of
rational argument and dropped the subject.

"I am sure that Tep has returned to his temple hideaway.
Maybe he still has a few slaves there who will look after him. I
still don't know who Mikhail really is, what he was doing up on
the plateau and what his connection to us and to Tep is. But I
think this strange Russian means to confuse. He has not played
his last card yet. I think it is best we cross into Thailand as quickly
as possible, to be safe. Then we will see what we can do."

Carissa embraced him, "Yes, Maier, let's check into a hotel in
Bangkok and not leave the room for a week."

"Do you have a passport?"

She shook her head.

"Rolf does not have one either. But I think we can cross at
Koh Kong."

The muddy road to the border led through the Cardamom
Mountains. The small group was forced to cross four rivers,
swollen by the rains, on improvised bamboo platforms operated

by skinny men dressed in rags. At nightfall, they reached the border town of Koh Kong.

Maier drove the car directly to the pier. The small town was – but for a handful of casinos where rich, gambling-addicted Thais lost their fortunes, and sometimes existences – a collection of wooden huts built on high stilts. The settlement appeared to slide slowly into the tepid dirty coastal waters of the Gulf of Thailand. Children and pigs played amongst the crumbling houses. Policemen sat on shaded balconies, drank beer and played with their guns. As soon as Maier had got out of the car, tough teenagers tried to sell him marihuana, opium, heroin and other teenagers. Maier grabbed the boy who spoke the best English, pulled him back to the car and pressed twenty dollars into his hand.

"What's your name?"

"Somchai," the boy lied.

"I need a speedboat to Thailand. My two passengers don't have passports. We have to avoid the Thai border post."

Somchai, hardly older than fourteen and already thoroughly disillusioned with life, grinned brazenly at Maier.

"Tausend dollar, mister... *Kein problem.*"

Maier laughed. "If you can get me a boat in ten minutes, I will give you forty thousand dollars. What do you think?"

Somchai laughed back. "I think you cheat me, *barang*. If you have forty thousand dollar in your car, you not need me."

Maier opened the door, pulled the keys from the ignition and dangled them in front of the boy's nose.

"Get me a boat to Thailand and the car is yours. It is not registered. It does not have plates and it is brand new. There is even some petrol in the tank."

The boy did not hesitate but skipped around the car and jumped into the passenger seat.

"No problem, mister, you drive."

Minutes later, they stopped in front of a small guest house. An old, toothless Khmer lay in a hammock next to the door.

Somchai beamed. "This my grandfather. He has boat. Small boat but very fast."

The boy woke the old man and implored him in Khmer. The alleged grandfather stared at Maier and the car and finally asked in French. "You are being followed? By the police? By bad elements?"

Maier shook his head.

"We were attacked and robbed in Sihanoukville. My friend is injured and needs a doctor."

The old Khmer took a long hard look at Rolf, almost as long as at the car. Maier knew that the man did not believe a word of his story. But that hardly mattered. This was business.

"OK, tonight I will take you to Trat in Thailand. Take a room in my guest house and buy new clothes in the market. If you arrive in Thailand the way you look now, you will be arrested."

Maier looked down his shirt front. The man was right. And sensible. He looked used up. His vest was torn and frayed, his trousers black with dirt and dried blood. He would not make it to Bangkok like this. The Thais would immediately stop three dishevelled blood-soaked foreign travellers and demand to see papers. Appearance was everything in Thailand.

He dragged Rolf to a small room. Carissa left to buy clothes, while Maier took a shower. Then he showered his client and gulped down a plate of *loc lac*, fried beef topped by a fried egg. After the long journey Maier felt like he was eating an exotic delicacy. Even Rolf swallowed a few bites in silence. The young coffee heir was still in shock.

Late at night, Somchai and his grandfather came to pick up the small group. Rolf and Maier had changed into loud beachwear. Maier had sacrificed his moustache. Carissa had dyed her hair black and Rolf had hidden his blank eyes behind mirrored sunglasses.

This time, Somchai insisted on driving. The boy could hardly see above the steering wheel, but he handled the heavy SUV like a champion driver. A few minutes' drive took them to a dilapidated wooden pier, which jutted out between two abandoned stilt houses into the Stung Koh Poi River. Maier grabbed the keys from the ignition, his only bargaining chip, and walked out onto the pier.

"Your boat."

Maier looked down at a plastic bowl, a tiny fibre-glass dingy with an ancient outboard engine. The contraption bopped precariously around in the filthy water. Maier turned to the old man with a doubtful expression.

The Khmer smiled widely at his client.

"No problem, Monsieur. I have done this trip many times. I drop you at a pier from where you can get a taxi to Bangkok. Avoid the buses, they are often stopped by the military close to the border. A taxi with three *barang* inside is no problem."

Somchai helped Rolf into the small vessel, which was tied off between the two houses. When the boy had jumped back up to the pier, he held his hand out to Maier. The detective gave him the keys for the car.

Maier did not turn around as they slowly oozed through the black water out into the Gulf of Thailand. The boat was a bit too small, but the old man was a good captain. As soon as they had left Koh Kong behind, he opened up the engine and they sped across the open sea towards freedom. An hour later, the small vessel was far from the Cambodian coast in international waters. As Koh Kong faded into the darkness behind them, Maier relaxed. Cambodia was done. The case had bled itself to death. It was almost time to lick the wounds and celebrate being alive.

Around midnight, the boat changed direction and raced towards the bright lights of the Thai coastline. Rolf had passed out next to him, but Carissa sat in front of the boat, wide awake, her eyes scanning the empty night.

THE CITY OF ANGELS

Carissa had fallen asleep, fully clothed, on the bed next to him. The TV spat silent images of crises in other places. The air-con was going full blast and sounded like a coven of witches, out of sight, flying circles, riding their brooms, exhaling arctic breath, somewhere above his head. It was breakfast time. Or 2am in Hamburg. Sundermann answered on the second ring.

"Maier, you hit the big city?"

"Yes, I just dropped Rolf Müller-Overbeck in hospital. He is almost safe and sound and will come out of this with a couple of scratches, both mental and physical."

Maier squinted into the morning. He was exhausted and not in the mood for a debriefing. He looked across at Carissa who managed to look beautiful even as she slept with her mouth open and her face drawn.

3000 miles to the west, his boss started congratulating him.

"Maier, we spoke to the family while you were en route. Frau Müller-Overbeck is as close to happy as she will ever get."

He knew that Sundermann's compliments sometimes came with a catch.

"You've done great work, but we aren't done."

Maier felt irritation rising in his throat. He was so completely done.

"The case is not closed? We've done everything the ice queen hired us for, haven't we?"

Sundermann took his time and chose his words carefully, "As I said, Frau Müller-Overbeck is virtually ecstatic that her son is back in what she calls the 'real world' and that he's well cared for. But you know these wealthy clients. Enough is never enough, Maier. Easy is never easy. I know you are fed up and exhausted, but this morning she paid a fat bonus, and asked that you visit Rolf in hospital when he is himself again. And the young heir will ask you to return to Cambodia, to find the woman and to get her out. The family pays, because Rolf has promised that he will return to Hamburg if Kaley is safe. I gather that she's back at that temple where they kept you prisoner. What do you think?"

Maier was sick to his stomach. He felt like a babysitter for Hamburg's rich again. Unnecessary. And not in the mood to return to the hell he'd just escaped from. Maier had seen enough of the jungle temple.

"I don't want to appear negative, but I think it's almost impossible to free Kaley from the twists and turns of her past. Her fate is so closely linked to Cambodia, that she's almost a mirror of the country's history. The distance between the two, it is enormous – cultures, mentalities, education, expectations. Rolf just does not want to see that Kaley comes from a different part of the world with different ways of thinking. He ignores the fact that she is so deeply traumatised by the war that she has an obligation to her past."

The sour hiss of the static between Hamburg and the Thai capital bled into Maier's dull, tired head. Some case. But Sundermann wasn't going to let his detective's sober assessment sway him. Maier could already hear the wheels crunching.

"Maier, none of this matters. We took the case and you've resolved everything this far. But now the family Müller-Overbeck is throwing more money at us in order to help their son close this chapter of his life. That's why you will visit him in hospital tomorrow."

"Were you threatened with the city council?"

"I was," the agency director admitted. "I have to be politician as much as I have to be businessman. Let's give the gods of Blankenese the feeling that they can rely on us. It's good for me and good for you. And for the German coffee industry."

Without a great deal of conviction, Maier consented.

"You know that I won't achieve what Rolf expects. He wants me to ease his guilt, because he killed the woman's daughter."

"Maier, do your thing. I know you can. Work your magic one last time. Go and see Rolf, check the water temperature and do as our client suggests while threatening to break my left arm and sticking money in the right one."

Maier hung up and looked across at Carissa. So much for her suggestion to spend a week in bed together. He guessed she would go back to Phnom Penh. He almost envied her for feeling at home there, for having somewhere to go.

Rolf Müller-Overbeck lay in a private suite in Crescent Hospital, a few minutes off Sukhumvit Road in downtown Bangkok. The hospital was one of the most expensive in Southeast Asia and served as a collection point for countless tourists and wealthy Thais, as well as a handful of dictators from neighbouring countries.

As Maier entered the room, four giggling nurses were making the bed. Rolf sat in a wheelchair and conducted the girls' efforts. Maier felt a quick flashback go through him – to the young girls, dressed all in black, who'd lined up by his bunk, needles in hand.

"Hello, Maier, good to see you. Sorry I lost it with you in Phnom Penh. You saved my life."

The young German had regained some of the colour in his face and almost looked like a hero. His hair had been cut short, his earring had disappeared and Maier noticed that the coffee heir was starting to cultivate a moustache, a little like his own.

"Rolf, you are looking good. I am glad we got you out. It would have been a shame to throw your life away in Cambodia."

Maier thought he could detect a more thoughtful expression on his client's face.

"Maier, I simply didn't know what to do after I'd killed that little girl. Pete took charge of the situation so quickly, there was no choice. I was...not assertive enough. I made mistakes. Now it's so long ago that it has become unreal in my memory."

The nurses lifted Rolf off the wheelchair onto his bed and waved goodbye, giggling on the way out.

"Do they help you go to the toilet as well?"

Rolf laughed. "Probably, if I asked them to."

Then he became serious again.

Maier sat down on the sofa that stood next to the patient's bed.

"Did Kaley ever tell you anything about her sister?"

The young man from Hamburg shook his head in surprise. "She told me almost nothing of her past. I only know that she was married to Tep's son."

"And you want me to go back there and find Kaley for you?"

"Maier, I want to know who she really is and why she took part in this terrible ceremony in the casino. I want to know whether anything can be done to change her situation. I didn't manage that but I owe her. I killed her child."

Rolf had tears in his eyes. Maier decided to tell Rolf no more about Kaley and the men and children in her life. Or about Daniela, her dead German sister. These stories were best kept in the files. Maier left. Outside in the leaden Bangkok heat, he stopped to catch his breath. As futile as so many things he had done since working on this case. He wasn't going to get around his last pilgrimage to Cambodia. Maier flagged a taxi and headed straight for the airport.

HER EYES SAID GOODBYE

Siem Reap, formerly a provincial French town, was on its way to becoming Cambodia's second capital. The world had rediscovered the spectacular ruins of the Angkor Empire, and the land-mines around the temples had been cleared. The tourists were back. Since the international airport had opened, investors, who circled like vultures above the UNESCO world heritage site, could not get hotels, restaurants, shopping centres, massage parlours, casinos and bars off the ground quick enough.

In the brand new Siem Reap International Airport, the immigration officer had photographed Maier, who was travelling under a false name on a new clean and French passport. Bangkok made such things possible.

Maier rented a motorbike and drove out to the temples. The town's first traffic light had just been installed and was guarded by three policemen with loudspeakers, who were giving twelve-hour-long lessons in basic traffic behaviour to passing motorists. In order to save trouble with the local authorities, Maier bought a ticket to the temples. Five minutes later, he circled the broad moat that stretched around Angkor Wat.

The largest temple in the world lay in the morning sun like a sleeping colossus, but the detective didn't stop. Instead, he opened the throttle and shot through the southern gate into Angkor Thom, the old Khmer capital, past the Bayon temple and its two hundred or so gigantic faces that smiled down stoically at Maier, challenging him to drive further into the jungle. It was too early for the tour groups and buses and Maier had the roads all to himself. Many of the ruins were surrounded by dense forest and Maier had to brake hard now and then, in order not to mow down one of the many monkeys who enjoyed sitting on the tarmac before it got hot.

Maier left Angkor Thom via the Victory Gate and ran past the eastern Baray, a huge reservoir built by the Angkor kings to help run the thousand year old empire's powerhouse economy. Village children jumped into the street excitedly as Maier passed, waving postcards and cans of Coke, hoping to make a few riel off this early traveller. Away from the temples and the tourists, Siem Reap was desperately poor. The Cambodian government and a private company shared the profits of the tourist dollars – virtually nothing trickled down to the traumatised population, for whom Angkor was the spiritual, cultural and economic heart of the country.

Beyond Banteay Srey, the Citadel of Women, the road turned into a red lateritic track, but Maier pushed on as fast as possible. He had planned to return to Siem Reap the same day and catch a night flight back to Bangkok. Small settlements stretched along the dusty road, huts on stilts, without electricity or water. Until recently, there'd been jungle behind the huts, but the poor who lived here had logged and burnt it all for rich landowners – the land looked like a wasted moonscape.

Beng Melea had been built in the twelfth century, following the same basic design as Angkor Wat.

Maier stopped in front of the overgrown temple. A CMAC crew, known to its international donors as the Cambodian Mine Action Center, was working close to the temple. Twenty young men in blue uniforms roped off a small piece of land next to the ruin and began to search the dry ground, metre by metre. It would take years, if not decades, to remove all the mines and explosives buried in Cambodia. Every month, innocent people lost their limbs. The war never ended. In almost all the countries Maier had worked in as a war correspondent, governments or opposition parties had mined parts of their own land. The result was always the same – the victims were mostly civilians, often children.

Maier drove along a narrow path into the forest, which forked several times. He followed fresh tyre tracks deep into the jungle of northwest Cambodia. An hour into his journey, the track broadened. Maier slowed as a crumbling stone tower emerged from the foliage ahead. He had reached his destination and pushed the bike off the track into the forest. Small green parrots chased through the canopy above and Maier could see a few flying foxes sleeping in the trees. The world was fine for the moment. For a while Maier sat at the bottom of a tree, letting the silence settle. This time he wasn't going to be overrun by murderous teenage girls.

The temple was smaller than Beng Melea and completely subsumed by the forest. Maier didn't see anyone, but he approached the ruin slowly and with care. He circled the building. The temple only had one tower. Two others had collapsed and pulled down part of the roof with them. An SUV stood parked behind the temple. The engine was still warm. The car was unlocked and Maier found a gun in the glove compartment. He stared at it for a moment, then left it where he'd found it. Partially-burnt suitcases crammed with cash filled the boot and the back seat.

Suddenly he heard voices from the temple interior and hunkered down behind the sandstone wall which surrounded the building. Something stank. Terribly. Slowly, ever so slowly, he raised his head above the wall.

Pete and Inspector Viengsra were barely recognisable. The two men grinned yellow teeth at Maier. The detective dropped back down behind the wall. Tep had brought the heads from Bokor, driven them onto wooden stakes and set them up at the entrance. Flies cruised in thick shape-shifting clouds around what was left of the two men. Pete's formerly red hair had turned rust brown and the eyes of the policeman were missing. Even on Maier's side of the wall, the smell was unbearable. He retreated to his bike, vomited into the bushes and sat in the shade until the sun dropped into the trees.

A couple of hours later, he picked a different entrance for his second attempt to enter the temple. This time he got lucky. He could hear the general's voice reverberate around the temple ruin. The old soldier spoke English.

"Cambodia no longer need you. Your men and your children are dead. All dead. Your power used up. The curse of the Kangaok Meas coming to an end."

Maier slid into an alcove that might once have housed an *apsara*. Inside, he could barely make out Tep in the semi-darkness. The general wore a bandage around his neck and had his hands up. Kaley pointed a gun at Tep's chest.

Would she shoot, if Tep attacked her?

Tep smiled and Maier knew that the old general didn't feel threatened. He continued in Khmer.

"Please come. I will take you back to the car. There's no need for the gun. We're both Khmer."

Maier couldn't work out why the old general had spoken English to Kaley. Did he know the detective had arrived?

Rays of sunshine poured through the partially collapsed ceiling. The dust that the two Cambodians kicked up snowed in narrow shards of light onto century-old dreams of withering stone. The might of the temples and the country's glorious past had to be a heavy yoke to carry for the Khmer, starved and crushed by endless war. The country would never be as proud again as it had been. Perhaps the burden of longing for past glories had contributed to the madness of the Khmer Rouge. Tep's madness.

Tep and Kaley had turned off into a narrow corridor. Maier followed slowly. He was still spooked by the young murder girls and desperately hoped he wouldn't meet one in the dark. But the temple was abandoned. Tep and Kaley were the only survivors of the Kangaok Meas Project. The general and his prisoner pressed on, with Maier following at what he considered a safe distance. He cursed himself for having left the gun in Tep's car. He could see no way of getting her away from the old soldier. He would have to jump the old man at the next corner. But the detective hung back too far behind the kidnapper and his victim.

When Maier finally stepped from the narrow corridor into the open, it was too late. Tep didn't make deals. The old man had led Kaley into a logged clearing and disarmed her. Kaley stood stock still, forlorn and confused. The general was already fifty metres away, limping back towards his car.

Suddenly he spun around, saw Maier and shouted, "We give life to Kangaok Meas, my friend Lorenz and me. And when we need to, we take it as well. Today I finish our dream."

Kaley stared at her tormentor without comprehension. Maier stopped on the lowest step of the temple stairway and called to her.

"Hello, Kaley."

She did not turn. He called to her again. More than ever he now thought of her as a ghost. What had he been thinking, trying to save this shattered woman?

"Kaley."

Tep raised his gun and fired a couple of shots at the detective. Maier dropped to the ground, looking for something to hide behind, but the old general was too far away and the bullets hit the temple walls a few metres away. Tep didn't come back for Maier, an easy target on the bottom step of the temple stairway. Mercy was hardly in the former Khmer Rouge soldier's repertoire of sentiments. So why didn't the Cambodian come and finish him off? Something was very wrong. The clearing in front of the Khmer ruin had gone dead silent. The general had stopped walking, his gun empty. As if waiting for something. For the end.

Maier waved at the woman and slowly started walking towards her, watching the general as well as the ground ahead. He didn't have to go far to understand how Tep had trapped Kaley and was using her as bait. But it was too late to turn back. A few metres to his right, a handful of warning signs for landmines had been thrown to the forest floor. Tep must have had them removed. The old general obviously knew how to cross the clearing without losing a limb. But Maier didn't. The detective suddenly had the feeling that the last unresolved questions of his case were about to be answered. Everything was falling into place. What had the Russian told him, before he'd left the roof of the casino?

"Don't forget, follow the sticks."

It had sounded like nonsense. But the Russian was not stupid and had never said anything unnecessary. Mikhail's remark suddenly burnt like a flame through Maier's mind and he took another look at the clearing.

Mikhail was a step ahead. He had known even then, on the roof of the casino, that Maier would end up in a minefield. And not just in any minefield. In this minefield.

At a distance of about two metres, small sticks rose from the dry forest floor. Some had been broken and kicked away. Perhaps Tep had tried to obscure the safe way out of the clearing, but after studying the ground for some time, Maier could see a clear route all the way to the petrified woman. One just had to know. Without worrying too much, Maier stepped onto the dusty ground and slowly walked towards Kaley, who looked at him in shock.

After a few metres, something like dizziness overcame him. He stopped, only to notice that his sweat-soaked shirt was sticking to his back. Fear. It was all in the mind, he told himself. The Russian hadn't killed him in Bokor. There had to be a reason. Mikhail did nothing without reason. Mikhail had foreseen this situation.

Tep still stood on the edge of the clearing and watched Maier. He was too far away to shoot them. But he did not want to walk back out into the minefield. Which didn't stop him cursing Maier.

"Maier, so good to see you so close to death. You will go a traditional way, I promise you. I tell you our first meeting, we not like snoops in Cambodia. But you difficult to kill. Have nice day with lady. Today is last one for you."

The old soldier turned in disgust and got into his car.

"Follow the sticks, what does it mean?"

Kaley shook her head. For the first time, Maier saw her, the Kangaok Meas, as a human being, fragile and vulnerable, without the aura, just like anyone else.

"And how do we get out of here?"

"Just the same way we came in. As a man in Bokor told me, follow the sticks."

Maier looked at the ground in front of him. On the way out of the clearing, Tep had torn away many of the sticks. The way they'd come, back to the temple looked more promising.

"Look at the small sticks in the ground. We have to follow their path. Here and there some have collapsed but we should be able to see my footsteps."

They began to walk back slowly.

Maier went first. Now and then he turned and looked back at Tep, who sat in his car, waiting for him or the woman to die. Thirty metres more.

Suddenly they reached open ground. Maier could not see any of the sticks. They were so close to the temple now. So close, fifteen steps, no more. Fifteen steps of death. Maier stood looking desperately for his footprints when Kaley passed him. She made directly for the temple. She almost had a spring in her step. Maier followed carefully and turned once more.

The general had been waiting for Maier's turn and waved from the car's driving seat before he bent forward to put the key in the ignition. The explosion threw the heavy SUV into the air. The heat of the flames was incredible. One of the axles came off and flew, tyres burning, across the temple wall. A second explosion ripped the car apart, perhaps the petrol tank had caught fire.

"Let's go, back into the temple."

Maier squeezed past Kaley and took up the trail through the minefield. The last few steps towards safety were clearly visible. A few minutes later he stood with Kaley on the broad stairs of the temple. Maier wiped the sweat from his forehead and sat down in the shadow of the narrow corridor that led into the temple interior. Kaley had a dreamy expression on her face. An expression that Maier had not seen before.

She stepped towards the detective and embraced him.

"Thank you, Maier, you are good man. Les is right."

The scene he had watched through the hole in the floor of the casino flashed through Maier's head. He never did have a chance to fulfil his promise. He had been deluding himself and the woman too. As she stepped away from him, he held out his hand, but he knew instinctively that she would not take it. Kaley was done with taking and had long given everything she had ever had. Just like Cambodia. All she expected him to do now was to witness her last pathetic, heroic act. She turned away from him and, no longer choosing her steps carefully, left the safety of the temple and walked into the morning. Maier did not try to stop her or follow her. But neither did he leave. He owed her that much, perhaps more, much more.

There were times when Maier liked to remember the gentle attempts by his friend Hort to make him laugh, especially when there was absolutely nothing to laugh about. Those were the moments when he thought he could understand his dead friend Hort. Then the exploding landmine ripped away all his thoughts. The ground shook briefly. A cloud of dust rose from the tired earth. It was all over.

Maier, stunned, sat down on the temple steps. Absentmindedly, he put his hands into the pockets of his vest and pulled out a strange object. After staring at his find mindlessly for a short eternity, he recognised it as one of Carissa's half-smoked, crumpled joints. The detective lit up and watched parrots at play in the canopy on the edge of the clearing. Rolf Müller-Overbeck was going to be distraught. As Maier followed the exuberant dive-bombing of the small green birds that squawked above his head, his mind drifted away from the carnage and he experienced a sudden moment of almost absolute certainty. It was time to go and see his woman.

A MIRROR FOR THE BLIND

Sundermann had sunk deep into his wicker chair and watched Maier and Carissa fight over the best parts of the dinner they were sharing. Eclectic world music dripped from invisible speakers through the Foreign Correspondents Club. A faint breeze from the river cut through the heat.

Maier was pleased. His mission was ending back where it had begun. Down in the street, the hustlers, the limbless and the hopeless congregated just as they had for days, weeks, months and years. Tourists stumbled along, avoiding the drug dealers and taxi girls as best as they could, who with the minimum exertion required, tried to separate the visitors from their cash. A little circus of cross cultural absurdities.

But things were looking up. Cambodia was coming out of its self-prescribed dark age, blinking, insecure, proud and with so little care for her past that her very immediate future would likely be a happy one. Beyond the next ten minutes though, everything was speculation. The culture of impunity was the only ticket in town.

Other guests kept looking back at Maier and his partner. Some men walked past them several times. Carissa looked stunning. Her hair had turned white once more and her shiny green dress, tailored from Thai silk, perfectly complemented the large red ruby, suspended from a thin gold chain around her neck, which wanted to get lost in her cleavage.

Maier detested paperwork and had debriefed himself over an excellent sea food salad, several ennormous wood-fired pizzas and many tall glasses of Vodka Orange. The orange juice was freshly squeezed and the detective was happy. Sundermann and Carissa were on their third bottle of Beaujolais, when Maier finally ended with his account of his moment in the mine field. Sundermann appeared to be as sober as at the start of the evening.

Maier had respect for his boss, who was ten years older, drank like a world champion and looked after the handful of detectives he employed like a kind uncle. And Sundermann had a discreet, if noisy style – suits by Armani, close shave, an expensive pair of rimless glasses, a tie for every occasion, a likeable open smile and a compliment or calming word for every client. Maier liked working with the best. He had learned, a long time ago, in his life as a war correspondent, that working with amateurs led to calamities. It was no different for detectives. He could trust Sundermann. Sundermann had come all the way to Phnom Penh to personally sign off on Maier's Cambodian adventure. And Sundermann always asked the right questions.

Just like Carissa. The journalist excused herself and Sundermann switched to German.

"Who is this Mikhail? A colleague?"

"First I thought he was just a cynic, a former mercenary, who wanted to take things in his own hands up there. But I guess he was a man with a plan."

"An investigator?"

Maier shook his head in doubt.

"That man is an assassin, not a detective. He didn't hesitate for a second in that jail and he almost shot me dead. He also didn't defuse the explosives on the hotel roof, he just moved the clock of the timer forward."

"So why didn't he shoot you?"

Maier hesitated, tried to process his thoughts from assumptions into usable information.

"It was a calculated risk. I am sure of that. This crazy Russian decided in that split second, with his finger on the trigger, that I could be useful to him. But how, I have no idea. Not exactly. I have my theories."

Sundermann nodded.

"No, Mikhail was no Russian Rambo. I think he was a sleeper who had been waiting for something near that casino. I am sure he has a military background." Maier looked doubtful. He knew that the chances of ever tracking down the Russian were minute. "Our research here in Cambodia didn't turn up a thing. Disappeared into thin air. Same at the borders, no sign of him. But that doesn't really mean anything, aside from the fact that he's a pro."

"I know that. But it makes no difference. Maier, I have heard, from a source in southern Germany, that someone else was after the woman. Perhaps an associate of the White Spider. Or our friend Mikhail. Perhaps you were used to provoke the events in the casino. The question is, was there another case, some kind of mission going, in connection with Kaley, while you were in Cambodia? And does it have anything to do with Lorenz?"

"We know some of the answers to this already. Kaley's sister, one Daniela Stricker, who was killed by Tep or his son, had lived in southern Germany for twenty years. She had a German passport, and then turns up after all these years on Cambodia's coast and promptly gets killed."

"That we know. But we don't know why she came back or whether she was connected to someone else in this story."

Maier shrugged. "Perhaps she hired the Russian to find her sister. I am sure he wired the car at the temple. He planted the sticks in the minefield. In a way I finished his job for him. And mine. Quite brilliant."

Sundermann didn't have to say anything. Maier knew his boss agreed.

"I have a feeling I will meet Mikhail again," said Maier. "But I doubt we will find out exactly what is role was in all this. He is a slippery customer."

Sundermann nodded thoughtfully and let it go. As he passed a sealed manila envelope to his detective, Carissa floated back onto the Foreign Coresspondents Club's terrace.

"The notes for Laos," Sundermann said. "Your next case. I trust it will be a walk in the park compared to your Cambodian mission. When you are done here, fly to Hamburg and meet your next client. I rely on you, Maier. Travel safely"

Maier made a grab for the case files and an almost full bottle of wine and pulled Carissa away from the table and through the club. The world turned around them and Maier knew that everything was OK, would be OK. He would beat his traumas. He would start right away. Carissa would help him.

"Let's go to bed and celebrate."

Carissa laughed, her eyes full of challenge. "Yes, Maier, let's party like never before, like there's no tomorrow."

Maier was too happy and too drunk to think about her words or to notice the dark look simmering beneath her smile as they descended the broad stairs into the rubbish strewn street.

They jumped a tuk-tuk to the Hotel Renakse, a charming former royal guest house opposite the palace, a few hundred meters from their dinner party, and for Maier perhaps the most romantic place in the city. They propped each other up as they slowly walked through the hotel garden up the pebbled drive and through the colonial-era building's sparsely furnished corridors. The night was dark and cool. The floor tiles danced under their feet. A bird called from the river, answered by the cry of a lone drunk. Everything was good and Maier wallowed in his illusions, throwing furtive glances at the journalist, who responded with the happy-sad looks of someone hopelessly in love. This was the closest he might ever get to it. To something essential. Once in the room, they fell into a fever. Even youth was somehow with them and the last thing Carissa said to Maier as he drifted into sleep, burnt itself into his mind like a rust-colored tropical sunset after the rains, "All through our dinner, I was on the verge of having an orgasm, Maier. You were the most handsome man in Phnom Penh tonight, no doubt about it. It's uncanny you came back here. And it's been good knowing you all these years. And so much more."

When Maier woke in the morning, he was alone. Her smell still clung to the sheets, but he knew that Carissa had said goodbye. His life was empty and without worry, just as he wished it to be. It hurt. He got up and went to the bathroom to examine his psyche.

With bright red lipstick, she had written one of his favourite quotes on the mirror. "We live as we dream."

ACKNOWLEDGMENTS

Thanks to my family, especially my wife Aroon Thaew-chatturat and my brother Marc Eberle – both played instrumental roles in getting me to finish *The Cambodian Book of the Dead*.

Thanks to my friend Hans Kemp for embarking on an adventure called *Crime Wave Press* and helping to get Detective Maier on the road. Lucy Ridout did a great early edit.

In 1995, I crossed from Thailand into Cambodia at Hat Lek, racing in a speed boat up the jungle-fringed Koh Kong River, with troops dug in on both sides. The other passengers besides my travel companion and me were a man who had a suitcase chained to his wrist and a sex worker on her way home from Pattaya. The sky was gun metal grey. I was hooked. Cambodia is a land of stories, both beautiful and beautifully poignant – an obvious location for the first job for German detective Maier, a former war correspondent who investigates crimes around Asia. Throughout my many subsequent trips, I was touched by the friendliness of the Cambodians and shocked by what they have to put up with.

Those who provided insights: Youk Chang (at DCCAM), David Chandler, Soparoath Yi, Poch Kim, Luke Duggleby, Gerhard Joren, Roland Neveu, Kraig Lieb, Barbara Lettner, Jane Elizabeth, Jochen Spieker, Joe Heffernan, Chanthy Kak, Julien Poulson, Kosal Khiev, Chris Kelly, Tassilo Brinzer and Marie Phouek .

The amazing Emlyn Rees and team at Exhibit A took the plunge and put the shine to it.

Maier will be back – in *The Man with the Golden Mind*.

  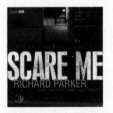